THE
SOUL
OF A
THIEF

STEVEN HARTOV

THE
SOUL
OF A
THIEF

A NOVEL

HANOVER
SQUARE
PRESS

HANOVER
SQUARE
PRESS

Recycling programs
for this product may
not exist in your area.

ISBN-13: 978-1-335-14457-7

The Soul of a Thief

For questions and comments about the quality of this book, please contact us at CustomerService@Harlequin.com.

HanoverSqPress.com
BookClubbish.com

Printed in U.S.A.

For my mother, Trudy, who survived, thrived and told me and Susie the stories. And for Lia, who loves and believes.

THE

SOUL

OF A

THIEF

AUTHOR NOTE

I DO NOT KNOW the origin of this story. One autumn night some years ago, I woke up and began to write it, as if compelled to do so. I am generally a practical man, but this tale flowed forth as if commanded by some otherworldly force, and I was just the vessel of its telling. Alarmed at first, I soon looked forward to each night of work, to hear the next part of the tale and honor it as best I could. I also realized then, that this memoir is more than an invention of imagination, as it first came to me in recurring dreams when I was still a child.

There is no one to thank, except perhaps the ghost who told it through my fingers, and all those who indulged me, as I wrote and wondered where it came from.

I

IN THE SPRING of 1944, I realized that I was not going to survive the war.

There was, upon this revelation resisted for so long, a sublime unburdening of tension, a sensation of relief and release I had not enjoyed since being expelled as a boy from a Catholic public school in Vienna. After all, my survival until this point had been predicated upon a carefully executed waltz of luck and deception. But now, rather like a skilled player of Chemin de Fer who wins too long at the table, my good fortunes could not but fade, and my fatigue was draining my abilities to deceive.

I should make it clear that I did not harbor what the famed Viennese psychologists then termed as suicidal tendencies. Quite the contrary, I was a survivor by strength of will and character. However, some factors made it clear that emerging in one piece from this worldwide conflagration, with myself at its epicenter, was highly unlikely.

I was the young adjutant to an SS colonel named Himmel, whose actions reflected exactly the opposite of his heavenly moniker.

I was also, on paper, a Catholic named Brandt, yet in fact the descendant of a great-grandmother named Brandeis.

And finally, I was in love with the Colonel's fiancée, a magnificent creature of my own age, who had just informed me that in fact my emotions for her were well requited.

No, it was not likely that I was going to survive this war. But inasmuch as the practicalities of shelter, sustenance and personal security can so easily be spurned in exchange for youthful and mad romance, I no longer cared. It had become very clear to me in the early months of that year, that unless I plumbed the depths of my courage and found the well of a reckless swashbuckler, the postwar world would be a morbid and cold planet, unfit for living.

And so, since I was unlikely to survive, I would make my dash for the gates with my love in hand. And, if I could hone every one of my strategic skills and adopt the soul of a thief, I would be very rich, to boot. Yes, in all likelihood, a rush of bullets would bring me to ground long before my escape.

But, so be it…

Colonel Himmel was a war hero, which made my status as his adjutant an envious position, if one viewed such employ through the eyes of a dedicated Nazi patriot. However, I was merely grateful that I had come to fill my position late in the game, for at barely nineteen years old, until the previous year I had been ineligible for more than cannon fodder on the Russian front or service in the Hitler Youth. This fine, upstanding organization I'd been forbidden to join in Vienna, as my ethnic background was in question. As for the infantry, my number had simply not yet come up.

Upon my expulsion from *Gymnasium*, I had been employed as a physician's assistant in a Viennese hospital, which delayed my being swallowed up by the Wehrmacht. Yet it was there, while visiting a trio of his wounded commandos, that Himmel spotted me. He was a pure combat officer, decidedly apolitical, and I believe that what struck him was my appearance. I was a fine youth then, blond and blue-eyed and wiry, genetic gifts owing to the Balkan Semitic lineage of my great-grandmother rather than to any inheritance of an Aryan bent. He whispered a few inquiries to the doctors whom I served, and I was promptly whisked away to a new position and adventures I had not dreamed of, or wanted.

I was thankful, however, for having come to Himmel's side at this latter stage of his commando career, because throughout the war his résumé had been quickly filled up with daring raids against Allied troops, mountaintop rescues of captured officers, and the long-range executions of enemy generals. The Colonel had a tendency to reward his support staff by insisting they accompany him on most such ventures, and so, a long list of previous adjutants, company clerks and even cooks had been killed in action on a number of fronts. My recruitment to the Colonel's staff in 1943 somewhat lessened the odds of my falling prey to foreign shellfire while shining the commander's jackboots, but it was in any event a nerve-racking assignment.

You see, Himmel had been twice awarded the Iron Cross, as well as the Knight's Cross for exemplary valor, on one occasion by Adolf Hitler himself. I shall briefly digress to say that I am not proud to have been in attendance for that ceremony, but it was most certainly a surreal dinner soirée I shall never forget, for it is seared upon my mind's eye. The awardees, more than two hundred officers from various branches of the Wehrmacht, Kriegsmarine and Luftwaffe, were invited to the Eagle's Lair at Berchtesgaden. Of course, I use the term "invited" with tongue in cheek, for these weary men were ordered to appear on the given eve, despite their presently distant locations or battlefield predicaments.

Thus, the towering antechamber of Hitler's *Schloss* was awash with men in dress uniforms, yet one must realize that so many of these previously perfectly tailored tunics and jodhpurs had been stowed now for years in Panzer tanks, Heinkel bombers or U-boats. The courageous officers had done their best to shine cracked boots, polish rusted buckles and steam the wrinkles from moth-eaten wools, yet even so, it all appeared much like a costume ball in the tenth level of hell. The submariners' beards were badly trimmed, the Luftwaffe pilots' eyes gleamed with fatigue, and some of the infantry heroes actually had caked spots of blood on their cuffs and lapels, as their most recent wounds still oozed. I hardly think now that many of them remained ardent worshippers of their Führer, yet like Roman legionnaires in the presence of Caesar, they managed to effect erect spines and the gunshot clicks of heels.

Hitler was customarily late, by I believe at least two hours, and I shall never forget his demeanor when he finally appeared. He seemed, quite frankly, completely surprised, and subsequently annoyed. He behaved like a man whose wife has invited guests to dinner without his consent, and it was only when Goering whispered a reminder in his ear that he dredged up the manners to stay the course. So quickly did he dispense the medals, with scarcely a complimentary word and absently offering that embarrassingly limp handshake of his, that I imagined his primary motive here was to finish with it and hurry to the toilet.

Of course, had I shared my view with a single soul, including any other young adjutant or even a castle cook, I most certainly would have found myself immediately en route to Smolensk, or worse. However, just after the Führer's departure, I offered Colonel Himmel a champagne glass from a silver tray and congratulated him for his courage, which I had too often personally witnessed along with an accompanying clutch of my sphincter. The Colonel received his drink, nodded his gratitude, and very briefly rolled his single eye. He then smiled at me for a millisecond and quickly issued me an order of some kind, yet the moment had been shared.

For an assassin, a brigand, a tyrant and a thief, my master did have his good points.

To me, Himmel's most endearing quality was that he never fully inquired as to my background. During the prewar years and throughout the conflict, it was incumbent upon elite Nazi officers to fully vet each member of their command, despite the assumption that the Gestapo had already done so. Yet Himmel had always been a career combatant, regarding Hitler's anti-Semitic diatribes as nothing more than a rallying point around which to galvanize the populace. Having not a bone of fear in his body, he dismissed the regulatory racial codes with a snort, and assembled his company of *Waffen Schutzstaffel* based upon performance, and nothing else. Thus, his command was peppered with a number of racially questionable men of swarthy complexions and altered family names, and I would not be surprised if it included a gypsy or two.

Of course, having none of this information upon being fairly kidnapped by the Colonel, I spent my first two months quivering in his presence. I was waiting for him to summon me and wave a Gestapo document in my face, some horrendously accurate accusation that there was, in fact, a wizened old Jewess concealed among the many branches of my family tree. That, in itself, would have been enough for any other such officer to have me shot. The full truth, in fact, was worse.

My beloved father and mother were devout Catholics, which one might think a guarantee of my immediate lineage. However, one must also realize that devotion to God, under the Nazi reanalysis of religion, was not viewed kindly by the authorities. Adolf Hitler had become the New God of Germany and its protectorates, with Christ a poor third to the Führer and his pagan symbols, such as Albert Speer's monolithic architectures and the towering iron statues of eagles, stag horns and the like. If you were a devout Catholic, you were expected to display your crucifix as nothing more than proof of your ethnic purity. In Vienna, the city of my birth and youth, the *Anschluss* had provided Germany's Nazis with a pool of deeply fanatical followers. Those who claim that the Austrians were so much worse than the Germans themselves are correct, for there is no one more obsessive than a convert.

My father would not, however, relinquish his religious beliefs. And although he supported the economic and political precepts of Nazism, he refused to rein in his attendance of Mass, regular confessions or charity efforts for the Church. Such behavior greatly frightened my mother, of course, who was edgy enough given our genetic status and the questionable position of her only son. Yet the authorities, recognizing my father to be a man of some age and granted eccentricities, declined to rigorously pursue his conversion to Hitlerism. That is, until he strayed too far.

My father was, by trade, a book seller. Adolf Hitler was, by choice, a book burner. It required no more than one massive, flaming pyre of the classics to set my father's inner rage alight, and thereafter he was a changed man. He quietly joined "O 5," the Austrian anti-Nazi resistance movement. On the evening after *Kristallnacht*, during which every Jewish shop and synagogue in Vienna was burned to the ground by the Brown Shirts, along with approximately twenty thousand copies of both the Old and New Testaments, three members of that thugly gang were found murdered in the Tenth District. My father returned late that evening, exuding an odor of fear and adrenaline, and he packed a single suitcase, hugged myself and my mother to him, and informed us that he would have to leave immediately or endanger our lives.

I never saw him again. But still today, there remains etched into the exterior of the great St. Stephen's Cathedral in Vienna, a white scrawled carving of defiance, the figures "O 5." I have been told that my father was the very chiseler of that message from the underground.

So, you can well understand why my first few months with Himmel were so fraught with the constant urge to pee, even though he appeared to regard my history as irrelevant.

The second trait which so endeared my master to me, as it were, was his choice of women. I refer not, of course, to the long line of prostitutes and desperately widowed wives we encountered in our travels throughout Italy, the Rhineland or France. Some of these Himmel paid well as he invited them to bed, and some he spontaneously mounted in empty castle keeps and haylofts. These he regarded as the spoils of war and nothing more.

The true measure of his good taste was revealed in the selection of Gabrielle. We had settled temporarily near Le Pontet, a village beside the fabled French town of Avignon, for a spate of rest and recreation. Much of the small ville had suffered from errant Allied bombs, and a large German field hospital had been erected in the meadows as a sort of waypoint and triage center for the wounded from all fronts. The slim bridges of the Rhone were constantly awash in horse-drawn wagons, with the local French girls essentially enslaved as nurses to transport and tend the injured. It was there, above the bloody river waters that would someday be bottled and sold by the shipload to American supermarkets, that Himmel spotted her.

She was virtually a child, barely eighteen years of age, the daughter of Le Pontet's mayor, who had been executed by the Gestapo. Despite the soiled appearance of all the other females employed by our army, Gabrielle's skin was pure and translucent, her fingernails unbroken, the flaxen blond hair that framed her diamond blue eyes falling straight and true to her slim waist. As she sat upon the bench of a caisson that contained the writhing forms of three wounded panzer crew, her chin erect and her hands lightly snapping the reins of her horses, it was clear that she had inherited a strand of royal French genes. Himmel ordered the driver of his Kübelwagen to halt, and he immediately fell in love. He was done with whoring.

The rest of how I came to know her, I shall leave for later telling.

And finally, the Colonel's third trait which I came to temporarily admire was his greed. Perhaps that is unfair, and a more generous description of his calculations might be called practicality. After all, his strategic assessments of any given situation were almost always correct, and his analysis of the war's progress, despite his own personal victories, was untempered by emotion. By the time I joined him, Himmel knew that Germany was going to lose this war. He also knew that the Allies were about to mount a massive invasion of the continent, the furious tide of which would not be repulsed. Despite the erroneous hunches of Hitler and the endless arguments of the High Command, Himmel would regularly spread a map of Europe across any makeshift dining table or vehicle boot, jab a finger at the coast of Normandy and state, "Here. It will come here."

Although I shall never be so immodest as to claim that I had become the Colonel's confidant, practicality dictated that he place his trust in my circumspection. Someone had to safe-keep the Colonel's papers, plans and plots, and inasmuch as I was imprisoned by my *Mischling* lineage and apparently no threat to him, he chose to trust me implicitly. Of course, be-fore actually doing so, he did remind me that any slip of my tongue would result in an instant and painful death, without benefit of a hearing.

Thus, I came to know that Himmel planned to finish out the war not only as a survivor, but as a very wealthy one. He surmised that there were other high-ranking officers who had made the same calculations, some of whom had access to the whereabouts of Nazi gold stores and caches of jewels and works of art accrued during various occupations. But as my supremely practical commander determined, gold and trinkets were simply too heavy and unwieldy a trea-sure; difficult to transport, impossible to conceal.

He reasoned that the Allies would storm ashore in France sometime in the summer of the year. He also reasoned that with so many hundreds of thousands of Allied troops on the march, their paymasters would not be far behind. With the end of the war nearly visible on the horizon, all cur-rencies in Europe would become essentially useless, save the American dollar, or the British pound.

The Allied Army's treasury corps would doubtless be following their troops in heavily armored convoys of some sort. This would be Himmel's swan song, his epitomal target, his final mission.

He was going to steal it from them.

And I was going to steal it from him…

II

In April of 1943, I first faced my death on the second week of my employment.

Lest you think me of a timid nature and overly dramatic, I shall relay to you the first of many such events which sowed the seeds of a conviction that my survival might be in question.

I had just commenced my tasks for Colonel Erich Himmel of the Waffen SS, and at first it appeared that serving as the Colonel's adjutant was certainly an insurance policy among the many uninsured. Himmel's Commando was presently hosted in one of the many glorious castles astride the eastern banks of the Rhine, not far from Rüdesheim, a tiny village nestled in a bend of the swollen waters of the river. Early spring had blessed the rolling hills with greenery and flowers, cool morning fogs caressed the church spires, and as we were far from any of the industrial cities, the Allied bombings were no more threatening than, or discernible from, the occasional spates of evening thunderstorms. Surely, no matter the dangerous adventures to be undertaken by the unit, I would remain here in this virtual paradise of tranquility, while the SS did its duty elsewhere.

Inasmuch as I was not a combat soldier, and had never been trained as one, at first I served the commander in the only threadbare suit I owned. It was a loose and comfortable gray tweed, hanging a bit on my scrawny frame, but perhaps it comforted me somewhat, offering the illusion of being nothing more than a civilian secretary. I began by simply serving the commander his coffee and cakes, meals of goat cheese and rough breads, tending to the condition of his uniforms and boots, and making sure that his supply of eye patches was in order. He had lost his left eye early in the war, a wound that he dismissed as a blessing, for it obviated the requirement to squint when he fired his pistol.

At first, the commander barely seemed to notice me, and he hardly spoke to me except to issue terse but polite instructions.

"Shtefan, bring me this. Shtefan, bring me that."

I responded quickly and efficiently, although it was difficult to click my heels along with my stiff bow at the waist, for I still shuffled along in a pair of church dress shoes, worn down to the soles and beyond.

The commander's captain and lieutenants rarely gazed in my direction, as if I were a ghost. But soon, a young, dark-eyed lieutenant named Gans approached me in Himmel's presence, carrying a carelessly folded uniform in his arms.

"You can have it," the commander stated, not looking

up from a sheaf of orders on his desk. "It belonged to Fritz Heidt, but he is dead."

"That is…most generous," I stuttered, while cringing at the idea. "But my suit is just fine, Herr Colonel."

Himmel glanced up from his paperwork, and seeing that narrow squint, I hurried off to don the filthy thing. The trousers fit adequately, aided by the thick braces over my bony shoulders, but in the tunic there was a neat bullet hole just above the heart. I swallowed hard as I buttoned it, then reasoned that the odds of yet another bullet striking the garment in exactly the same place were in my favor. The high boots that were issued me were small and damp, but manageable. As yet, I had no army stockings, and my left heel kept sticking to the leather. It was not until that evening that I realized there was still blood in the boot.

I did not then surmise, until the castle began to bustle, that the issue of my fresh costume was the portent of an upcoming mission.

Until that eve, the men had been relaxed, at least when protected from Himmel's view. At night they stood the watch or slept within the castle walls, but during daylight they pursued the business of elite combat troops in respite: meticulously cleaning their weapons, shining buckles and boots, replenishing ammunition, and occasionally rough-housing with each other like a pack of wild pups. As their uniforms had all sustained various degrees of damage, they would summon the local Hungarian refugee girls and, assuming that every female possesses the inherent traits of a seamstress, oblige them to cut and sew and repair loose buttons.

If a girl was particularly comely, a younger member of the troop would be posted to alarm if an officer approached, while a trio or so of his comrades raped her in the wine cellar. These assaults were horrific in nature, yet strangely devoid of violence, and once I witnessed a rumpled teen leaving the quarters with tears tracking her face, yet grinning a quivering smile. She carried a pile of breads and cheeses in her arms, along with two bottles of port, the apparent rewards for submission without a scream. The next time I saw her, she appeared in the courtyard and made straight for the cellar, unbuttoning her blouse as she clipped along, eyes cast downward, a happy quintet of SS on her heels. These incidents assailed my sense of honor, gentility and romance, yet I dared not object. It would be some months before I understood that war and the proximity of death could make beasts of even princes.

Occasionally, the troops would test their weapons immediately after repair. I admit that it took quite some time for me to acclimate myself to this practice. The violent activity would be barely prefaced with a warning shout of *"Ich schiesse!"* and then the racket of a machine pistol would echo much too close. On the first time this occurred, I hurled myself to the ground, sending the Colonel's tea tray spinning as I flopped into a miasma of mud. The group of commandos who witnessed my squirming shock regaled themselves with laughter for many minutes, and I, red-faced and smirking like a fool, was instantly baptized with the nickname "Fish."

In any event, it was late in the eve after acquiring my uniform when Himmel suddenly stomped into the small maid's chamber in which I'd fashioned my quarters. I lay upon a straw mattress, wearing my trousers, braces, a rough undershirt, and reading a Hans Christian Andersen *Märchenbuch* by the light of a candle.

"Up, Shtefan! Up! Up! Up!"

The Colonel had an unusual spring to his step and a strangely euphoric glint in his eye, traits I would come to recognize and fear as the harbingers of action with the enemy.

He disappeared and I dressed quickly, still buttoning my tunic and working my tender feet into my boots as I hurried to his makeshift office, the grand salon of the castle. A fire was crackling in the hearth, and a wooden door had been laid upon a pair of sawhorses, making for a plotting table. A large map had been laid out, with hand grenades serving as paperweights to stay the corners. Officers surrounded the table, including Captain Friedrich, a nearly white blond and frightening creature of extreme height, and three lieutenants. The company armorer, a husky, gaptoothed sergeant named Heinz, was in attendance as well. I would also come to learn that his presence at any briefing boded ill for the faint of heart.

"That is all," Himmel was saying. "Have the men ready in ten minutes."

The officers responded with heel clicks and those robotic bows, and they rushed off to their assignments. Himmel quickly turned to a wooden footlocker at the base of his desk and, without looking to confirm that I was actually present, spoke to me.

"Fold up the map," he ordered.

I carefully removed the potato-masher grenades, lifting them with the timidity of a novice butcher extracting his first entrails, and I folded the map along its creases. I noted that it was a detailed terrain of a section of the northern Italian border, which was far away to the south.

"Put it in my rear pouch."

He meant the leather satchel that was affixed to his combat webbing, that heavy harness that contained his pistol ammunition, grenades, a water bottle and his SS commando blade, engraved with a swastika and the words *Meine Ehre Heibt Treue*—My Honor's Name Is Loyalty.

"Come here."

I turned to him then. He was standing next to the footlocker with a strangely mischievous grin on his face, as if he was attempting to suppress a private joke. In his hands was a leather pistol belt. I walked to him.

"Hold out your arms."

I extended them, expecting him to lay the belt across my wrists.

"Not like that, you little idiot! Out to the *sides*."

I blushed, and then the embarrassment quickly turned to another sort of flush as I began to understand. Somewhat like a proud father fitting his son with his first pair of soccer shorts, he flicked the belt around my waist and fastened it. In the next moment, he had a heavy pistol in his hand.

"The Walther P-38," he stated crisply. "Usually reserved for officers, but you will only knock yourself silly with a rifle." He held the pistol up for me to view it laterally, and I can only imagine how my eyes must have bugged terribly wide. "You pull back the slide here," he instructed, "release it and a bullet enters the chamber." The spring-loaded steel made me wince as it struck home. "This is the safety catch," he said, then wagged a callused finger at me. "Never put it on. You will only forget and wonder why you cannot fire."

I am sure that I gulped at that point, screaming inside my head, *Why? Why do I need to know this?!*

Himmel continued. "The magazine goes in here." He rammed it home, then came up with another long rectangle of steel. "Here is an extra one. Put it in your pocket, not in a pouch. You are not a soldier yet, and you will forget where it is."

Yet? I wanted to shout. *Yet? I'm not a soldier now, nor do I ever wish to be!*

At this juncture, I began to perspire profusely. It was clear that the troop was about to embark on some disastrous adventure of which I wanted no part. I searched madly for a way out, the one turn of phrase that might free me from this avalanche.

"Herr Colonel," I stuttered. "I doubt that... I mean, Sir... I think that I might be more a danger to your venture than an asset..."

"Nonsense!" Himmel boomed, and it was then that I understood his view of the world, the war, and the rites of passage. He was offering me an honor which could not be declined. "I do not expect you to contribute anything worthwhile, Shtefan, but I do expect you to keep yourself intact. And this as well..."

He reached into the footlocker and brought out a small leather case, slapping it into my palm.

"It is a Leica and two extra rolls of film. Take photos, and stay close behind me."

I must have been regarding him with the same expression of a child who first witnesses his parents' fornication. He actually grinned at me.

"British commandos have captured a staff officer of the 1st Panzer. We are going to free him. Just before dawn. Get yourself a helmet."

With that, he strode from the room, shouting orders to Captain Friedrich. With a trembling hand, I managed to slide the pistol into my holster and snap it shut, and as instructed, I slipped the extra magazine into my trouser pocket. Then, for a moment, I considered running straight for my chamber and the servants' entrance and not stopping until I had swum the Rhine and walked all the way to France. Unfortunately, we still occupied all that part of Europe, and what might befall me in the embrace of some other Nazi officer could make this impending fate seem attractive by comparison.

There was an open bottle of wine on the commander's desk. I drank a quarter of it quickly, and followed after him...

The castle was nestled upon a small soft meadow, in the cleavage of a pair of high peaks, and we wound away from it in utter darkness. The company cook's fires danced dimly from a lower window, and I never had thought to regard that cold, bleak stone edifice as a home from which to regret departure.

I sat stiffly in the rear of Colonel Himmel's staff car. The winter months were still fresh memories, and a harsh chill made the black air brittle, yet the Kübelwagen's folding roof was not deployed, and I had to set my jaw against my chattering teeth. Behind us, two medium troop trucks with canvas roofs followed close, and despite the rutted road and trundling engines, I could hear the raiding complement of twenty-one men chattering and laughing from within. I had no doubt that I was the object of their mirth, for they had passed me by en route to debarkation, as I stood behind the Colonel clutching the camera and his map case. I no doubt served up the image of a martial jester, wearing a coal scuttle helmet too large for even an average man. Its rim fell well below my earlobes, and the commandos, sporting leopard camouflage smocks, hauling their machine pistols and light machine guns and even an anti-armor *Panzerfaust*, had unabashedly jerked their thumbs at me and howled as they boarded their trucks.

Himmel's driver, an older, mustached corporal named Edward, deftly maneuvered the car along the winding mountain roads, without benefit of headlights. Beside him the Colonel sat, erect and silent, puffing a short cigar whose smoke wafted directly back into my face. Himmel was not wearing a helmet, but only a *Feldmütze*, the SS field cap angled smartly over his bristle of gray-blond hair, and every other member of the troop was similarly cavalier. But I was grateful for my steel hat, and certainly unconcerned with being out of fashion.

After two hours of a spine-numbing drive to the south, we rose from between the copses of mountainside trees and onto a higher road bordered by gently waving grass. A sliver of moon then peaked a distant crest, and Himmel turned his head to stare at it in disgust, as if his expression might convince the orb to retreat. Yet it only rose higher, throwing some small farmhouses and cattle fences into sharp relief. Soon, we were traversing a large flat meadow, and I realized we had climbed upon a lip overlooking the winding silver waters of the Rhine so far below. On any other night, in any other life, I would have noted the beauty of such a stunning vision. Yet something else caught my attention.

Sitting at the very top of the meadow were three large forms, silhouettes the likes of which I had never seen. They appeared to be enormous iron wasps, with faces of curving glass, ugly fat tires for feet, and above, double umbrellas of long glinting sword blades. I leaned forward in my seat, my mouth certainly agape, and Himmel turned his face to me and grinned.

"Hubschrauber," he yelled above the car's engine roar. "Helicopters. Have you never seen one?"

I believe that I slowly shook my head in disbelief. I had, of course, heard that someday there would be such an airplane, one that could lift straight up into the sky without benefit of wings. But as yet, I was certain that such things existed only in the ancient notebooks of Leonardo da Vinci.

"Skorzeny prefers a Storch," Himmel continued. He meant the light aircraft favored by the infamous commando leader, Colonel Otto Skorzeny. "Scarface Skorzeny," as he was often called, was a personal favorite of Hitler and clearly a competitor for Himmel's glories. "But I managed to elicit these from the Luftwaffe. They're Dragons, experimental."

I did not know why Himmel seemed to be informing, or

rather, confiding in me. Perhaps he expected me to some-day write his memoirs? I had not long to consider this, as the staff car raced toward the first of the iron monsters. There are historians who swear that no such functional machines existed until years later, but I bear witness to the contrary. A low-pitched whine began to emanate from its massive engines, and its drooping blades began to slowly twirl. From that moment on, I was gripped by an icy fist of fear that set me to a sort of paralysis. The staff car slammed to a halt, and I sat in the back, staring and immobilized.

"Raus!" Himmel snatched at my tunic shoulder and fairly dragged me from the vehicle. I slipped and fell into the mud, and then he was pulling me along as he shouted orders to his men and to the pilots. I vaguely recall the trundle of many boots as the raiding complement ran and leaped into their respective helicopters, while Himmel pushed me to the wide open doorway of the first machine and kneed my buttocks as if I were a cow. I climbed in clumsily, already hyperventilating, gripping the Leica case as if it might save my life. Himmel stepped directly over my quivering form and squatted in the iron cavern just behind the pair of Luft-waffe pilots, and immediately the space was filled with the first seven SS of his forward element. They jockeyed for positions, falling hard on their rumps and tucking up their legs. Someone's binoculars swung and struck my helmet with a resounding ping, and I saw Himmel twirling his fin-ger in the air between the pilots and I felt my stomach leap for my throat as the horrible device left earth for heaven.

I do not know how long we flew, yet it certainly seemed forever. And I did not see very much, as for most of the

journey my eyes were clamped shut. The engines roared
like a carpenter's lathe and a freezing wind sliced through
the rattling compartment, and I remembered as a child
being forced by my father to ride the great carnival wheel
in Vienna's *Prater*, and how I had peed in my trousers, an
urge I barely contained at this moment. At one point, long
into the horrible flight, someone slapped the top of my
helmet, and I opened my eyes to see the grinning face of
Captain Friedrich, his steel blue eyes merry and his flaxen
eyebrows arched in utter thrill. He suddenly pinched my
cheek with what one might suppose a gesture of comradely
affection, yet it hurt so much I nearly yelled. But it was
then I looked to the fuselage's windows, and realized we
were in fact skimming at breakneck speed through a deep
and winding valley, and we were well *below* the peaks of
its sides. I groaned and squeezed my eyes shut once more,
and it required every muscle of my stomach not to regur-
gitate its contents.

We flew on into a breaking dawn; I could feel the growing light upon my eyelids. I heard someone bellow, "Stukas!" and I managed to take a peek. We were flying much
higher now, and astride the helicopter was a pair of the
Luftwaffe's ugly fighter-bombers. I managed to twist my
head a bit, achieving a glimpse of our other two transports
bobbing in the cold blue air not far behind, and then the
Stukas flipped over and dived away from us. Understanding
nothing of such raiding tactics, I did not know that they
were there to first bomb the perimeter of the target, with
the intent to shock the British commandos and force them
to take shelter. Nor did I realize that in order to maintain

this tactical advantage, we would immediately assault into the still-raining debris of the bombing.

I yelled then, for the helicopter suddenly tilted nose downward, and I believed we were crashing. I flung my arms out and actually hugged myself to Himmel's back, like a girl gripping a reckless horseman, and I cared not what the men would think of me or call me later on. Then all at once the horrible machine swooped up again, seemed to stop in midforward motion, and settled to the hard ground with a resounding thud of steel.

Still gripping the Colonel, my cringing face pressed against his battle harness, I was dragged from the compartment as he leaped out. I smashed to the ground, a rag doll of flopping arms and legs, and then someone yanked me up, and I saw that Himmel was already running away at full tilt and I chased after him. Following that madman into battle was not an hour before the very last intent I had, but now I wanted nothing more than to see his back filling my field of vision, and absolutely nothing else.

I do not really know what happened on that peak that morning. I was the poorest witness to history, for I saw little more than my master's form, his waving arms, the spent brass shells spinning from the chamber of his pistol. I heard nothing of distinction to remember, save the gunfire that began almost immediately upon our birthing from the helicopters, muffled and unrecognizable shouts, punctuations of screams and thudding explosions that filled my quickly deafened ears with a sensation of cotton fiber. The stench of ordnance scorched my nostrils and throat, but my ham-

mering heart pumped my lungs to take in every breath of
oxygen that would surely be my last.

All around us the men were sprinting forward in concert with Himmel's incredible pace, firing their machine
pistols and hurling their grenades. It struck me at once
that he ran with the utter arrogance of a man in his own
backyard, though he certainly had never set foot in this
place before. At one point, he suddenly stopped before a
huge concrete bunker, and of course I smashed right into
him and bounced off his pelvis. When I gained my footing again, I saw through the heavy smoke a wide entrance
to the redoubt. I bent over to try and catch my breath, and
just then a figure wearing a Tommy helmet suddenly appeared from around the corner of the edifice and Himmel
reached out his arm and shot the man point-blank. I did not
see the victim fall, for my eyes instinctively shuttered, but
when I opened them again Captain Friedrich was emerging from the bunker. He was grinning from ear to ear, his
face spidered with streaks of blood that flowed from his
now hatless blond hair, and his hand gripped the elbow of
a Wehrmacht Panzer general.

The man was clearly in shock. He was middle-aged and
gray all over, from his hair and through to the pallor of
his skin, with his tanker's tunic torn and blood spattered.
I saw his jackboots angle forward as he began to crumple,
and then Himmel gracefully stepped in, bent and slung the
officer over his shoulders like a bear rug.

"Nach Hause!" the Colonel yelled, and then he was running back toward the helicopters, the entire complement of
men close behind, spinning and firing their weapons madly

as cover. I thought I had nary a breath left in me, but my legs instructed that now was not the time to quit, and I managed to shadow my master as he ran, the general's form bouncing upon his shoulders like the fallen victim of a house fire.

The men hurled themselves into the helicopters, whose blades had never ceased to whirl, and some of them took to a knee and fired their machine pistols without end at the enraged survivors of the British hideaway. My teeth were set like those in a naked skull and my back compressed with every shot, my heart pounding in its anticipation of a bullet from behind.

Himmel suddenly stopped just at the lip of the helicopter compartment. Then he turned quite casually, the general limp upon his back.

"Did you get a photo?" he yelled at me.

Only then did I realize that the Leica had never left its pouch. I stared at it, amazed that it was still in the death grip of my fingers, and I looked up and wagged my head from side to side. The helicopter pilots were shouting, something was banging repeatedly off the iron sides of the machine, and I knew it was the impact of British bullets.

"Well?" the Colonel shouted again. "Take one!"

My mouth fell open. He could not possibly be serious! But I quickly saw that indeed we would not leave this hell unless the master had his souvenir. Somehow, my fingers managed to open the pouch and I extracted the camera. Something kicked at the mud next to my boot and I leaped a bit, while my quaking hands lifted the Leica; yet I could not even see through the viewfinder, as my eyes had filled with the tears of the absolute conviction of my death. More bullets rang off the helicopter, the blades were churning up a thunderous wind, the pilots were shrieking, and I saw Himmel grin like some ungodly and calm white hunter in the African veldt as I clicked the shutter.

And then I fainted.

In June of 1943, I became a corporal in the Waffen SS.

I shall not insult the reader with a host of limp excuses, or in any way deny that I coveted the rank and title which only months before would surely have repulsed me. However, I do beg patience in the hearing of my explanation.

Had I remained in all technicalities a civilian in the employ of the army, I would have continued to receive the concomitant pay, which amounted to essentially nothing. On the other hand, as a field draftee, and instantly granted a rank suited to my tasks as Colonel Himmel's adjutant, I would be rewarded the monthly stipend stipulated by Wehrmacht rules and regulations. Most of that pay would be recorded in my *Soldbuch*, yet issued directly to my mother in Vienna, while I retained some pocket money for the occasional purchase of a black-market treat. One might say that my motive here was purely mercenary, although the benefits to my mother, especially were I to fall in battle, assuaged my discomfort upon being issued the *Rottenführer* collar tabs.

Thus were the rewards of becoming an official member of Himmel's Commando. The drawback, at least so far as I considered it at the time, was Himmel's stipulation, which he informed me of prior to my promotion.

You see, I was still a virgin.

And the Colonel refused to have a virgin serving in his order of battle.

He was not, as far as I could assess, a sexual deviant of any sort. He simply believed that a sexually naive soldier was an incomplete man, spending too much time engaged in fantasy and wonder, carrying a needless mental burden that could prove a dangerous distraction.

"A man who has not bedded a woman spins in circles," he explained. "The hormones remain unreleased and his potential bottlenecked. Take care of this, Shtefan, and you shall receive your rank."

He was ever surprising me with some unexpected and outlandish task. But this one surpassed all other previous orders. I had by then survived three additional combat adventures with the unit, admittedly all of them barely witnessed as I crouched in the lee of the Colonel's charging silhouette, yet the prospect of my deflowering summoned a fear beyond that of physical wounding.

On that glorious summer weekend, the troop, under temporary command of Captain Friedrich, was enjoying a brief rest and recreation in Munich. It was only the Colonel, myself and his driver, Edward, who traveled the bomb-pocked Autobahn down to Salzburg. I had never been to this magnificent city of medieval castles, classical concerts and springtime carnivals, and initially I felt blessed at having been selected for the venture. The Colonel was to attend a conference of high-ranking SS officers, hosted by Heinrich Himmler himself, and he had even invited his wife to join him at the Schloss Reichenhall Hotel.

Have I failed to mention that Himmel had a wife? Oh yes, the Colonel was married, and had three young daughters as well, all of whom lived on the outskirts of Munich. I had foolishly anticipated a rather relaxed episode, full of high-born officers and their gowned wives, all dancing Viennese waltzes and sharing feasts excavated from some secret privileged stores. Yet now, the summer excursion filled me with foreboding.

Arriving in the city, which did not at first glance appear to be suffering the later stages of the war, Edward and I escorted the Colonel into his hotel. We remained some paces behind, carrying his modest valises and map cases as Himmel strode into the wide lobby, stamped to a stop and threw his arms wide to the sides. A trio of small blonde girls in white frilled dresses ran to him and leaped into his arms, and as he laughed and kissed and tickled them, his wife approached as well. She was extremely small and trim, wearing a prim gray suit, with her dark blond hair pulled tightly into a bun, and she placed a white-gloved hand upon my master's shoulder and offered him a taut cheek. In turn, he slipped a hand behind her head, angled his chin and kissed her hard upon the mouth, and then he roared with laughter as she stepped back, blushing and smoothing her suit coat as if it had been soiled.

A pair of bellmen quickly recovered the Colonel's valises from our hands, and Himmel turned and strode to us.

"You will stay at the SS barracks on Wandersee," he said.
Then he looked at me with a harsh squint. "Execute your
assignment, Shtefan, and report to me in the morning."

I saluted and clicked my heels, Edward mimicked me,
and we departed as I blew out a long, trembling sigh…

I sat stiffly beside the aging corporal in Himmel's staff
car as a cool night breeze wafted from between the dig-
nified edifices of Salzburg and the wheels trundled over
rain-polished cobblestones. I released the stay of my collar and pushed my field cap back onto my head, scratching
my brow and trying to imagine just how to go about this.
Edward was silent, though he smiled a bit and smoked as
he drove, and initially I thought him not to be privy to the
true nature of Himmel's order. But then, he spoke.

"So, Shtefan. I assume you've been ordered to fuck."

I looked at him. "You know?"

"Of course. It happens to every virgin in the troop,
though there aren't a lot of them by the time they get to us."

He was clearly enjoying this and speaking loudly above
the engine rumble, and I wanted to shush him, even though
certainly none of the pedestrians we passed could possibly overhear.

"I…but I…really know nothing about this." I fidgeted
in my seat. "How to go about it…"

"Well, you've stroked your own cock, haven't you?" he
posed as he finger-brushed the tips of his graying mustache.

I must have blushed a deep purple crimson, for the corporal glanced at me and nearly choked on his own laughter. I had meant that I had no idea how to go about locating a willing volunteer, rather than the exact physical logistics of sex. Of course, that knowledge evaded me as well, but he went right on before I could explain.

"It's pretty much the same," he said with a shrug. "But here, once you get hard, you just stick it in and pump until you squirt. If she isn't wet, you can slap some hair oil on her. But believe me, as soon as you see your first pair of tits you'll come to attention right quick!"

I began to perspire, my heart palpitating. I wiped my palms on my trousers. We passed a pair of pretty young women in long dresses and high shoes, and I imagined in my panic that even if both of them stood naked before me in the most luxurious and inviting of bedroom suites, my body would simply freeze and refuse to do my bidding. What would happen if I were, somehow, somewhere, able to find a cooperative woman, and then be unable to perform? Would Himmel have me summarily shot? Would my war record file read, in summation after so many life-threatening combat excursions, "Executed for refusal to perform his duties"?

"The very first time can be hard, though," Edward continued. "No joke. If you've never had your hand up a girl's dress before, you can panic and shut down, and your cock'll just hang there like an earthworm." He paused. "Have you?"

"What?"

"Stuck your hand up a girl's dress?"

"No." I swallowed.

"Outside? Ever felt one's tits?"

"No." I was growing sullen at this point.

"Well, then, you might have to drink some schnapps and loosen up. Of course, sometimes drinking too much can make you soft as pudding."

"Edward." I was gritting my teeth. "This isn't helping. And where shall I supposedly find this sort of woman anyway? At this hour? In a strange city?"

"Listen, boy. All cities have whores, and I know where the whores are in every city. I can smell them from ten kilometers out."

"Whores?" My nose bunched up in disgust.

"Yes, whores! Of course, whores. What'd you think, that you're going to fall in love in one hour, buy her a ring, marry her and fuck her by dawn?"

"Gott im Himmel," I groaned, and I reached up for my cap brim and pulled it down over my face, folding my arms and pouting.

We did not speak for a while. Edward smoked and hummed an annoying ditty as he drove, and although he issued no lyrics to accompany the melody, I was rather certain it to be some lewd rhyme which made him merry in his head. His gay mood depressed me even further. My mission seemed utterly impossible, no less than being ordered to steal a ring from the Kaiser's finger while he bathed in a tower of his palace, surrounded by armed footmen. Yet I was determined, in my stubborn adherence to the slim precepts of romance, to at the very least seduce some young, lonely, comely, and desperately charitable female of my own age, or thereabouts.

"So?" Edward finally said. "No whorehouse?"

"No." I pouted. "Never."

"Fine, then." He shrugged. "You can try here."

The Kübelwagen broke out into a large cobblestoned square. In its center was a towering statue of Beethoven, and as the night was pleasant and devoid of the threatening drum of aircraft engines from high above, the Salzburgers had come out to stroll and chat. Small groups of various ages milled about, and surrounding the square were a number of brightly lit taverns, their music and the laughter of their patrons echoing between the edifices.

I fastened my collar, set my cap smartly on my head and disembarked from the staff car. Edward fixed the hand brake and exited himself, brushing cigarette ashes from his tunic.

"Where are you going?" I asked him.

"With you, of course."

I frowned. The odds of my finding this night's love dropped like a brick from a Bavarian steeple, as I imagined his crude and portly form accompanying me.

"I think I can manage alone, Edward," I said as sternly as I could.

"Maybe." He arched his brows in doubt. "But if you make a pass at some officer's daughter and wind up in the clink, it'll be my ass as well as yours. So, I'm coming along, for my own safety."

I placed my hands on my hips, mimicking one of Colonel Himmel's most infamous postures.

"And how am I to succeed with you shadowing my every effort?"

He smirked at me then, shaking his head. "Don't worry.

I'll stay in the shadows and just watch your back. At any rate, in two hours you'll be begging me to help you find a nice, clean little whorehouse and get it over with."

"Humph." I straightened my shoulders and strode away toward the first tavern that presented itself, hearing Edward's boots clicking on the stones close behind. I would certainly show him. Yes, I would. I would march into one of these merry little enclaves and have a drink at the bar and strike up a conversation with one beautiful young miss. And I would charm her with my Viennese gentility and regale her with jokes and compliment her person and her scents and her magnetism, and soon she would be batting her eyelashes at me and blushing and whispering hints of a private room nearby in the servants' quarters of a town councilman. And long before dawn we would be making mad and passionate love, for perhaps the third or fourth time, upon all manners of furniture and with utterly ecstatic abandon!

Two hours later, I emerged from the fourth such establishment. I was utterly defeated, and hoping that the sheets of brothel beds were at the very least turned over after every ghastly visit.

"I told you," Edward said without genuine reproach, but rather a melancholy tone in concert with my defeat. After all, he knew that the Colonel expected him to guide me in my quest, and to assure its success.

We stood in the square just outside this latest tavern of disaster. Edward was smoking, and as always he instinctively offered me the cigarette tin. Though I had always declined before, in this instance I succumbed, and he nodded and lit my smoke with an army lighter. I coughed terribly, waiting for the rancid substance to somehow calm my nerves.

There had certainly been an abundance of suitable women in all the establishments. Of all sorts of ages, shapes and sizes, they laughed and danced and drank from deep steins of watery wartime beer. They leaned upon the shoulders of rough-looking army officers, and they pressed their cleavaged bosoms against coarse uniforms and lifted their legs to show their calves. And although in the course of two long hours I managed to elicit a dance from one matronly, middle-aged, half-drunken farm woman, essentially I felt like a boy on his first deer hunt, staring wide-eyed at the potential prey and clutching a weapon I had no idea how to use correctly. Utter disaster.

Simultaneously, Edward and I crushed out our cigarettes, sighed, and remounted the staff car. He did indeed seem able to follow the scents emanating from some distant house of ill repute, though in fact he was simply observing the direction taken by wandering army troops of the lower ranks. A quartet of half-inebriated panzer drivers sang *"Ach du lieber Augustin"* as they staggered along a narrow road, elbows locked and joking about the deleterious effects of alcohol on proper erections, and Edward knew to simply tag along with the car.

He stopped as we approached a row of tall, narrow, three-story apartment buildings. Their faces were of broken brickwork, and they were squeezed together like gravestones in an overcrowded cemetery. Two of the buildings had large street-front windows, with heavy brocade curtains and a reddish lamp glow bleeding through the frays.

Apparently, this was a signal which clearly spoke to the corporal, though it was unrecognized by me.

"Come, boy," he said, and I steeled myself and followed him into the first such building. He passed through the heavy front door without so much as flipping the iron knocker, and immediately we found ourselves in a dark and decrepit sitting room, occupied by an elderly matron cocooned in a threadbare housecoat and woolen slippers. She sat upon a worn purple divan, reading a pfennig novel by candlelight, and I prayed that this gray-haired matron was not the only prospect in the house. She looked up and grinned, her mouth a garden of broken teeth.

"*Guten Abend!*" she croaked. "Your pleasure, gentlemen?"

"Yes, that," Edward snapped. "If there's anything here to please us."

"*Einen Moment.*" The old woman struggled to her feet and hobbled away somewhere, while I jammed my hands into my pockets, looking about at the fading portraits of German composers and Alpine apple orchards, and attempted to summon my most casual whistle. It was nowhere within me.

A pair of women sauntered into the room. The first of them was black-haired, middle-aged, and powerful in the appearance of her musculature beneath a heavy emerald dress. The thick makeup upon her face looked almost clownish, her lips heavy and blood red, her eyes outlined in inky borders, and the upper portion of her dress was unlaced, revealing a bosom that appeared to me to be as large as the rump of a pig. The second woman was somewhat more youthful and substantially smaller of stature. Her dark blond hair was braided into "strudel" coils astride her ears, and her attire resembled that of a beer-garden waitress, replete with its white bodice and billowing short sleeves. Upon her feet she wore high black boots, laced up the center to her shins, and her face was also overly masked with paint. I tried to blur the image of her mouth, for its lipstick was somewhat askew and I dared not imagine the cause.

"You take Sylvia?" The old woman, who now peeked from behind her prostitutes, gestured at the larger of the two women and winked at Edward.

"All right," he said, and I was immediately grateful, as he was clearly volunteering to mount this creature in deference to the better choice for me.

"And you want Heidi, *ja?*" The old woman lightly slapped the rump of the blonde "waitress" as she jutted her trembling chin in my direction. Heidi smiled, showing a chipped front tooth and the tip of her tongue.

I managed a nod, even as I experienced an icy chill throughout my spine.

"Twenty reichsmarks apiece," said the madame, very curtly.

"Ten." Edward snapped a reply.

"Fifteen!" The old woman raised a gnarled finger.

I was then engaged in turning my trouser pocket inside out, and counting some rumpled bills and coins.

"I am afraid I have no more than ten," I stuttered.

"Ten it'll be, then," Edward said to the old one. "Or nothing."

"All right." The madame stuck her thumbs in the belt

of her housecoat. "But you can fuck them for fifteen minutes. No more."

"Half an hour," Edward shot back.

"Twenty minutes!" She returned his serve.

I was certain I would require no more than a paltry minute myself, and only that if my already rebelling penis would suddenly take flight in an Olympian miracle.

Edward took the black-haired wench by her wrist and immediately moved toward a creaking stairway, and as he passed me by he whispered, "Just think of Ava Gardner."

I stared after him. I did not know who that was, and was lost for a substitute image. I found myself temporarily immobilized, while Heidi lifted the hem of her dress and too mounted the stairway. She stopped after a meter's progress, turned to me and beckoned with a finger, and I swallowed hard and followed.

Within a minute, I found myself standing before her in a small and dimly lit room, rather like the cabin of a steamship. There may have been a washstand, a small desk and a single chair, but I do not really recall, for my eyes were locked on the narrow bed covered with rumpled and graying sheets.

Heidi immediately plopped herself down on the edge of this newlyweds' paradise, sitting quite erect and spreading her boots. She regarded me with what she might have supposed to be doe's eyes, and placed a flirtatious finger in her mouth. With her other hand, she quickly lifted her dress and gathered its hem about her waist, revealing short, puffy white bloomers encasing her bare thighs. Then, with the practiced grace of a magician's assistant, she quickly dragged them off, down over her knees, and allowed them to hang about one ankle, while I stood there and stared at her in utter shock, as if the furry mouth that now presented itself to me was the maw of a dragon.

I could not move. My hands were clenched into tight fists, angled straight down astride my trouser legs, as if I might be at attention on parade. My breaths came in short rasps of panic through my nostrils, and although I tried with every muscle to summon some sensation in my groin, in truth I seemed to be utterly paralyzed from the neck down.

The woman giggled then, which quickly shot my face through with a roaring blush. She seemed to believe that my paralysis was simply a temporary lack of ardor, perhaps akin to a stubborn auto engine requiring coaxing on a winter morn. And so, she quickly unlaced her bosom bodice, slid her hands inside her upper dress, and scooped her breasts out into the air, where they settled upon her torso like a pair of cycloptic jellyfish. This attempt had no effect whatsoever, other than to further widen my eyes and tremble my knees.

For a moment, Heidi cocked her head at me, then quickly leaned forward and reached out for my tunic. I watched her hands as they deftly flashed the flaps aside, unbuttoned my braces, and within an instant I was standing there with my trousers and shorts about my boots. As she gripped me in her hand and opened her mouth, I confess that I squeezed my eyes shut and prayed. But it was all to no avail, as her enthusiastic tongue and lips managed only to soak me in a warm sort of slime, through which nothing worthwhile of me emerged.

"No, my dear?" She finally spoke, perhaps thinking that some romantic lingual engagement might encourage me. "Then let's try it this way, *Schatzi*!"

She suddenly fell back upon the bed, raising and separating her legs as she dragged me down, my body stiff as bone in every place but where it mattered. And I fell upon her, bumping hair muff to hair muff, flesh to flesh, and she twisted and bucked and ground her hips and gripped my buttocks and bit down onto my earlobe. But we remained unjoined, and I felt nothing more than sublime humiliation.

At last, she ceased her futile efforts and turned her head to regard a cuckoo clock on the wall. "So, that's it, poor boy!" she exclaimed as she jumped up.

Within a minute, I was fully dressed and outside on the street, waiting for Edward as I cursed Himmel and Hitler and the entire Reich, not to mention God, who was equally the culprit…

"You didn't?" Edward was driving once more and regarding me, post-confession, as if I had failed to feed my own starving child. "What do you mean, you didn't?!"

Silence for a moment.

"I couldn't."

"You didn't even try?"

"*I* tried. *She* tried. *All* of the angels in Himmel's version of *hell* tried."

"Was there something wrong with her?"

"I have nothing with which to compare."

"Well…did she have some hideous scar or something?"

"I believe she was biologically normal."

"Then what the hell was wrong?"

"Nothing happened. I couldn't… It wouldn't…"

He paused for a moment, shaking his head slowly and sadly. "And you paid her as well."

"Yes."

"Ten reichsmarks. And now you're broke, to boot."

"My poverty is hardly of great concern at the moment."

We drove in silence, like a disenchanted couple, both pairs of eyes forward yet seeing little more than images of our Colonel's express disappointment, which was bound to rise along with the morning's sun. We found ourselves headed back to the Beethoven Square, which seemed as appropriate as Napoleon's return to kick the corpses at Waterloo.

"Ohhh." I finally blew out a sigh. "I want to get drunk."

"That's certainly not going to help."

"At this point, Edward, it does not matter. I am hardly going to attempt this again." I fished in my pocket and found a few remaining pfennig.

"All right, then. What the hell."

We soon found ourselves once again in one of the taverns on the square. At this juncture, Edward seemed quite spent, and I was not surprised given the physically hardy appearance of his recent paramour. He wandered over to a table in one corner, collapsed into a chair and waved at someone for a large beer.

The establishment was full of Wehrmacht officers, all laughing and drinking and hurling jokes across the room at their compatriots. Many of them were crowded about large round tables, some with local women pulled onto their laps, and more than one enthusiastic game of cards was being played out. Crackling music was loudly expressed from a gramophone atop the tavern bar, and the open floor between the bar and tables was full with quickly prancing couples, some swaying and clutching enormous beer steins. All in all I must have saluted twenty times as I carefully shouldered my way between these men, the long oak bar eventually appeared through the crowd, and I swam to it like a drowning sailor spotting a bobbing timber.

Exhausted in spirit and body, I climbed up onto an empty stool at the very farthest corner of the bar, placed one elbow on the polished and puddled wood, and rested my forehead in my hand. I had arrived at a very dark place in this stage of my life. It seemed that, until this night, my adventures in the army had been, although life-threatening, also exhilarating in some sense. Yet now I wanted none of it, and the reality of my predicament had come tumbling down, the realization triggered by the failure of my most basic libidinous necessity. I was hardly a man, and what made me think myself capable of surviving in the world I now inhabited? If I could not meet this most simple challenge, what might my master next present? Some task that would surely mean my death, instead of my humiliation. I began to plan my escape, knowing full well that desertion would also mean certain execution if I were ever caught. I nearly sobbed.

"And what can I do for you, handsome boy?"

I lifted my head. The barmaid, whom I had not heretofore noticed, stood directly in my vision. I noted first her smile, for it was warm and very wide and replete with fine teeth, without a hint of decay or breakage. Her long brown hair was pulled behind her neck, and her matching eyes were wide and friendly. She wore a very modest dark blue dress, buttoned tastefully to her throat.

I grimaced more than smiled, and I touched the brim of my cap and then removed it. "Is the beer expensive?" I asked.

"I don't think so." Her smile warmed further. "Five pfennig."

I frowned and shrugged. "I am afraid I have only three."

"As I said, three pfennig." She winked.

She turned away for a moment, and her movement appeared to be nearly a pirouette, for in an instant she faced me once more, a high glass mug with a snowcap of foam in her hand. She plunked it down on the bar before me, and I pushed my last scraps of pay across the wood.

"*Danke,*" I said as I pulled the heavy glass closer.

"*Bitte.*" She nodded. Then she glanced up at a clock on the wall behind the bar, and she smoothly removed a white apron, folded it and tucked it away somewhere. "I think I'll have one as well." She poured herself a similar helping of beer from a huge keg, then pulled up a stool from her side of the oak and perched upon it. She raised her glass in my direction.

"I do not want to make trouble for you," I said, glancing about for her employer.

"I'm off now. A girl deserves a rest, don't you think?"

She clicked her glass against mine and sipped her foam, and I watched her as I did the same. She grinned as she swept a slim white line from her upper lip with her finger.

"I'm Francie," she said.

"I am pleased to meet you. I'm Shtefan."

She looked at me then, slightly tilting her head. One must realize that we were forced to speak very loudly above the din.

"You are wearing SS tabs, Shtefan."

"Yes." It was curious to feel that I was unworthy of such a dastardly coterie of warriors.

"I always think of them as older, and larger. And killers. You don't seem to fit the image."

"I'm just the commander's adjutant." I was desperately uneasy with this young woman. She was pretty and very open, and I was the world's most pathetic fraud on every front.

"Ahhh." She nodded and sipped some more, and I did the same, and we watched the room and were silent for a moment. Then, "And how old are you, Shtefan?"

"Nineteen."

"I am twenty-three."

"I wish I was twenty-three already."

Naturally she did not understand my wish, being unable to connect it to my sexual status.

"And what are your tasks, for your commander?" she inquired, then suddenly touched her finger to her lips. "I should not ask you that. It might be a military secret."

She was not joking, but I suddenly began to laugh. It came from somewhere deep and melancholy, a well of irony in my groin, and I had no control over the bitter mirth that racked my body as I threw my head back and tears actually sprang to my eyes.

"Why is that so funny?"

"My *tasks*..." I could not breathe, I was laughing so hard. "I...I must..."

"You must what, Shtefan?"

"I must lose my virginity!" At this point I was holding my chest, and I had to replace the mug upon the bar or spill its entire contents. "That's the horrendous secret that must not be divulged! That is the shame for which my Colonel will not stand!"

I do not know why I vented my pain thusly to a stranger, but perhaps I could no longer contain my frustration, and she seemed a likely creature to sympathize. Eventually I calmed myself and settled back into silence. I held the mug with one hand, and with the other I rubbed my brow, and as I dared to look up at her again, I found her regarding me with the empathy of a kind nurse.

"Yes." I nodded. "So foolish, isn't it? That's what's important in the military social scale. To be one of the men, to be undistracted by adolescent fantasy. And it's an *order*, not a request. Isn't that so cruel?" I paused and sipped, then raised a finger. "Believe me, I've *tried* to obey. I have tried all night this very night, but it seems the pathetic, romantic images of my youth have enslaved me with an inability to execute this task on command. I wish I were such an animal, but I am not." I restrained myself then, my voice falling to a murmur. "I apologize. I should not be so crude."

Another long moment of silence passed between us, such as it was among the raucous music and laughter. Francie seemed to be thinking, looking off into nothing, and slightly nodding her head as if a rush of warm memories passed before her eyes.

"And, so?" She regarded me again. "What shall happen to you now?"

"Who knows?" I shrugged. There was no point in humiliating myself further.

"Did you try a prostitute?" she asked plainly.

I blushed so deeply then, a wave of shame washing from my neck and up to the roots of my hair. "Yes… But it was no good."

"I did not expect so." She nodded once again. "Young men want to be gentle, although they will never admit so. Young men must pretend to be virile and uncaring and always prepared to take such a reward, paid for or not, but we know it is all a lie." She placed her fingers lightly on my sleeve as she drank a long pull with her other hand. "The truth is, young men just want to be kissed."

I nodded in agreement, although I was utterly mortified at this juncture. Her words comforted me little, as I did not need a psychologist, but rather a miracle.

"Where are your comrades, Shtefan?" She looked over my shoulder and around the establishment, and I confess that my heart sank a bit. I did not expect this pretty young woman to volunteer herself on my behalf, but her question clearly indicated a wish to change the subject.

"I am only here with Edward, the commander's driver," I answered, as I glanced over my shoulder and jutted my chin in his direction. He was yet perched in his comfortable corner, downing his third stein of beer.

"Is that him?" Francie pointed. "The gray one with the belly?"

"Yes."

Francie dismounted her stool and smoothed her dress, and without saying another word to me, she made off from behind the bar. I watched her with a frown, having not a clue as to her intentions. Yet, as she made her way through the crowd toward Edward's table, I could only imagine some sort of horror. Was she a Gestapo agent? Was she determined to relay my dismay at the unfair commandments of my master? Did she have some sort of ticket book in which she had to maintain a recorded quota of inebriated betrayals?

The facts, which I did not know until much later, were thus. Francie marched right up to Himmel's driver, smiled and offered a small curtsy.

"Edward, where does Shtefan have to be tonight?"

He was apparently quite drunk, his eyes shot through with crimson spiders and his lips drooling. "Shtefan? He has to be buried in something...or wind up *really* buried in something!"

"Where is the commander headquartered, Edward?" Francie was a patient girl, having dealt with thousands of drunkards.

"At the Reichenhall," he slurred.

"Shtefan shall be there in the morning."

And with that she walked away from him and returned to the bar. Somewhere en route, she had recovered a white shawl, and she hooked her fingers in my elbow and stood still for a moment and smiled at me.

"Come, Shtefan," she said firmly, though with her gentle smile. "Apparently, someone has sent you a gift…"

Francie lived in a single room, at the rear of a large house that had once been a luxurious private home, but was divided up into apartments for the course of the war. She had her own entrance, and it revealed a small hallway, a small bath and a cozy salon in which her perfectly made-up bed was the overbearing feature. Absolutely everything was neat and in place, from her books to her framed family photographs to her rack of pressed clothes and a small dresser of her private things. I confess that at the time I did not really take much of this in, as en route to her abode along the silent cobblestone streets my heart was keeping up a drumbeat. We had hardly spoken at all, while she held my hand and seemed as light-footed as I was light-headed.

When we entered her room, we stood for a moment, very still. Next to me, she held my fingers lightly, and we faced the bed. It was very silent here, save for the occasional vehicle swishing by outside, and at last she nearly whispered, "This is a safe place for you."

And I believed her. She turned to me then and reached up her hands to touch my face. She was shorter than I, and she came to her tiptoes and lightly brushed her lips over my furrowed brow. And then, her hand removed my cap, while the other held my chin, and she touched her mouth to mine. I closed my eyes. Her lips were like warm silk, and my own lips seemed to melt slowly into hers, like bars of cold pewter surrendering to a blacksmith's fire.

She kissed me deeply on the mouth, for a very long

time, and at last I allowed my fists to open, and my hands to venture up to her waist. She pulled me somehow closer, and I felt her hand reach for mine, and when she placed it, gently upon her breast, I felt a shudder flash from my knees to my neck.

Somehow, she never really stopped kissing me, as she managed to pull her dress up and over her head, and as she deftly helped me to lose my uniform. She was young, but precociously wise as I view her now, for she knew that my attention would be focused on her mouth, while by way of sweet deception she revealed the secrets I had heretofore so feared. It was not long before we stood there without any clothes at all, and the very first true caress of my body to a woman's, that incredible softness of her full breasts pressed against my chest, is a sensation that comes only once, no matter how often it be repeated in life.

She did not touch me below the waist, until we lay together upon the bed for a long, long time. She helped my fingers explore her body, moving with each new moment of my learning, and if her quickened breathing was a practiced strategy I did not care, and all of it soon had its effect. And when at last she reached down for me, the touch of her cool fingertips caused me to fairly leap to her attentions, and before I knew what was happening I was inside her, and I groaned as if my last breath was being expelled from my lungs.

She hugged me then with all of her strength, and she swayed beneath me and used her folded legs to help me, and she kissed my mouth and my cheeks and my ears, and as I lost control and the room swayed and a profound joy and dizziness overtook my body, she whispered hoarsely, "Yes, Shtefan. *Yes.*"

And it seemed that the explosive release that then coursed through my entire being was matched only by her happiness that, somehow, she had managed to find one good thing about this war...

IV

IN SEPTEMBER OF 1943, my master became a hero.

It was in the autumn of that year that we made our pilgrimage to Berchtesgaden, during which my commander was dubiously blessed by the personal, though quite absentminded, bestowment of the Knight's Cross by the Führer himself. The summer months had been deceptively languid, while interspersed with four more lightning raids into Pantelleria, Palermo, the Italian Alps and Corfu, where Himmel's reckless courage seemed only to blossom further. The men of the Commando whispered that he would surely be rewarded very soon.

Yet given the dismissive and disappointing nature of this coronation of the nation's bravest men, I felt a certain sorrow for Colonel Himmel, that he should give so much of himself and receive barely a nod in return, despite the medal itself. Yet in viewing the graceful manner in which the commander absorbed this reality of state, I realized that he, most certainly like all the officers present, had long ago accepted the fact that his courage was simply an integral part of his makeup. He most probably knew, already as a child, that he would accomplish great deeds of daring, and the trappings that would someday result were to be thought of as no more than diplomas. Medals were merely signatures upon the histories of dutiful deeds, which would have transpired with or without them.

And so, with the black Maltese medal and ribbon draped about his collar, Himmel withdrew from this elaborate and melancholy ceremony as quickly as protocol would allow. Edward and I had to fairly chase after him as he fled the *Schloss* and quick-marched down along the curving entrance drive, slapping his leather gloves into his palm and smacking his jackboots on the cracked concrete. He reached the staff car, hopped into the compartment without opening the door, turned and raised his arms high.

"*Schnell!* Back to work!" he yelled, and I thought that his grin was twisted up at its edges by force of will. It was difficult even for a man such as Himmel to accept the clay feet of his mentors.

We drove now to Bad Tölz, that quaint Bavarian town astride the Isar, where the Waffen SS held its headquarters and central barracks. In preparation for some special assignments, the unit had been relocated to this hub of commando activity, awaiting further glories. The trip from Berchtesgaden, while less than 150 kilometers, began after midnight and required considerable maneuvering over pocked peasant roads. I sat next to Edward, with the commander perched in his proper place behind me, and after an hour I began to nod off despite the trundling of the wheels over deep ruts. Himmel swatted me on the back of my cap.

"You shall not sleep, my corporal, while your commander plots!"

I snapped my head up, rubbed my eyes and saluted smartly without turning. I was also grinning, as was Edward, and I knew my master was doing the same. This had become rather a joke between us, for our strange trio had traveled thousands of kilometers together, and our humors had found a way to intersect despite the ranks.

Our quarters in Bad Tölz were not inside the SS buildings nearby the ancient spa, for our unit's tasks were considered exceptionally secret even within this environment. Unfortunately, this meant that the Commando temporarily resided in a row of giant field tents, and although these were outfitted with iron woodstoves and sufficient bedding upon our canvas cots, the now constant rains chilled us from our boots to our bones. To a man, myself included, we were anxious to receive a new assignment and an improved residential position, even if that meant a shattered bunker at some remote and thunderous front.

As we finally approached the encampment this night, it was clear that something strange was afoot. Rising from the eastern valleys along the curving cattle road, there was a strange glow in the sky above the camp, and as we neared it an enormous bonfire appeared amid the horseshoe arrangement of tents. Torches had been fired up and staked about the perimeter, and all three of us sat up in our seats as we squinted at an honor guard comprised of the men.

They embraced the final roadway entrance to the camp,

standing stiffly at attention in two long rows, face-to-face. Their jackboots and black helmets were polished, their buckles sparkling and bayonets held high to form a nuptial canopy. I could see the corpse of a fat wild boar being turned on a spit above a crackling fire, and a large plotting table had been laid out with bowls of fruits, piles of cakes and kegs of beer.

If Hitler himself had casually dismissed the courageous exploits of my master, Himmel's men had not. The Colonel raised a fist and whispered something, and Edward stopped the car. The commander slowly disembarked, smoothing his tunic and setting his SS officer's Death's Head cap as he would hardly do for any officer of the General Staff. He carefully pulled his gloves onto his hands, and I swear I saw him swallow hard as he began to march toward his men, and they began to sing the Horst Wessel song with enormous and fervent power, their voices echoing off the surrounding hills.

Edward and I slid out from the staff car, looked at each other, and fell into pace behind our master, though at a respectful distance. He marched crisply up along the access road, approaching his roaring honor guard, and the sight of these warriors under a black sky tinged with fire would have imbued even Leni Riefenstahl with a chill. Before Himmel reached the mouth of this canopy of bayonets, a ginger-haired lieutenant named Schneller stamped up to his side, saluted smartly and spun to escort the Colonel through the steel cordon. Simultaneously, at the far side of the tunnel of troops, Captain Friedrich mounted an ammunition crate. In one hand he clutched a large SS banner mounted

on a makeshift flagpole. With the other, he snapped and
unfurled a small scroll.

The men finished their chorus. Himmel stopped before
Friedrich, clasped his gloved hands behind his back and
looked up at the captain. Friedrich began his recitation, and
from my position well back of the ceremony, the scene was
reminiscent of a wedding, contrived by Dante.

"A Colonel by rank, a King by courage,
A Shepherd to wolves, an Angel of warriors,
Lead us forth into temptations, of blood and fire,
Have no doubts of our duty, sacrifice or desire,
Be there medals or none, until death's final knell,
We shall follow you, Commander, to the bowels of Hell."

I raised an eyebrow. Clearly, the captain was a crude
poet, yet the men thrice shouted, "To hell!" in thunderous unison as Friedrich stepped off his perch and presented
Himmel with a perfectly polished Prussian cavalry sword.
He also handed him the scrolled recitation, signed by each
of the unit and now bound by Schneller with a crimson
ribbon, and all three men saluted each other and clicked
their boot heels.

Himmel turned to his complement of commandos. I
could see, even at a distance, that his smile quivered a bit,
and his one eye shone as if he had imbibed a liter of alcohol. It seemed that he wished to speak, but he could not
manage it, and so instead he thrust the cavalry sword high
into the air and the men shouted and cheered and surrounded him, each clasping his hand and gesturing at his
Knight's Cross. Lieutenant Gans, who had a scar across his
full lips that foiled every smile, grinned as I'd never seen,

and the giant Sergeant Meyer's soft brown eyes and baby face glowed with admiration. They then raised the Colonel upon their shoulders, like the captain of a champion soccer team, and carried him to the table of food and drink.

From somewhere a hand-cranked gramophone began to crackle Bavarian folk bands into the chilled air, and the party carried on for over two hours. There was considerable taking of beer and wine, and the men joked and danced and even held an impromptu wrestling match between a pair of light machine gunners, and wagers were made and lost and I was certainly pleased to be well included as a member of the troop. "Drink, Fish!" became a constant rallying cry as so many in turn forced a steel cup of beer into my hand, and before long I was laughing and celebrating as if I had been born into this brood of unpredictable panthers.

At 3:00 a.m., a dispatcher on motorcycle interrupted the festivities. The roar of his BMW approaching the fires quelled the laughing and shouting, and he dismounted, raised his goggles, marched straight to Himmel and offered a stiff-armed "Heil Hitler." The Colonel, who was now sweating and red-faced from spinning out a Bavarian jig, immediately stilled himself, scowling as he tore open the envelope.

He stepped closer to a torch and squinted for some time at the missive. Then, he folded it and placed it into his tunic pocket. The men watched him, quietly drinking their beers, and he shrugged and smiled wanly as he dismissed the messenger.

"Well, my comrades," he said at last. "There is a time to laugh, and a time to kill..."

★ ★ ★

The Commando traveled from the onset of dawn, and all throughout the following day and well into the evening. With our staff car in the lead, we first set out northeast for Regensburg, then made northwest for Erlangen, and Himmel hardly spoke at all but to issue short directional orders. Save the cook, Heinz the armorer and a single private, the entire complement was along, yet none of us but the master knew our destination. This in itself was unusual, for once a mission was afoot, the Colonel customarily shared each detail that might aid success in martial tactics. Yet on this terribly long day, Edward and I suffered in his silence, left to ponder only the bomb-ravaged countryside and count the horses drawing caissons and supply carts toward the distant fates of other men.

I had, by this juncture, enough experience to assess a task by virtue of its preparation. When the Colonel ordered lightweight loads of personal battle harnesses, weapons and field caps, it was likely to be a lightning effort and mercilessly short. And by counterpoint, should he insist on satchel explosives, support mortars and helmets, my bowels cringed with the certainty of artillery and heavy resistance. However, on this day the unit was posting far from its headquarters, and it might well be tasked additionally while en route, so everything but the kitchen trough was aboard our trucks, making an educated guess quite impossible.

However, what chilled my spine and set my mind to racing over every imaginable fantasy on this excursion was the order Himmel had snapped at me just prior to embarkation.

"Leave your pistol, Shtefan."

I had looked at him then, touching the butt of my holstered weapon possessively. The sidearm that I had so initially despised had become something of an amulet.

"Might I not need it, Herr Colonel?" I asked.

"Leave it. I do not want you to have it today."

I obeyed, of course, and had reluctantly relegated the tool to my footlocker. And based upon some instinct, I did not even attempt to carry the Leica that had made itself a necessity heretofore.

With dusk, we were on the road to Schweinfurt, carrying on deeply into the heart of Germany. With each kilometer, we extended the range from any possible front, a fact that further stirred my curiosity into a whirlpool of discomfort. At last, and sometime close to midnight, the moon rose above the hills and hued the high, frothy clouds with fringes of silver, and we turned from the main road and wound our way up into the deep forests of the Hassberger. There, thousands of pines stabbed at the pale night sky with black and spiny spears, and it seemed that there was nowhere left to go but the looming cap of a windswept mountain.

A pair of dim headlights flashed then, a signal that briefly illuminated a broken road among the forest. Edward slowed the staff car and picked his way along this rising passageway, its shoulders eerily shadowed by the towering trunks and needled branches of the enormous trees. Our headlights then fell upon the flanks of a similar car, yet unlike our own field Kübelwagen, this one was enameled in a deep and polished black, its swastika emblem perfect and unmarred, its chrome fixtures buffed to a gleam. Four officers sat like expressionless mummies inside the car, their heavy leather coats and black peaked caps the calling cards of Gestapo. One of them raised a gloved finger and crooked it, and their car turned and made up the slope, and we followed.

We broke into a large grassy clearing at the crest of this height. A cold wind ruffled the wild meadow, and the moon made its greenery into a ghostly pale blue, and in the distances far below the dim lights of townships flickered like star clusters in undiscovered galaxies.

The Gestapo vehicle halted at the fringe of this clearing. Edward parked a bit to its rear and flank, as if avoiding some sort of infection by contact. Our lorries slowly gathered to the left, and I could hear the canvas flaps snapping up and the men mumbling and stretching their cramped limbs as they hopped to the wet ground. For some unexplained reason, there were no shouts of command, only whispers as if in a rectory.

Edward and I stayed in place as Himmel got out of the car, meeting his Gestapo counterpart halfway between the vehicles. My master pulled his orders from his pocket, and the conversation that was carried to me on the wind I shall not forget.

"What is this exactly about?" Himmel asked without so much as a greeting.

"You have your orders." The Gestapo officer looked not at my commander, but simply gazed out over the night's panorama.

"And I shall follow them, as always," Himmel growled. "And as always, I will know the intent of my mission before its commencement."

The Gestapo officer did not turn his head nor change his expression. He merely placed his hands behind his back, and lifted his nose as if sensing something foul on the wind.

"These men are British and Canadian flying officers," he said. "They have escaped from Stalag Luft Six."

"Then why not simply return them to Stalag Six?"

"They have escaped four times. The rest are to be furnished a lesson."

Himmel lifted his chin a bit, then nodded once in understanding, if not heartfelt compliance. He snapped open the order sheet and pulled a pen from his pocket.

"Sign the orders, Hauptmeister," he said.

The Gestapo officer turned to him, raising an eyebrow. "They have already been signed by the Führer."

"Then you should have no issue with signing them as well." Himmel's tone left no quarter for quarrel. He extended the papers and the pen. The Gestapo officer snatched them up, signed them with a scrawl and handed them back. He then marched to his staff car, leaned inside and placed a radio handset to his head. I watched my Colonel as he turned and strode off to Captain Friedrich, who had now formed our men into the ranks, where they waited with their weapons slung, stamping their boots a bit to ward off the bitter chill.

It was not long before the strain of heavy engines reached us. More headlights appeared from the far side of the wood, and a pair of unmarked trucks made their way into the clearing. As they stopped, a small unit of Luftwaffe field security guards hopped from the trucks, opened the tailgates, and began helping the passengers down onto the grass.

These men, perhaps thirty in all, were dressed in all manner of civilian coats and sweaters, some with torn woolen trousers and more than a few missing a shoe here and there. A pair of the prisoners had apparently been wounded somehow, as white soiled bandages were tied about their arms and thighs. None of them had shaved or washed in at least a week. All of them were blindfolded.

It was then that my heart began to hammer in my chest. Until that point, I had not truly fathomed the conversation between my master and this arrogant secret policeman, and now my mind could not accept what my intestines began to grasp. This was not possibly the mission that had been thrust upon us at the climax of our merriment. It could not be that a hero such as Himmel would be rewarded for his gallantry and glories by this horrible staining of his honor. This Germany that I had come to know within a cocoon of dedicated patriots could not in any way acquiesce or participate in cold-blooded murder!

The scene before me began to blur then, like a half-remembered nightmare on the edge of waking. My eyes began to fill and I could not breathe, and my hand gripped the ledge of the vehicle door, my knuckles white and my nose snorting steam into the air. I watched as Himmel issued an order to Friedrich, and the Commando moved silently forward, taking up a long position in line abreast. Across from them, atop the rounded summit of the clearing, the Luftwaffe troops almost gently formed the prisoners into a similar line. Himmel then strode to the Gestapo officer, who frowned at him, and then the two were engaged in some sort of row. Yet at last, the leather-frocked policeman hissed at his own adjutant, and this young man hurried to the Luftwaffe guards.

He returned leading a tall Allied pilot by the elbow. This man was clearly the ranking officer of the prisoners, and he stepped carefully and with the lanky North American grace I'd observed in films, until at last being left off to one side, alone.

Himmel approached him. The blindfolded airman lifted his head as my master spoke, so quietly that none of us could hear the exchange, nor whether it was in English or German. Though transfixed by the scene, I realized that in the background the Luftwaffe guards had quickly withdrawn, leaving nothing between the prisoners and our troops, who were now silently unslinging their weapons. I saw the flash of a cigarette as Himmel offered it to the tall Canadian pilot. He touched the man on his forearm, and my throat constricted as I was swept with the vision of my father once treating our mortally ill German shepherd just so. And I remember something of a small smile appearing on the pilot's lips as he declined the smoke and said something, and then Himmel suddenly drew his pistol, cranked back the slide and shot the man directly in his forehead.

I believe that I yelled. I do not really remember. But I do recall that Edward's hand smacked down onto my leg and gripped me so hard that I bit my lip. Yet my exclamations were irrelevant, nor were they heard, for in concert with the Colonel's gunshot our commandos cocked their own weapons and opened fire. I squinted and groaned, and my entire body shook as if I in fact was the recipient of every bullet, and the entire meadow exploded with hundreds of horrible flashes, and I wept as the silhouettes of those men danced macabre pirouettes and smashed to the earth.

It was over in less than ten seconds. The wind quickly snatched away the echoes of gunfire and the stifling smoke, and all that was left were our troops; erect, silently lowering their weapons, clearing and checking their breeches. Himmel stepped forward toward the ragged line of corpses, and Friedrich made to join him but the Colonel waved his captain back into place. My master strode carefully; I could see his back bend a bit here and there. Something moved then among the tangle of bodies, and he walked to that slim evidence of life and quickly snuffed it out with another pistol shot, and I jumped and gripped the door ledge once again.

"Wipe your eyes."

Edward was whispering something.

"What?" I could barely breathe.

"Wipe your eyes, damn you!" he gritted.

I swatted my gloves at my eyes, and then my cheeks. They came away wet and I smeared them on my trousers.

Himmel was striding back toward the car, his face set in an expression I had never witnessed as he holstered his pistol. The Gestapo officer was standing alongside his own car, his fists to his hips, and he jutted his chin at our commander as he passed.

"What about the burial, Herr Colonel?"

"That is not my department," Himmel snapped, and immediately he was flinging open the door to our car and slamming himself into the rear seat. Already our troop was remounting the trucks, the engines revving. The Gestapo officer was an ignorant and foolishly brave man, for he was shortly beside our staff car, thrusting a hand and an envelope into Himmel's lap.

"There will be more of this," the secret policeman said, and I fought the urge to thrust my own hand out and choke him as he nearly smiled. "The program in the camps is falling behind. You and your ilk will be expected to help out."

"Drive, Edward," Himmel nearly shouted as he snatched the envelope from the Gestapo man, and Edward gunned the engine and spun the wheel, and I heard a spew of curses from that horrid fascist as he was engulfed in a spray of mud.

But I did not look back. And I was frozen in that physical pose and paralyzed state of mind for so many hours, that I absorbed nothing of the return trip to Bad Tölz. In those few minutes on that windswept hill, everything had changed, and nothing in my life or in that of those around me would ever recover to dance or sing or celebrate anything again, as we had done only so few hours before.

We stopped once en route, so that the men could stretch and relieve themselves and partake of some cold combat rations. There was none of the usual roadside banter customary to these excursions. The few men who attempted a joke were met with cold stares through clouds of cigarette smoke.

I stood shivering at the roadside ditch, my fists clenched inside my trouser pockets, staring off into nothing. Himmel turned me around with a hand on my shoulder, and a small shock coursed through me with his touch.

"A letter arrived for you yesterday, Shtefan," he said. He was not looking at me, but watching his troops for the signs of cracks in their demeanor. "It had been opened by

Field Security, but I returned it. I said it was an error, that it must have been intended for some *other* Shtefan Brandt."

I looked up at him, watching his face, waiting. His black eye patch had frayed at the edges, and I reminded myself to furrow in his cache for a fresh one, then felt a wave of nausea sting my gullet.

"This war has turned to something else," Himmel said quietly. "But it will not matter. There will be more of such crimes, yet some of us must execute our duties." His gloved hand gripped my shoulder briefly, and I winced, though not from any physical pressure. "You know, Shtefan," he stated, "a warrior may send out his falcons. But he also knows that they may well come home to roost." He paused for a moment, exhaling through his nose. "In the end, your kind will find my kind. Yes, you will."

He turned from me then, and I was left attempting to decipher in a rush the intent of his words. It was as if he were assigning to me the care of his soul, or perhaps, the role of his judge in what might come to pass. He already knew that, in time, he would receive his due for his crimes, be they reluctant or not. Yet I could not fathom that I would be his paymaster.

"Herr Colonel," I managed to say. Himmel stopped in his tracks. "What was in the letter, Sir?"

I faced his back, and it rippled with a sigh.

"The Shtefan Brandt, to whom it was addressed," he said flatly. "He received a note from a cousin in Vienna. Apparently, *that* Shtefan Brandt's mother was sent last week to Dachau."

V

In January of 1944, I began to covet my master's mistress.

As I regard the past now with a well-worn eye, I marvel that the time from September until January was comprised of so few days. Yet I know that there are periods of a young man's life, some of them lasting for years, in which much of his person remains in an idling gear, without great changes or altered views of the world. Then, there may be only a few months of compressed time, during which adventures and occurrences can alter his character forever, as if the urgent hands of some greater power have suddenly pounced upon a half-formed statue of clay and chosen to madly remold its shape. Such was this period of my life, when the hesitant youth that had been Shtefan Brandt became a young man determined to rein in his own fate.

I never loved my Colonel, no, but trembling in the presence of his professional courage, I will confess that I regarded him always with awe and respect. He engendered a sense of loyalty, induced by his charismatic manner and his own dedication to his profession and his men. I shall not deny also, that his protective attitude toward me automatically returned a dedication in kind. Yes, of course I observed the fissures in his character with dismay, and at times, even disgust, but I saw him as no less entitled to faults than any other man. When he betrayed his wife with whores of convenience, he did so without a wink or murmured excuse, displaying no more apology than would a wild dog for snatching up a rabbit. When he fought and killed his enemy, he did so with a sense of enthusiastic accomplishment, though without taking glee in the blood of the vanquished. And from the date of the murders at the Hassberger Forest, though he was ordered to execute more such assignments, I thanked him silently and many times for assigning me to other duties and forgoing my witness.

One night, just prior to the Colonel's departure for one of those shameful killing fields, he was clearly distraught with the assignment. I supposed this to be the result of a twinge of conscience, yet in truth he regarded such tasks as beneath the dignity of soldiers of SS caliber. Mistaking his mood for one of troubling guilt, I imposed upon the armorer, Heinz, to provide me with half a dozen rounds of blank ammunition, which we used occasionally in training. I then retrieved Himmel's spare pistol magazine from his combat harness, loaded it up and waited for a moment to be alone in his presence. I trembled a bit with emotion as I showed him the magazine, clearly topped off with the ineffectual rounds, and entreated him to use it and absolve himself, at least once, of a crime.

He took the magazine from my hand, and for a moment he turned it and stared at the blanks. He nodded slowly, and then he slapped me across the face with the force of a lightning bolt.

I was stunned and speechless. My cheek flamed with pain and humiliation, and I could not help the tears that sprang to my eyes.

"Would this not be a betrayal of my men, Shtefan?" Himmel demanded quite simply.

"Yes, Sir," I barely muttered.

"Would this not be a dereliction of my duty, as a German officer?"

"Yes, Sir."

My head was bowed, the tears ran down my cheeks, and I was quivering, awaiting at the very least another slap. But instead, the Colonel grasped my shoulder.

"I thank you for your gesture, my young corporal," he said in a hoarse growl. "But this is a soul you cannot save, nor should you try."

He placed the magazine in my hand, squeezed my fingers around it, and left without another word. I understood, then, that these few months had brought irrevocable changes upon only me, for Himmel himself would never change. The time for the construction of his character had taken place long ago. He was a being of power, an example to be beheld, for its rejection or embrace of my choosing. He was an Abraham to my Isaac, and I had no doubt that he might give up his life for me in combat, or sacrifice me in the wink of a second, should the Gods of Battle deem it so.

Watching my master fall in love, then, was a new chamber of his complex mind to which I became privy. I believed already that he loved his wife and daughters, but I was also convinced that said affection did not approach his feelings for the army or his troops. His caring for other beings seemed compartmentalized, each dependent upon the role played by that person in the larger scheme of life. He appeared to have a fixed lexicon of manners and displays for various individuals. His family received the gentler, though hardly sentimental, Himmel. His men received a harsher and more brittle love, though deeper in its devotion. And I received something of a mix, and I knew not why.

As for Gabrielle, when I first realized my master was smitten with the girl, I winced for her inescapable fate, for I assumed it to be the lust I had witnessed once by virtue of my own indiscretion. We had, by that time, repositioned ourselves to France and had occupied an abandoned farmstead south of Dijon. The main house of this once lovely estate had been partially burned, though its ground floor was essentially intact, and Himmel occupied the large salon, while I was relegated to the separated kitchen, along with "Mutti" the cook, whose corpulent form and wild beard seemed anything but motherly. The commandos had taken over the empty barn.

On the very first day of this occupation, a sunny and bright winter morn, Himmel had ordered Edward to stop the staff car as we passed a pair of young French farm girls walking along the access drive. The one was brunette and puffy, while the other was comely and freckled and sprouted a mane of carrot hair. Neither of them appeared to be yet eighteen. Himmel produced a pair of red apples and, presenting a charming grin rarely seen, chatted a few words in French and made his gift. The redhead returned his smile, curtsied, and apparently agreed to a nocturnal "chat."

That night, I was well into my second hour of sleep in the kitchen when the screams of an animal surely being skinned alive snapped my head up from my woolen bedroll. I dragged on my trousers, yet some instinct prevented me from lighting a lamp. I glanced back at the snoring form of Mutti and then followed the rhythmic echoes of torture. Tiptoeing in the dark, I pushed through the kitchen door and reached the frame of the entrance arch to the salon, and there I stood, transfixed.

There was a large, rough wooden table in the center of the room. During the day, it had been spread with tactical maps and plotting pens and compasses, which were now strewn about the floor as if having been swept off by a wave. Upon the table, the redheaded girl lay on her back, completely naked, her young pale skin mottled pink and gleaming with sweat. Her arms were flung above her head, her small fists clenched and her sinews rippling, as her wrists had each been buckled into a leather belt, then tied off to the table legs. Below, Himmel stood at the edge of the table, his breeches about his boots, his braces quivering on the wooden floor like beached eels. He was gripping the girl's ankles in his hands, spreading her legs too wide even for a ballerina, and for want of a more eloquent description, he was fucking her with all the delicacy of an oil derrick.

My mouth dropped, and I was totally immobilized by this vision and its accompanying, unearthly score. I had never seen my master's nude form, and his muscled back displayed a pair of puckered pink nipples, clearly the exit wounds of an enemy marksman, while upon his left shoulder was a long white scar, no doubt from the blade of a cadet duel. Shining rivulets of sweat slithered from his neck and over his skin, and his rump bunched over and over as he pistoned himself in and out of the girl, and with each piercing her young breasts bounced and she jerked her head upward and squealed with nothing like pleasure. Her eyes were slammed shut and with every wrenching twist of her neck, her tears were flung across the stained wood of the table, and as Himmel's iron thighs bucked against the furniture and his purpling penis plunged again and again into her flesh, the table legs thumped the floor, adding a chorus of thunder to the girl's aria of pain.

I suddenly felt myself being dragged backward, and nearly losing my footing, a momentary fright stabbed into my chest. Yet I found Mutti's fist gripping my forearm, and I did not resist as he silently pulled me through the kitchen door, closed it carefully and released me. We stood there, toe to toe, and my shocked expression did not amuse the cook for even a moment. He quickly flung a finger to his pursed lips and then drew that same finger across his throat. Then, he pointed at my bedroll, and I nodded and skulked back into my cocoon, as he did the very same. For an endless hour, we each lay there in the dark, listening to those ungodly cries, until at last they crescendoed and subsided into stuttering weeps, and we stole into sleep before another round might commence.

Thus, you can well imagine that when only one month later, as Himmel's hardened gaze was trapped by the beauty of Gabrielle upon that bridge near Avignon, I immediately imagined him shortly pummeling her in our new quarters astride the ville of Le Pontet. Once again, we had occupied a countryman's former estate, although this trio of mansion, carriage house and stables was almost completely intact. It had once been the country residence of a local French prefect, and had subsequently been occupied by three Nazi administrators. However, with the beginning of 1944 and the Allied armies sure to pounce upon France within the half year, the bureaucrats had fled to Berlin, leaving their accommodations to the combat officers.

Yet my master, whose pattern of sexual pursuit most often resulted in a "quick kill," surprised both myself and Edward with his digression. Upon spotting Gabrielle driving her caisson of wounded across the bridge, he ordered Edward to halt the staff car, and we held up there on the left bank of the river, watching the crowded and pitiable procession. I did not at first understand his reason for halting there, for in most such cases he was of little patience and would order the way cleared. But at last I turned round to him, and found him gazing with an unfamiliar and gentle ardor, and he raised a gloved finger and pointed.

"Look at that magnificent creature, Shtefan," he said.

I took her in then as well, her golden hair, glowing skin and perfectly regal posture, and I felt for her the pity reserved for a beautiful doe in hunting season. Yet Himmel produced no apples here, nor did he invent some pretext to have Edward order the girl to his quarters. He simply sat there, breathing and watching, and almost immediately I understood that he was not going to rape her, but to court her.

"Look at her very carefully, Shtefan," he instructed, and then, after a moment, "Will you remember her?"

"She would be difficult to forget, Sir."

"Exactly. This afternoon, I want you to return to the town and find her."

This would not be complex, as she was clearly in the employ of the local Wehrmacht field hospital.

"Yes, Sir. And then?"

"Just find out who she is and where she lives, and report back to me."

I wondered, then, if Himmel's uncharacteristically delicate approach was the result of the recent visit to France of his wife and daughters. Upon our occupation of the French country estate, he had almost immediately sent for them, realizing that such accommodations would unlikely present themselves again in the near future. Thus, he and his family enjoyed a private week in the main mansion, while those of us in support staff were quite comfortable in the carriage house, and the commandos were, as usual, satisfied in the barn. I thought now that perhaps the master's wife had quite sated his lust during that familial lull. On the other hand, her brittle and cold demeanor certainly did not conjure images of carnal passion. Perhaps, with her leave-taking, he was waxing nostalgic for the romantic courtship long departed?

That afternoon, I did not impose upon Edward to drive me into Le Pontet, but instead saddled a horse from the barn. There had been two healthy stallions still residing on the estate, yet one had since escaped, and as I blanketed and leathered the larger chestnut, Captain Friedrich and his crew of noncommissioned officers gathered about me and attempted to shred my ego.

"Fish!" Friedrich began the chorus of catcalls. "What are you going to do with that animal?"

"*Ja!* Fishes are supposed to swim, Brandt, not ride!" the giant Sergeant Meyer chimed in.

"I think he's going to bring it to Mutti and cook it up for the Colonel!" someone else yelled out.

I continued to dress the horse, smiling slightly and ignoring their taunts.

"He's going to throw you, Brandt," Friedrich warned. "And then you'll wind up facedown in the mud, as always!"

Of course, I was unoffended that the commandos assumed me to be less than a novice horseman. They could not know that as an integral part of the extracurricular requirements of my former *Gymnasium* in Vienna, we were required to provide services to the Spanish Riding School.

As I lifted my left boot into the stirrup and quickly mounted the steed, someone from behind decided to amuse himself and the troop by slapping the horse on his rump. The stallion jerked the bridle then and leaped forward, but I quickly reined him close, turned him in a tight circle, and raised his pummeling hooves into the air, which caused half a dozen of the SS to fall back on themselves in alarm. Then, I quickly turned him again for the open barn doors and heeled his flanks.

He exploded from the barn like a Thoroughbred, and hearing the commandos rushing out behind us, I chose to give them a bit of a show before my departure. I galloped him at breakneck speed, and leaning hard to the left, we thundered a perfect circle around the entire circumference of the barn. When again we rounded the forward corner, Friedrich and his men were standing there openmouthed, in a clownish clump, and I raced right for them until they split into perfect parts and leaped for safety. I admit that I grinned from ear to ear as I bent over the stallion's neck and raced away for the town, the shouts and applause of the commandos echoing behind.

It was nearly dusk when my mount and I approached the large Wehrmacht field hospital on the outskirts of Le Pontet. South of the town, rumbling Junkers transports delivered wounded from northern Italy and other Mediterranean catastrophes to the aerodrome at Châteaublanc, who were then tumbreled to the sprawling facility. The hospital was situated in a wide pasture, intentionally distant from any major crossroads, as such always provided enemy bombers with convenient map coordinates. Thus, there was no facile access for vehicles or wagons, and the former grazing field had been churned into a sea of mud.

Central to the hospital stood an enormous surgery tent, bordered by smaller tents for triage, support, equipment, kitchens and the like. Then, there was an outer ring of half tents, merely canvas roofs upon staked poles, and each of them crowded with flank-to-flank cots, occupied by freshly sutured soldiers and moaning amputees. Throughout the grid of narrow, muddy lanes laid out between the tents, bandaged soldiers hobbled upon makeshift crutches, local women in bloody aprons hurried to and fro with pots of medicines, and caissons of all sorts trundled. The steamy breaths of the pained and frightened rose into the January air, and from the main surgery tent could be heard the shouted orders of overworked and exhausted physicians, as the blanketed evidences of their failures were carried off on stretchers to the nearby graveyard.

I dismounted at the perimeter of this hellish circus and, wrinkling my nose from the stench of gangrene and alcohol, tied the steed to a broken post. I began to walk along a wide lane toward the surgery tent, focusing my eyes on the way ahead and trying to take in as little of the suffering as I could, when a captain of the medical corps suddenly appeared before me, and I automatically saluted. He did not bother to return the gesture.

"We have no SS here, Corporal," he snapped. "And if you're complaining of gout, go back to your troop."

"I have no complaints, Herr Doktor," I replied. "I have been sent by my Colonel to seek out a French orderly."

"We have none to spare." The doctor was wearing a long woolen coat over his bloody whites, and he rubbed his bruised and exhausted eyes.

"No, Sir," I continued as politely as I could, feeling genuine sympathy and no envy for his profession. I had worked for physicians in a much more pristine environment and could not imagine functioning in this miasma of unquenchable suffering. "This is a young woman I must locate only for the purpose of passing a message."

"Oh, don't tell me." The doctor threw up his hands in disgust. "Another officer who wants to fuck Gabrielle."

"I beg your pardon?"

"She's a small blonde beauty with blue eyes and the carriage of a princess, correct?"

"Y…yes, Sir."

"Well, every officer who spots her comes round here wanting a piece, but you can tell your Colonel it's not on. She's integral to this hospital and much more important to my wounded than to some Schutzstaffel strutter with a lonely prick. You can tell him she's our amulet, a gift from the Nazi Party, and she's not for plucking."

I was more than a bit stunned by this doctor's ire, and although it was instantly clear that Himmel would not likely be a more successful suitor than the myriad who had gone before, I still had my orders.

"Herr Doktor," I responded in as soothing a tone as I could. "I am only required to confirm her whereabouts. Thereafter, our commanders can dispute the results as they wish."

The doctor sighed, realizing that he had been firing at the messenger.

"Gabrielle Belmont. She lives in the old mayor's residence in Le Pontet, by the clock tower of Notre Dame de Bon Secours."

"Thank you, Herr Doktor." I clicked my heels, bowed and turned away to head for my horse, and I did not respond as I heard the doctor call after me.

"I hope you don't find her, Corporal. And if you do, I trust she'll have the good sense to slam the door!"

I wondered, as I left, if every man this Gabrielle passed had not fallen madly in love with her. Yet almost immediately, I was gripped by a profound depression that occasionally ambushed me now, as just the image of a female form would remind me that my mother had also once been young and beautiful. No, I had not forgotten that she had been taken away to Dachau, not for a moment, yet in order to survive I had been forced to embrace an unlikely optimism. I had taken to believing that this "correction facility" might be the best of the Party's secret enclaves, and that she would in fact survive better within this environment. After all, while the Allies had taken to bombing industrial centers and civilian cities alike, they had yet to target prisoner of war or relocation camps. Vienna would certainly fall target to American or Russian ordnance, but Dachau might remain unscathed, the eye of a hurricane.

I had very little information about the Nazi death camps, and given my ethnic background, I did not dare demonstrate curiosity, but only absorbed the occasional comments and held my peace. I did not know the whereabouts of my father, nor the true nature of my mother's predicament, but the concept of being orphaned was just too much for me to bear, and so I swept that fate into a dormant cave of my mind, focusing instead on my own survival.

I did so again as I mounted the stallion and trotted off for Le Pontet, maintaining my personal pact to fulfill each and every of Himmel's assignments to perfection. I had gained the girl's name, and now would simply confirm her address, and report back to my master.

It was nearly dark as my horse clopped along the damp and shiny cobblestones of the town. Few of the French were about now, as they had returned to their homes to build the evening fires. The windows of the quaint houses were cracked and patched, some glowing with the flickers of oil lamps within. Tufts of snow sat upon the street corners like arctic turtles, and I shivered upon my stallion.

I stopped as I approached the clock tower of Notre Dame de Bon Secours. It was tall and peaked, with its spire of dark wooden timbers and tiles raking upward, and the large round clock itself had ceased to keep the time. This was no surprise, as the roof of the tower had been pierced at a downward angle by some vicious spear of air ordnance, the exit hole a splintered wound of cracked wooden bones. My eyes followed the trajectory, and my mouth fell open as I spotted the unexploded aerial bomb.

It was there in the front garden of a small stone house, its fins jutting up into the air, its trunk half buried in the frozen soil. Not four meters from the frightening projectile, a young woman in a woolen coat was turning the barren earth with a pitchfork. She wore high galoshes on her slim ankles, and her hands were encased in fingerless woolen gloves. Her long blond hair was pulled back behind her neck and tied with a dark yarn. It was Gabrielle.

I urged the stallion forward and stopped astride the garden's fence, a broken weave of posting. She glanced up at me with a twist of her head, then continued turning the brittle earth as she spoke.

"*Guten Abend.*" She greeted me without warmth. The Germans had been in her land for years, and she was undoubtedly fluent, though the lilt of her French accent suddenly gave my harsh native language hues it did not deserve.

"Good evening," I replied as I removed my cap. "Is this not very dangerous?" I gestured at the bomb.

"It fell over a month ago." She continued her work. "It has no timing mechanism. We have come to terms. We are sharing the garden."

I was tempted to dismount the horse, but I somehow felt that any sort of polite gesture would be dismissed as insincere formality.

"Why are you gardening in winter, may I ask?" I said.

"Hope," was all she replied.

In mere seconds, I had assessed her. She had courage, optimism, and incredible beauty. Though she was offering only her profile in the near dark, I could well discern her very full lips, her slim nose and the ice blue of her eyes. I quickly returned to my task.

"May I inquire, are you Gabrielle Belmont?"

"I am she."

"I have been asked to obtain your name and address, mademoiselle."

"For which officer?"

"My commander. SS Colonel Erich Himmel."

Gabrielle halted her raking then. She straightened up, holding the fork with one hand, while she placed the other at the small of her back and arched a bit, as she exhaled a sigh. She faced me and looked up, and I confess that her expression chilled me further. I somehow did not want to be judged by her, yet it was too late.

"What is your name, young man?"

"Shtefan Brandt." I briefly dropped my forehead.

"And what do you suppose your Colonel Himmel wants of me?"

I blushed deeply and looked away, playing for a moment

with the reins as my horse snouted in the ground for a tuft of grass.

"I am not at liberty to ask him. I must only follow orders."

"That seems to be the rallying cry of your race," she said, and she returned to her gardening.

She was quick, and cynical as well, and I was completely humiliated. I was only grateful that I had given her no reason to smile, because I sensed that such an expression on her face might have completely shattered what remained of my false composure.

"Well, you have my apologies..." I began again.

"Your apologies?" There was something of a short laugh in her exhortation. "For destroying my country? Or for interrupting my evening?"

I said nothing.

"Tell your commander that I am Gabrielle Belmont, and I live at Number 3 Rue Lavoisier, and I spend my days and often my nights attending to the needs of his wounded and fallen brethren. And unless he also happens to be the conductor of the Berliner Opera, I cannot be had for a song, or for anything else."

I nodded, and set my cap back on my head, but she was not finished with me.

"Tell your Colonel Himmel that I am the daughter of Charles Marcel Belmont, the mayor of Le Pontet, who is no more. Tell him that my father cared for the people of this town above all else, and that when he tried to prevent the shipment of so many of our children to your murder camps, he was executed by the Gestapo."

At this point, I snapped the reins and turned my horse, for I could bear no more. We began to clip along the cobblestones, though I felt the young woman's gaze upon my back, and it pierced me no less than a red-hot blacksmith's tongs.

"And Shtefan Brandt." She called out to me, and I was forced to rein in the horse, and I turned in my saddle to face her, at least now comfortably at some distance.

"You can also tell him that my mother, Monique Belmont, was executed along with my father. She was a Jewess of Paris. *That* should certainly quench his erotic fantasies."

With this, she thrust the pitchfork deeply into the icy garden, and she turned and strode into the house, and she did not slam the door, but closed it quietly, with utter grace. I sat there for a moment, staring at the trembling pole of the garden implement, and just beyond it, the sharp fins of the bomb.

I rode back to the farmstead, enveloped in a cloud of my own silence, and so slowly that even my horse was impatient with my despair.

VI

In February of 1944, I was shamed by a woman's courage.

It was the undaunted and arrogant spirit of one Gabrielle Belmont of Le Pontet, Arrondissement d'Avignon, which forced my realization that heretofore, and for nearly one year, I had survived only by virtue of my own self-deception and the practical thinking of a Standartenführer of the SS. Himmel was not a man of kindnesses. He was a creature of expedience, a professional who placed the military objective above all else, and it was merely luck that the Nuremberg Laws did not at this juncture appear on his personal scale of priorities. Should the truth of my racial heritage have been somehow brought to fore by any potential enemy within the troop, my presence within my master's ranks could well have brought the full wrath of the National Socialist German Workers' Party crashing about his head, yet we shared this secret in a conspiracy of silence. More than once I was tempted to raise the issue, if only to demonstrate my grati-

tude, yet such urges I suppressed, choosing instead to endure the sensation of being a convicted felon in the employ
of a police detective.

Gabrielle Belmont's proud rejection of Himmel's advances then, by virtue of her open declaration of her heritage, was enough to make me regard myself as so much
less than an earthworm. I reasoned that perhaps she felt
well armored by her position as a nurse, or the coveting
of her form, or perhaps her parents' fate had overcome her
instincts for survival. But if in fact she survived at all after
taking such a bold and reckless position, I did not expect
to witness a further demonstration of her striking character. Yet there was to be so much more.

The events which transpired during the ensuing weeks at
first confounded my still-naive nature. On the very night
after my first encounter with the French girl, I recited her
words by rote in the presence of my master, experiencing a
great discomfort as I did so, for her unabashed truths raised
the issue of my own lineage. Yet Himmel only blinked his
single eye as he listened, then smiled and waved me on to
my other tasks. I found myself wondering if my own character might ever be so resolute as his, that my utter rejection by such an angelic creature would also result in no
more than a bemused expression.

On the next day, the Colonel snapped a sealed envelope
into my hand. Apparently, it contained a missive prepared
by him in private, which was very curious, as Himmel had
come to rely on my honed typing skills, and only in very
rare occurrences of highly secret communications did he
resort to hunting and pecking of his own volition. The en-

velope was addressed to the resident Gestapo commander in Avignon, and my orders were to make delivery and await a reply in kind.

So, once again I saddled my horse, whom I had renamed *Blitzkrieg*, in keeping with my obsequious habits of attempting to demonstrate my martial enthusiasm. I assumed correctly that the Gestapo officer would be occupying the desk of Avignon's former chief of police, and indeed found him residing in the station house astride the main thoroughfare. I remained at attention in the office of this middle-aged, bespectacled Berlin bureaucrat, while he studied the Colonel's message. He thought for a moment, jotted no more than a numeral on the original page, resealed it and handed it back to me. It was a crisp and sunny day, and during my ride back to the estate I was sorely tempted to hold the envelope up to the glaring light. Yet I feared being spotted en route by some member of the Commando, and declined to tempt a breach of Himmel's trust. He received the return message and perused it with no more than an additional smile.

On the next day, the Colonel bade me gather a straw basket, a bottle of French wine, two loaves of bread and a sprig of wildflowers. Indeed my curiosity was piqued, as Himmel was not prone to such demonstrative table dressings, and I assumed he had found a new target for his affections. Yet I undertook my task, which was no easy feat, being forced to beg a bandage basket from the staff of the Wehrmacht field hospital, whereupon I spent some time washing bloodstains from the straw and drying it in the sun. The other items, although rare, were less difficult to acquire, as I had learned that to merely mention the title of an SS colonel would send the local French scurrying to fulfill such orders. Mind you, I was overly polite and accompanied my requests with an apologetic smile, as if that might diminish the undercurrent of hatred engendered by my uniform.

That evening, Himmel received the basket, complimented me on its arrangement, and awarded me an evening's rest. He then ordered Edward to fetch the staff car, but he did not include me in his travel plans, as was nearly always custom. I saluted and returned to my quarters in the carriage house, yet in truth I felt rather like a pouting child denied a parental outing. And when after an hour or so Edward returned, he declined to share the evening's events, which further stirred the embers of my sense of rejection. Yet I quickly swept such foolishness aside. After all, the Colonel was entitled to some semblance of privacy, even from myself.

During the next two days my musings were stifled, as I labored at my master's feet from dawn till dusk. Despite the theoretical respite of the Commando, Himmel never allowed the men to slip into a state of comfortable sloth. He structured many hours of intense training and review, during which the men simulated assaults over various types of terrain. Using live ammunition and hauling every item of heavy gear that might be required in long-range combat, they sprinted across open fields and leap-frogged through snow-swept woods. They vaulted over fences and hurled live grenades and detonated abandoned buildings, while Himmel sprinted along with each participating element, shouting corrections and berating those who lagged or erred, somewhat like a hard-bitten soccer coach with an endless supply of energy and oxygen. Of course, I was forced to match my master step for step, recording his grades and comments in a log, until my leg muscles twitched, my lungs felt afire, my fingers were utterly frozen and my head pounded from the din.

At the end of each day, he bade me join the troop in accuracy drills, and in truth I felt a swell of pride when he ordered that I familiarize myself with the MP40 machine pistol, a frightening device our foes had dubbed the "Schmeisser." However, throughout these efforts I found myself continuously returning to curiosity, wondering if in fact the basket of treats meant that the Colonel had attempted another courting of Gabrielle Belmont. If this was the case, I had no doubt that he had failed to crack her resolve, and found myself wishing to see her once more, if only to be sure that she had not been summarily executed for her stubborn pride.

And so, when I did see her again, the circumstances stunned me.

That Friday eve, I drew Himmel a steaming bath, and he washed away the grit of a training day and dressed carefully in his cleanest uniform. He then ordered the staff car brought around, this time with myself accompanying, and summoned a light truck with four armed privates as well.

"Intelligence reports indicate a growing French resistance in the area," he explained as I presented him with a fresh eye patch and tried not to stare into the awful black hole of his missing orb. "Make sure the guard stays at a polite but effective distance, Shtefan."

I did not inquire as to the nature of the excursion, as I was temporarily overwhelmed by the realization that the Colonel was placing me in some sort of charge. The burden of his trust at once swelled my head and frightened me, and I quickly speculated that the small bodyguard of SS might scoff at any attempts on my part to herd them. However, being the Colonel's adjutant, and in effect the ranking noncommissioned officer present, afforded me with some power I would not hesitate to effect.

The small convoy of the staff car and light truck then wound its way toward Le Pontet. The canvas cover of the following lorry had been stripped away, and the four privates sat beneath the skeletal canopy, their "Schmeisser" machine pistols facing outboard, their helmets gleaming in the moonlight. Himmel sat in his position behind me in our Kübelwagen, humming and tapping on his knee, and Edward seemed to have run the route before. We soon entered the eastern fringe of the town, and when I again saw the finned bomb in the front garden of Gabrielle's home, I realized that this was no secret rendezvous with some undercover Abwehr agent. This was a date.

Himmel dismounted the staff car, set his officer's cap at a slight angle, and strode up the slate walk to the door of the house. He rapped twice with his gloved knuckles, about-faced and immediately returned to the car, where he stood as stiffly as a chauffeur. I confess that I felt both a thrill and a surge of dismay as Gabrielle emerged from her house. Had she so quickly succumbed to my master's charm? Had it required no more than barely fermented wine, stale bread and dried flowers to break her stalwart

spirit? Yet if Gabrielle was in fact defeated, that surrender
was unexpressed in her proud demeanor. She was wearing
a long black cloak belted at her small waist, a pair of short
laced boots and woolen gloves, all somewhat threadbare
to be sure, yet her golden hair piled atop her head and her
perfect posture drew attentions to her rose-cheeked face
and nothing else. She walked to the staff car and entered
gracefully as Himmel bowed briefly, and I felt myself blush
as her gaze did not, even for one instant, fall upon me.

The convoy then moved off to the market section of the
town. No matter the dire circumstances of hardship and
hunger, the French somehow managed to ignore the war,
and each night a pair of Le Pontet's cafés remained open,
whether or not there were sufficient foodstuffs or drinks
to be served. Edward pulled up to a small establishment
called L'Ours Blanc, the White Bear, which had clearly
been no more than a pub prior to the war, but was now
the prime restaurant of the town. It had a pair of large
multipaned windows astride a heavy wooden door, and
the glow of table candles from inside set the frosted glass
to wavering with golden hues. The crackled voice of some
French chanteuse seeped from a gramophone through the
wooden timbers.

I was out of the staff car before Edward had set the hand
brake, and I opened Himmel's door and stood smartly aside
as he emerged and turned, offering a gloved hand to Gabrielle. She was shortly beside him, and I carefully avoided
meeting her eyes, focusing only on my master as he quickly
perused the area. He then faced me and placed his left
hand on my shoulder, while pointing with his right hand

first to one outside corner of the White Bear, then to the other, and then to the recessed doorway of a house across the street. I clicked my heels, and he and Gabrielle walked off to their dinner.

My heart was hammering now as I smoothed my uniform and set my courage in its place, for I had never before issued an order to anyone else on earth, unless it was such as relayed on behalf of the Colonel. I took in a long breath and walked to the light truck, where the four privates had taken to lounging in the back and rolling cigarettes. I stood there looking at them for a moment, and in perfect impersonation of my master's postures, joined my hands behind my back.

"*Ja*, Fish?" The eldest of this group, a large Berliner with a granite jaw named Rolf, regarded me as if I was disturbing his Sunday morning slumber. I had to be quick, or be lost.

"One man at that corner," I said curtly as I gestured. "Another at that one, and the other two over there in the alcove."

Rolf slowly sat up on the truck bench, piercing me with a steely gaze as he licked the flap of his cigarette.

"Are you giving us orders now, Fish?"

"Yes, I am," I snapped. "And tonight, it is not 'Fish.' It is Rottenführer Brandt, and if you are not on guard within thirty seconds, I can summon the Colonel and have *him* issue the order."

I did not move or change my expression, mostly due to my frozen state of utter terror. Yet my stance seemed to have its effect, and after regarding one another for a moment or two, the four commandos muttered some curses, hopped to the ground and made off for their posts.

"And no smoking," I added without looking at them as I walked back to the staff car to join Edward.

"Very impressive," he grunted as we stood beside the Kübelwagen. "God help you if they catch you alone this weekend."

"God help *them* if they fail to follow a superior's orders," I replied, feeling quite besotted with my newfound power. Edward looked at me, pursed his lips, and nodded his approval.

I did not, for the remainder of the evening, glance even once inside the establishment. I could not bear to witness the ease with which Gabrielle had surrendered her spirit, nor could I entertain images of her further conquering to come.

During the fortnight that followed, my master continued his courtship apace. Thus, I was privy to a different Himmel, a polite and mannered gentleman, albeit one whose concepts of romantic seduction even seemed strategized and structured. He would train the men very hard for two days, and on the second night he would repeat the exercise of dinner with Gabrielle. One evening we escorted the couple to a mountain château, where the Wehrmacht's 19th Army subsidized a Vichy family's dinner establishment, and Himmel was proud to parade his newfound beauty among so many of his envious peers. On another unusually mild eve, Mutti the cook was sent out to a sheltered clearing in a pretty wood, where he prepared a roaring bonfire, a roasting pit of chicken, and a perfectly dressed table so that the Colonel and Gabrielle could dine in comfort beneath the stars.

During each of these excursions, I played my role as commander of the guard, and apparently the task began to fit me well, as my orders were no longer met with challenge from the troop. I never witnessed the social exchanges between Himmel and his beauty, focusing only on the immediate environment, alert as a rottweiler to any threat, and refusing to admit to myself that this professional enthusiasm might stem from some other emotion. As for the training days between, I began to embrace them and look forward to them, my physical strength and ability to keep up growing from some inner well of rage not yet comprehended. There was even one long day of a forced march in full battle dress, which lasted for nearly twenty hours, and during which I marched beside my master step for step, surprising both him and myself and certainly the commandos who labored to keep pace.

After a week, Himmel summoned me and handed me a folded note, ordering me to deliver it to Gabrielle's home. As I bowed and made to leave his office, he barked from behind his desk.

"And no flirting, Shtefan," he said. "She's mine."

I turned to him, blushing and about to protest, and I found him smiling hard, then bursting into a fit of laughter with my expression. I summoned a grin to match his own, clicked my heels and went off to saddle Blitzkrieg.

Approaching the closed door of the barn, I stopped short and stood very still, listening to a raucous exchange coming from within.

"You think Himmel's going to bed his blonde bitch?"

"Which one? Gabrielle, or Fish?!"

When the laughter receded, there was this.

"Don't make light of Brandt. He's doing well."

"Well? He's doing *too* well. He thinks he's regular SS."

"*Ja*, the fucker's been ordering us about like a Reichs-führer."

"Leave him alone. He just follows his orders, like any of us."

"You think so? One of these days he's going to put a bullet in your skull and take over your platoon!"

This last comment evoked so much laughter that I chose that moment to enter the barn, suppressing my own smile as I did so. On the heels of their discussion, the commandos looked at me and blinked. Then, a wiry corporal named Noss came to his feet and stood at attention, his sea green eyes gleaming merriment. The rest of them quickly followed the joke, all coming erect and standing straight and stiff, and as I blushed a deep crimson and hurried to my horse, they collapsed in a flailing pile of twitching mirth.

When I arrived at the home of Gabrielle, I did so sporting my newly developed air of strength and reserve. Once again, she was working in the garden, and Blitzkrieg trotted up beside her fence and stopped. I greeted her politely yet with a studied chill, and handed her the note as she approached. She read it briefly and nodded, placing it in the pocket of her coat.

As I lifted Blitzkrieg's reins to flick them, Gabrielle cocked her head at me and spoke.

"Do you judge me, Shtefan Brandt?"

I could not reply at first. Because I did indeed judge her. I was furious and frustrated and felt an amorphous sense of betrayal, and I had no idea why.

"It is not for me to judge, mademoiselle," I said.

She nodded slowly twice, and she reached up to stroke Blitzkrieg's glossy neck, and he looked at her.

"Do you judge your horse, then?" she posed.

"For what?" I frowned.

"For whinnying when you shoe him."

"No." My brow furrowed further.

"Of course not," she said. "Because you can imagine what it must be like, to have a blacksmith's nails driven into your feet."

She was shortly gone, and with her analogy echoing in my brain, I galloped home like a race jockey.

Himmel's note had been an invitation to dinner, but this time at his quarters, and the next evening Edward drove to fetch Gabrielle. I was gratefully excused from attendance to this soirée, a task left to Mutti, who was ordered to concoct a gourmet repast of goods scrounged far and wide. I remained in the carriage house, feeling edgy and cross, and I sipped from a bottle of cooking schnapps and reread the same passage over and over again, from a book whose title I do not recall. When at last, sometime after 11:00 p.m. Mutti returned, both Edward and I looked up from our bedrolls, expecting an order to escort Gabrielle back to Avignon. But the cook only shrugged, and forming a circle with one hand, he pumped a long finger back and forth within. Edward laughed and covered his head with his blanket, soon to snoring.

For over an hour, I could not sleep, but only tossed and turned in those tortures of insomnia which are rarely physical. At last, I decided to visit the latrine, a long deep ditch dug in the ground beyond the barn, and I somewhat staggered there in my boots and braced trousers. My body beneath a long-sleeved undershirt quaked with the cold, and having buttoned up my trousers again, I intended to hurry back to my bed. Yet as I looked at the main house in the distance, my feet defied my good sense, and I was drawn to quench my morbid curiosity, or something else.

I moved in silence across the soaked slim grass, past puffs of glistening snow, and my eyes flicked over the estate. The Commando always posted a guard outside the barn, but on nights such as these he was permitted to stand inside the door for stretches of defrosting, and there was no human shadow about. I stopped in the lee of a large tree, watching, listening. The main house was dark, save a single window that barely flickered with a candle's glow, and I deftly moved to one corner of the mansion like a burglar. My breaths were coming hot and quick, and I strove to limit the plumes of steam emerging from my mouth, taking the frozen air through my nose. I waited, listening again, yet here no squeals pierced the night, no tortured grunts. It appeared that my master had continued his courtship in gentlemanly fashion, perhaps offering Gabrielle the small second-floor anteroom as quarters for the night. There came to me only a faint and rhythmic knocking, perhaps the swing of a cellar door in the wind.

I nearly bolted then, and well should have, but I could not. Instead, I slipped silently along the rear wall of the house, until my nose touched the frame of one large window, and just the pupil of my eye inched around to the glass.

Indeed there was a single candle glowing on the dining table. The plates and glasses had not been removed, and a pair of empty wine bottles stood their posts. Closer to me, I saw the back of a small divan, and Gabrielle's small fingers gripped the curved wooden molding there, while her head, facing me, hung down between her hands. Her flaxen hair was unfettered now, and it seemed to whip in constant, milky waves. She was kneeling on the sofa, and behind her Himmel stood, shirtless and sweating, gripping her naked waist and making the cheeks of her buttocks quiver as he slowly plunged in and out of her.

My eyes bulged as I was rooted to the spot, and my heart began to bang so loudly in my constricted chest that I was certain it would be heard. I watched the rape in utter horror, only glad that I could see little of Gabrielle's nude form, that I could not see her breasts below the divan's back, surely swaying with each painful degradation of her body. A fury unlike any I had ever sensed rose up inside my bowels, I felt an overpowering urge about to propel me through the glass, and my hand twitched for my pistol, but it was not there. And then, at the very precipice of my rage, my mouth suddenly fell open. I slowly turned away from the window, nearly swooning, and I leaned my back against the frozen wood of the house and stared up at the moonless sky. For certainly, I had just seen Gabrielle turn her head to Himmel, as with one hand she reached back and gripped his thigh, helping him to penetrate her...

What awaited me thereafter was a week of numbness. All semblance of illusion had been stripped away, all fantasies of good and right and romance, merely a joke. The strong took what they wanted, and the weak resisted, if at all, only symbolically. My brief sense of shame upon Gabrielle's initial vent of courage, and the urge to match it with my own, had been shattered, and I viewed her now with no more sympathy than for any other of my master's whores. I was grateful for my life, which I might have easily lost in a split second of insanity, had my adolescent fantasies not been choked at the root.

There were more such "dates" between Himmel and Gabrielle, all held now in his quarters, yet my empathic feelings for her had been supplanted by disgust. On these evenings, I slept quickly and well after my dismissal, the one remaining hint of my true emotions being a morning's tender jaw, no doubt from a night of grinding my teeth in my sleep. On the morning after one such evening, I reported for duty to find the Colonel and his mistress taking breakfast at his plotting table. I bowed at her with studied manners, even offering a careful expression of welcome, then quickly turned to the business of carrying out my orders. At one point, Himmel rose and left the main room to fetch his dispatch case, and I felt Gabrielle's studied gaze upon me. I looked at her, my face expressionless, while she sipped her coffee and regarded me with her stunning eyes. Her one small fist was clenched upon the tabletop, and I was sure that her eyes began to glisten, but then she looked away and stared into nothingness.

She was now my master's lover, or at best his concubine, and I fully realized that my dealings with her must be proper and polite, without a hint of my true opinions. Any careless word or even revelatory expression might reach the Colonel's ear, and I was not about to risk my position with such carelessness. When occasionally Edward and I were sent to fetch her from her house or the field hospital, I spoke to her only when spoken to, and in studied and mannered replies, always accompanied by a pasted smile. I had returned to my very private war of survival, and principles were only for the doomed.

Then, our period of respite ended, as operations were about to recommence. One evening, Himmel hosted a small conference of commanders slated to participate in joint operations. These were ten officers of equal rank, from the infantry, Luftwaffe and Panzer divisions, and after their three-hour strategic discussions, they dined upon a meal we had prepared for the previous two days. Edward and I, along with Mutti, were called upon to serve the men throughout, and as they opened their collars and loosened their breeches, supping on wild pig and wine, they became quite raucous and began to sing. Even we the staff were invited to drink, albeit from our removed positions as servants in waiting, and standing, of course.

When it was over, and the officers had left, the pile of soiled dinnerware was too much for the country kitchen sink. Edward and Mutti piled the pots, pans, plates and saucers into a large washbasin, hauling it out to the farmstead well pump, where they began to labor by the light of a lantern. I remained in the kitchen, scrubbing at the wineglasses with a brush. Himmel was quite drunk, though jolly, and he placed a Strauss record on the windup gramophone and began to waltz with himself throughout the salon. His partner was a fresh bottle of Branntwein, delivered by a resourceful panzer commander.

My back was turned to him as I sluiced cold water from the faucet, but I could see his reflection in the kitchen window, his open tunic swaying as he danced.

"Do you think she loves me, Shtefan?" he called out as he closed his boots together, opened them, and spun.

My spine stiffened, yet I continued scrubbing.

"I beg your pardon, Herr Colonel?"

"Do you think she loves me?"

I had to respond quickly, for any delay would become its own answer.

"I have only just lost my virginity, thanks to you, Sir," I called back to him in a jolly tone to match his own. "Love is something I know nothing about."

Himmel laughed heartily, and he continued his waltz.

"She does not love me, I assure you," he said, yet without a hint of disappointment. And then he added, "Not yet."

I said nothing, but I somehow desperately wanted the exchange to continue, and I washed each glass very carefully.

"She is magnificent, don't you think?" He had crossed the threshold into the kitchen, and now he was improvising some new step certainly unimagined by the Viennese composers.

"Yes, she is." It was not something I could lie about.

There was a moment's pause. Then Himmel was just behind me, poking his finger into my shoulder.

"Then *why* do you think she sleeps with me? Eh, Shtefan?"

What then stabbed through my mind was, *Because she's an opportunist and a whore and she eats and drinks very well here,* but I turned my head to him and smiled.

"Well, you are obviously an attractive man to her, Sir."

"Ha!" Himmel threw his head back and roared, and I was grateful that he staggered away and recommenced his pirouettes.

However, shortly he was beside me again, and this time he set the Branntwein bottle on the sink counter, steadying himself upon his elbows as he looked at me from very close. His one eye was shot through with pink lines, and his eye patch was askew.

"I'll tell you why she sleeps with me, my young corporal." He waved a finger up and twirled it. "Do you remember that message I sent to the Gestapo commander?"

"Yes, Sir." I continued washing, glancing at him only briefly.

"Do you know what was in it?" he asked, and I thought that he might actually giggle.

"No, Sir."

He turned his back to the counter then and leaned upon it for further support.

"It was a question. Only one question. 'How many children, between the ages of eight and fifteen, and who are the orphans of former French Resistance fighters, remain here in Avignon and Le Pontet?' Of course, that Gestapo bastard knew the answer right away, Shtefan. All of those secret police finks know these things."

"Yes, Sir," was all I replied. I did not know where he was going with this. He moved away for a moment, then staggered back to his place beside me, now puffing on half a cigar.

"So, do you know what my message to Gabrielle said, hmm? The one I delivered along with your basket?" He was very pleased with himself at this juncture, and his face was again too close for my comfort.

"What did it say, Sir?" I ventured, although my heart was beating a bit too quickly now, and I could feel the sweat gathering beneath my hair.

"It said… 'My lovely young woman. There are twenty-two orphans of former Maquis fighters still living in the environs of Avignon. Their fates are now in your hands. Please join me for dinner tomorrow evening.'"

Not of my own volition, my hands froze in their activity, and the shock upon my face must have been comically apparent, as I turned to Himmel and blinked. His eye widened, and then he tossed his head high and roared with laughter, and he pounded the counter with a fist and snatched up the Branntwein bottle, taking a long swig as he danced away from me. I slowly returned to my task as I listened to the rest of his soliloquy.

"Yes, my Shtefan Brandt! Yes!" he called out to me. "Mademoiselle Gabrielle Belmont does not love me, but she *understands* me, which is more than I can say for my wife! She has a heart and a soul, the poor wretched thing, and a magnificent figure, and I don't have to pay her or force her. She fucks me, because she is a *French patriot*. Is that not poetry? Is that not *romance*?!"

At this point, my blush of shame was so hot in my face that I felt it like lava rising up from my feet. My ears had pricked up like those of a bloodhound, hungry to take in every morsel of this new evidence. And Himmel returned to my side, bracing himself once more and wiping a tear of mirth from his eye. His voice quieted to a confiding tone as he raised a finger again.

"Of course, Brandt, you will learn that love comes after. Yes, most of the time it's all chemical at first, and whether you force it or buy it or seduce to get it, it's all the same. She doesn't love me now, no. But she might. She might! A woman's completely different from a man. A woman has this biological reaction... It's all in the textbooks... If you fuck her enough, she starts to think you're her mate. Yes..."

He trailed off then, and he dropped his head, as if something foul was rising up inside him and he had to cope for a moment.

"You know what, Shtefan?" he whispered.

"What, Sir?" I braced myself for some new revelation.

"I think I'm going to have a good vomit and get to bed. In two days, we're back in action."

He pushed himself away from the counter then, straightened up and marched off through the salon, skidding the gramophone needle from the record as he passed.

I turned off the water and stood there in the ghostly silence, my arms quaking, as was my chin. A flow of emotions coursed through me then, and it took every ounce of composure to remain steady. I had had my world turned inside out, once again. And I was grateful, yes. I thanked a God in whom I had not heretofore believed.

Gabrielle Belmont was not my master's mistress.

She was not his whore.

She was not his lover.

She was not the Princess to an Evil Prince.

She was his hostage.

VII

IN MARCH OF 1944, I was mistakenly awarded the army's Iron Cross.

I should be quick, however, to counter the impression that the granting of this medal was, in any way, some typographical error on behalf of a flummoxed headquarters clerk. In fact, it was bestowed upon me as a result of a formal submission by Colonel Himmel to the General Staff, with all the appropriate requisitions and pomp in concert. And my description of the event as an "error" is less a result of modesty than of a clarified view of the events, as fermented by the passing years. Upon reflection, I have realized that with most soldiers, acts of bravery are often reflexive responses to the crises at hand. In short, I was awarded the Iron Cross not because I was thinking under fire. I was running, and I happened to be running in the right direction.

Himmel often referred to the SS as "The Führer's Fire

Brigade," and although he used the phrase with tongue in cheek, it was an apt description. The various divisions and battalions of SS rarely fought in static positions for very long, or even remained at the spearheads of successful campaigns. Once the effect of such elite troops had been felt by the enemy, the High Command would often pull these units out and send them off to where they were most sorely needed next. Our particular Commando was a small and mobile striking force, utilized as the tip of the blade on a surgeon's scalpel. Thus, my master would monitor the progress of the war, and wherever things were going badly for the Reich, he would correctly assume that a visit to that hellhole would be shortly in order.

"The Russian front is a total disaster, Shtefan," he muttered to me through the haze of a hangover, on the morning after his commanders' conference and personal confessions.

"Shall I practice my Russian, Sir?" I queried as I poured him his sixth cup of coffee.

"You are beginning to learn the game, my young adjutant."

However, in fact my deductions required no tactical brilliance on my part, for a pair of heavy transport trucks had arrived that very dawn. In addition to the crates of ammunition, hand grenades, antitank weapons and satchel charges, the trucks contained a full uniform of white winter camouflage anorak and trousers for every man. Further to that, for each squad came an unusual piece of equipment called a "Krummlauf." This was a curved barrel extension that could be fitted to a Sturmgewehr 44 assault rifle. On the top of the extension was a mounted mirror, and thus the weapon's operator could shoot around corners, while remaining behind cover.

We were going someplace very, very cold, and we would be fighting house-to-house. This conclusion did not require the brains of an Einstein.

I shall not pretend that this realization failed to cause me some alarm, as had all news of impending operations heretofore. Yet gone were the near mortal, coronary palpitations that had immobilized me in the past. My character had apparently undergone another subtle shift, somewhat like the skin of a chameleon, adjusting to new emotional hues. I think now, that observing the minute cracks in my master's demeanor, his tiny weaknesses coming to fore like the crow's-feet around an ancient's eyes, somehow added proportionately to my own strength. As I accepted the fissures of his humanity, my own were shored up. Of course, what I would not admit to myself was the fact that Gabrielle Belmont's sullied virtue had been repaired in my eyes, and there existed in my mind a sense of hope as yet undefined.

That evening, a pair of Luftwaffe pilots and an army intelligence major appeared at the estate. They huddled with Himmel and his officers until midnight, poring over maps and peering at aerial reconnaissance photographs through stereoscopes that showed the detail in relief. The troop was sent to bed early that eve, and after clearing the dinner dishes and leaving the officers to their strategies, Edward, Mutti and I sat together in the carriage house, playing a game of cards upon a mortar shell crate. The two men, who usually fell quickly into competitions of bawdy jokes, were curiously silent. They smoked and swigged schnapps and squinted at their hands, while occasionally eyeing me from beneath furrowed brows. I recall the conversation was somewhat like this.

"You shouldn't be going on this one, Shtefan," Edward muttered.

"I shouldn't?"

"No. This one's for the hard corps."

"You don't say." I bridled a bit, not really wanting to be thought of as genuine SS, while simultaneously offended at the exclusion.

"*Ja, das stimmt,*" Mutti agreed with Edward. He slapped a quartet of useless cards on the wooden crate, swigged from the schnapps bottle and wiped his bearded mouth on the back of his hairy hand. "You look a little sick to me."

"I'm not sick. I'm fine."

"He looks sick, doesn't he, Edward?" The burly cook poked the corporal's shoulder.

"*Ja*, very pale," Edward agreed. "Maybe we should tell the Colonel he's unfit for duty."

"Nonsense," I protested.

"You should stay home for this one, Shtefan," Edward continued. "Be sick and stay here and just check up on Gabrielle for the Colonel."

The two men exchanged a certain look, and small smiles, and I blushed very deeply and got up and went out from the carriage house to pee. I walked for a bit in the shallow snow under a pale moon, composing myself, and of course wondering if these men who had become my de facto uncles might indeed be right. Yet I managed to shake off the foreboding, for I did not know then what I know now.

Youths are chosen for combat precisely because they are unable to fully imagine their own mortality. If armies were composed of the middle-aged, there would be no wars.

When I returned to our quarters, the lamps were extinguished, and Edward and Mutti were curled up in their bedrolls. The cook was already snoring, but as I slipped into my woolen cocoon, I knew that Edward still lay awake.

"It's the Russian front, Shtefan," he murmured after a few minutes of oppressive silence. "It's not a fucking joke."

"I do not have a choice, you know," I replied quietly. "He expects me to go."

"Well, then, this time stay right behind the old man and don't let him out of your sight."

"I will," I said, and I shivered in my blankets.

"And maybe you should write a letter home," Edward added ominously.

And with that, the danger of this enterprise finally struck me, but I only managed to whisper, "I have no one to write to."

Edward turned over and went to sleep, leaving me awake and wide-eyed, staring at nothing but horrific images of my own concoction.

Well before dawn, Captain Friedrich assembled a select platoon of thirty-two on the field before the barn. The white camouflage uniforms were issued, and the men, who had donned double pairs of stockings and their warmest underclothes, struggled into the bulky anoraks and leggings. I joined them in the ranks, pulling a new woolen cowl over my head, and while strapping on my helmet I was not pleased to see the commandos doing likewise.

When they sought the protection of steel, it meant that steel would soon rain.

Heinz the armorer appeared then, followed by a trio of privates hauling the additional crates of ammunition, grenades and satchel charges. He spent a great deal of time checking over grenade heads and magazine springs, which was rather a silent ritual reminiscent of a priest placing wafers upon the tongues of the damned. Jolly by nature, his occasional jokes and those of the men echoed feebly in the frozen air.

Himmel strode from the main house then, replete in his white regalia, and I suddenly wished to be skiing in Graz. For the very first time, he, too, was wearing a helmet, and the only things to distinguish him from the rest of his officers were his eye patch and his very black Knight's Cross, which poked out from the collar of his tunic and looked much like a target against the white of his anorak. His gloves were gripped in his right hand, and he slapped them into his palm and grinned.

"*Guten Morgen.*"

The troops snapped to attention. I remember very well that just then, the sun peeked up from a bank of horizon fog, and it gleamed from the barrel of a light machine gun perched upon its bipod.

"We are going to Russia," he announced. Then, after a beat, "As if you didn't know."

The men laughed softly, and I realized that the real talents of command were very subtle and psychological.

"The 48th Panzer Corps is in the shit near Kamenets Podolsky, just over the Dniester River. They are going to attempt a breakout. But, in Chernovtsky, the Russians are assembling a full company of tank busters. We're going to go into the town, kill as many of them as we can, and get out. It is going to be strictly house-to-house, and strictly ugly. No prisoners, please. Any Russian you leave alive will surely be killing German panzers on the morrow. If I am killed in action, your captain and lieutenants have studied the route and target area, and you will complete the mission. Any questions?"

There was none. There was not even a murmur. Himmel nodded his approval, and then he clicked his boot heels, saluted his troops and snapped, *"Glück auf!"*

"Good luck!" They all shouted in unison, but no more than a croak emerged from my own dry mouth...

Our convoy wound its way first toward Le Pontet via Vedène, where the earliest of the French workers briskly clipped along the cobblestones, wearing fingerless gloves and blowing steam from their nostrils like horses. We had welcomed an additional truck into our complement, as our troops were ballooned like snowmen in their coveralls and could not all fit into the transports at hand. A Luftwaffe reconnaissance car led the procession, and in our staff car just behind, the Colonel and the army intelligence major continued to peruse and mark a pile of aerial photographs.

As we passed the Wehrmacht field hospital, I found myself sitting a bit more erect in my seat, and I could not help but let my eyes cast about, perusing the nurses and aides already scurrying about with their bandages and pails. I did not really expect to see Gabrielle, and when I did see her,

I felt a strange constriction in my throat. She stood upon a small mound of sandbags near the hospital's perimeter, and she was wearing a white nurse's apron and a white woolen scarf, and I thought for a moment that she surely had become the angel of some Wagnerian god, bearing a message as yet to be deciphered.

She watched us as we passed. I fully expected Himmel to look up, and to offer a smart salute or a cocky grin of departure. Yet in the staff car's rearview mirror, I observed him glance briefly in Gabrielle's direction, and immediately return his attention to his work. I envied his compartmentalization of his emotions, for my own were a swirling pool of fear and longing. Her eyes met mine for a long moment, and from where her hands clutched a bandage basket to her chest, she raised a single finger. My mouth made a very small smile as I then refocused on the road ahead, determined to return alive, and wishing for perhaps just a minor wound.

Beyond the field hospital were some humps of rolling hills, and below them a wide cow pasture, and upon that sat a Luftwaffe Junkers Ju 52 transport airplane. Its sides were flat and corrugated, its fuselage and wings painted white and striped with slim green snakes of camouflage, and its three large engines were already sputtering and coughing black smoke. The plane was designed to accommodate a limited number of paratroopers, but its benches had been stripped away and our entire troop turtled up the ladder and squeezed inside, sitting knees to rumps upon the freezing metallic floor. The arsenal of assault equipment was piled upon us, slipped beneath our legs and stuffed between our bodies, and as I realized that even a moderately rough landing would purée the lot of us like apples in a baker's mixer, we were quickly airborne.

I have, since the night of that "Vol Du Nuit" from France, experienced perhaps scores of airplane flights. Some have been luxurious, and most of a certain discomfort, yet no simple excursion of cramped calves in coach class or less-than-gourmet airline repasts shall ever compare to that most unforgettable journey.

It was a day without end, as we flew from a clear French dawn into a chowder of clouds above the Italian Alps, and trundled through thickening storms above Czechoslovakia. The Junkers's steel skin was so cold that frost formed upon the ceiling, and the engine heat piped through thin floor channels was entirely ineffectual. Only the tight packing of our trembling bodies served as enough insulation to prevent hypothermia, and as our breaths rose in the air and melted the frost above, the dangling droplets quickly froze into taunting icicles. The thrum of the big tri-motors was maddening, although I am certain that each of the troop prayed fervently to his private deity that it should carry on without a sputter.

At the rear of the Junkers there was a small steel waste commode, yet being so tightly packed and obstructed by our equipment, there was no hope of forging one's way to the toilet. And so, a small iron kitchen pot was passed from man to man, accompanied by much laughter and bitter curses as the commandos tried to locate and extract their shriveled penises. As the pot filled, it was passed to the rear, where a private named Donau, who resembled me in form and age, inherited the misfortune of spilling urine into the commode tube. The men chewed dry crackers and took small sips from their water bottles, and so many smoked that soon the cabin air turned into a rank, swirling fog. After a few hours, the inevitable occurred.

"I have to shit," someone groaned.

"Then shit in your pants and sit in it," Captain Friedrich ordered. "It'll keep you warm."

I do not know if any of the men took his instructions to heart. Thankfully, my nostrils were frozen beyond all sensation.

Colonel Himmel was perched in the cockpit with the pilots, yet at some point during the afternoon he sensed the sullen silence that had by then overtaken the cabin, and he bent his head and made his way among the troop. He carefully stepped between the men, reviewing assignments with his officers and stopping to joke with the lowest of the ranks. And as I watched him, I wondered. Had Gabrielle refused his bed, would he in fact have had those orphans of Avignon executed? Perhaps one by one until she relented? Yet I came to no conclusion, and when at last he returned to the cockpit, he paused to look down at me, amused by my effort to smile through my chattering teeth.

"Did you bring the Leica, Brandt?"

I froze momentarily. I had completely forgotten about the camera.

"No, Sir." I shook my head. "I apologize."

He squatted then before me, yet still smiling. "Don't worry. It will all happen in the dark at any rate, so you couldn't use it. Besides," he added as he slapped the top of my helmet, "I expect you to shoot something more than pictures tonight."

Sometime after dusk, when I believe we were above the southern wastes of Poland, the airplane entered a monstrous bank of winter storms. It shook and rattled and pitched and rolled, and the wings moaned like banshees and flexed to nearly snapping, and we were forced to grip each other's shoulders and thighs to keep from being tossed about the cabin. In the few small open spaces between our bodies, our ordnance slid and scraped across the floor like dinner plates in a submarine's mess, and very soon, the first man began to vomit. Someone crawled to a fuselage window and managed to crack the ice with a pistol butt and slide it open, but the terrible wind that screamed through the cabin did little to stem the infectious tide of nausea, and soon the piss pot was filled with bile. I do not know how I managed to keep my own stomach from regurgitating its meager snacks, but I concluded then that every army designs its sea and air transports with a precise objective in mind: the more horrible the trip, the more anxious will the troops be to debark and charge into the face of enemy fire.

I believe that it was sometime close to midnight when we finally landed outside Chernovtsky. I had only recently acquired my very first wristwatch, bartered from a badly wounded soldier at the field hospital in exchange for a bottle of schnapps. Yet the many hours aboard our flying ice box had crippled the hands of the timepiece, which hardly mattered since the precise hour was relevant only to Colonel Himmel.

My stomach rose toward my throat as the Junkers dipped

into a gliding dive, the pilots throttling the engines back to reduce the noise and enhance our chances of a surprise arrival. The pair of dim light bulbs that had heretofore glowed in the cabin were extinguished, and only a crimson combat lamp gave eerie silhouette to the pilots in the cockpit. The raven dark inside was matched by the blackness from without, and I could only surmise that we were weaving very low between the mounds of a hidden valley, as the nearly silent airplane banked this way and that. My master did not bother to warn us to brace for landing, for we knew full well it was about to pass, and more than thirty sets of teeth gritted hard as the wheels finally smacked once, then again, upon some unforgiving surface, and the tail settled as waves of powdered snow washed over the wings and whirling propellers.

We stopped.

"Thanks be to God in hell," someone muttered.

"Raus!" Himmel snapped from up forward, yet he had no need to coax. The door was sprung immediately, and the entire Commando abandoned the airplane like convicts from a prison fire, scorning the ladder and leaping into the snow, then turning quickly to receive their hurled equipment from the next in line. Those whose bladders were already empty quickly loaded their weapons and covered the flanks, squinting into the white flakes swirling from a black sky as the rest of us pissed and groaned with relief. And more than a few trudged off and squatted in more elaborate efforts, or rubbed the stench and taste of vomit from their mouths with gloves full of ice, and all of us cranked our cramped arms and stamped out our aching leg muscles.

The airplane had set down upon a very narrow country road, and I marveled that just a few meters beyond the cockpit, that road made a very sharp turn around a high embankment, which would have abruptly terminated our venture if not for the precision flying of the pilots. Already a panzer officer in a long, frayed greatcoat had rushed out to greet Colonel Himmel and the pilots, and the four of them conferred in whispers beneath a wing. A small squad of panzer soldiers were gathering their now extinguished landing beacons, while another struggled with large petrol drums, rolling them toward the Junkers across a flat expanse. Tightening my trouser cuffs against the shin-deep snow, I turned wide-eyed when I heard the copilot chuckle to the panzer officer.

"We didn't *have* to cut the engines. We were out of fuel."

Within minutes, the commandos had assembled themselves into a pair of long spaced lines, their weapons loaded at the ready, their equipment strapped upon their backs and buckles tightened. Beyond our small landing area the visibility was nil, as shallow hills rose all around, yet soon a pair of reconnaissance scouts appeared on slim skis, their iced fur caps and goggles making them appear otherworldly. As Himmel strode to the head of his column, I trudged quickly to his side, remembering the exhortations of Edward. A scout approached the Colonel, but he did not salute.

"*Guten Abend, Herr Standartenführer,*" he said. "The Russians have gathered mostly in the cathedral tonight."

"Good," said Himmel. "We'll give them something to pray for."

He turned to the troop, waved his gloved hand, and we were off.

At the crest of the very first rise, Chernovtsky appeared immediately in the distance, mostly a dark complex of low buildings, with a very few windows glowing in the snow. It was, perhaps, not three kilometers away, yet after only a sixth of that quick march, I was utterly exhausted. I had no idea that one could sweat so in the midst of this frozen and bitter landscape. My winter costume, whose insulating abilities had seemed nonexistent aboard the Junkers, now transformed itself into a fireman's suit in the midst of a house blaze. My woolen cowl was soon soaked with salty drippings from my scalp beneath my helmet, and rivulets ran down my arms and slithered between my legs. I was breathing like an asthmatic, barely able to keep up with Himmel's careless long strides through the snow, and I wished for nothing more than to strip myself of every piece of clothing and make the raid in my shorts alone. The reconnaissance men skied easily along at the point of our columns, and at last I began to fully appreciate the level of training of the SS to my rear. Not one of them flagged or strayed or fell behind. There was not a single grunt of effort or complaint from their ranks. I felt rather like the aging mascot dog to a team of Olympians.

Yet I managed to take heart, for certainly as we approached the town, Colonel Himmel would halt the troop. He would have us gratefully lie in the snow as he made a final assessment, and I could catch my breath and allow the winter night to cool my fevers. Yet this respite was not to be, as Himmel had clearly chosen aggression above care. There would be no careful crawling into positions, no tiptoeing along alleyways to lengthen the surprise. As we neared Chernovtsky, my master abandoned stealth, and without another word, he began to run.

And I remember it all quite clearly, every bit of it, for unlike my first venture into combat in Italy, this snippet of my personal history is seared into some corner of my brain. Like a strip of film engaged upon a continuous loop, it replays itself for me to this day, without warning, flicked on with the scent of an impending snowfall, the sounds of aircraft engines on a winter night, or even the sensation of harmless woolen gloves.

We charged directly into the mouth of the enemy's cauldron. Perhaps we were merely two hundred meters short of the town's perimeter, yet even as we gathered speed that distance seemed to stretch, like an agonizing pull of licorice. We were facing directly down the tunnel of its main thoroughfare, a long wide street of trampled snow and mud between dark edifices of stone. There were no outskirts of the town to speak of, not even a suburb of hovels. In less than half a minute, we would be in it.

Shocked by this discard of sanity, I tucked myself up behind the Colonel's back, trying to keep erect in the accursed snow as I ran. My helmet slipped back upon my head, its bouncing brim retreating to fully expand my vision, and as I glanced aside, the troop fanned out to the flanks, their figures blurring with their tremendous forward speed. Each squad knew precisely its objective, and they passed our spearhead and flew over the snow, heading directly for the streets and alleyways they'd memorized from the aerial photographs. Our pair of reconnaissance scouts fell away from us like pilot fish abandoning a shoal of sharks, and me, I felt merely a hostage rider on this cavalry charge into hell.

A jolt of pain shuddered through my shinbones as our boots struck the first street stones, and I inhaled a gasp through gritted teeth as I saw a cluster of Russian trucks and motorcycles parked along the thoroughfare. The relative silence of our boot heels upon snow had instantly become a thunderous stampede, accompanied by the racket of bouncing ammunition pouches and rattling weapons slings. The first to hear our onrushing storm was a huddle of tethered horses, and they flicked their heads about with widened eyes as beyond them I first saw the cathedral at the center of the town on the left. Its flat stone face appeared enormous to me, its thrusts of pointed onion spires like gleaming papal hats. Below, yet so much closer, were the first of the Russian troops.

A cluster of them stood in the very middle of the street, wearing heavy fur hats with earflaps, and long coats that nearly swept the ground. From their shoulders, the heavy wooden stocks, round magazines and gleaming perforated barrels of their PPSh-41 submachine guns still hung casually, and the glows of their cigarettes made orange arcs as they slowly turned from their chat.

It was Himmel and myself and Captain Friedrich and seven more in our gang of onrushing madmen, yet in that agonizing and endless moment on the precipice of discovery, I felt utterly alone, like a naked thief discovered in a bank vault. Yet certainly to those unfortunate Russians, we were at first an apparition, an unexplained arrival of their own troops, our haste a curiosity. And then, as our speed even doubled again, they discerned our helmets and our weapons and their eyes flew wide and they unslung their guns, and it was far too late for them.

Himmel roared like some wild animal as he began to fire from the hip, the explosions from his Schmeisser barrel blinding me, and I went instantly deaf as all the other guns joined his. The buildings flashed with the lightning of bursting machine pistols, the spent shells spinning through the air as one hot brass casing struck my frozen cheek and I winced as it hissed against my flesh. I saw one Russian thrust his gloved hand against a comrade's shoulder to save him, yet as both men flung themselves wide apart Himmel's bullets lifted them high and backward and they smashed down upon the muddy street. I found my pistol extended at the end of my quaking arm, yet I dared not fire as my master's form bobbed so close before me. A Russian leaped out from behind a stone escarpment and I saw his machine gun barking white gouts of flame, and to my right beyond Friedrich one of our men grunted and fell to his face as if his ankles had been struck from under him, and his helmet rim banged and echoed on the cobbles as all of our guns spun to that lone Russian and his long coat was shredded from his body by a vengeful hosing of bullets. A horse, perhaps his tether split by an errant projectile, thundered past our flanks, and as we passed the others they reared and bucked, their eyes huge and white and their nostrils spewing steam and panic. One of them was down in a pile of bloody snow, his flanks split open and drooling entrails, and he kicked his hooves and screamed an unearthly howl.

Himmel suddenly leaped into the air, his left arm slicing out for balance and his legs tucking up like a hurtler's, and as I saw his boots sail above a twitching corpse I attempted to mimic his grace. Yet my body twisted clumsily and I looked down to see my heel smash into a pale, ungloved hand, and with the horror of flesh and bone crushed beneath my weight I tumbled forward. But someone snatched at my battle harness, and I was instantly up again and running.

For only the briefest moment, there was a respite from the gunfire, yet it seemed to me that my pounding heart and the ragged spew of air from my lungs would certainly obscure even a cannonade. I reached up to tear my woolen cowl away from one ear, yet the fleshy drum within had already been so pounded that its cottony deadness was little improved. Still, I heard the heavy ringing of bolts as the men around me deftly changed their magazines on the run, and from somewhere ahead came the muffled shouts of calls to arms in Russian. The cathedral's arcing edifice grew larger, and as we passed the black tunnel of a cross street, I glimpsed another of our elements racing along a parallel thoroughfare.

We neared the church, and for an instant I fantasized that the company of Russian tank destroyers had in fact abandoned the town. Yes, this small group of men we'd slaughtered was the lot of it, all that was left, and we would shortly gather together in wonder and Himmel would kick the cobblestones in frustration and we would retrieve our wounded and be off to home. And just then, one tall wooden door of the cathedral's entrance swung open.

They burst from it in a wave of flying cloaks and weapons whirling about, the red stars on their fur caps glinting as they charged down the wide stone steps. Perhaps there were twenty of them, perhaps more, and without waiting to discern a target they opened fire, forming a ragged arc of men and sweeping across the street before them as they yelled in chorus and their bullets sparked and chunked off shards of building stones. And it was then, as those exploding barrels turned inexorably to us, that I knew it was the end. We were charging into a hornet's nest, and it was here in the frozen wastes of Asia that I would be stung to death with all the rest.

Himmel abruptly stopped and dropped to one knee, yet somehow I managed to avoid crashing into him as I flung myself to his right and smashed facedown into the street. The impact crushed my lower lip into my teeth, and instantly a rush of hot blood flowed over my chin, yet I lifted my head and gripped my pistol with both hands, and yes, I began to fire, to live, somehow, if I could. Our element knelt in a ragged line to both my master's flanks, caressing their Schmeissers to their cheeks and jerking rapid bursts, and as someone's spent shells clanged off my helmet, my own shells were being flung from my pistol and pummeling some comrade.

I could not see who I killed, or in fact if I harmed a soul at all, for my target was nothing but a blur of smoke and flashes beyond my squint. I grunted when something thumped into my back, then realized it was the Colonel's fist as he snatched a grenade from my belt, yanked the igniter from its bottom and hurled it, and he was up again and running before it exploded out there beyond with a heavy thump and flash.

He was yelling something now, a cry of warning I could not discern, and as I dragged myself up I saw that my pistol slide was open and I struggled to discharge the spent magazine. Yet being left alone was more a ghastly thought to me than any other, and I staggered after our element as I fumbled with the accursed weapon. Half of the Russians lay upon the wide stone church steps in a steaming twisted pile of limbs askew, while the survivors still fired, yet not at us. Just beyond the church and across the way, Lieutenant Schneller's squad had emerged from an alley, and he stood there flailing away with his machine pistol while his machine-gun crew lay in the street, their MG-42 rattling like a jackhammer, slicing through the Russians and pocking up the cathedral's face. And then I saw what Himmel had already seen, an open window of the church just astride the large entrance, and from it poked a strangely shaped green phallus. All at once the anti-tank grenade boomed a spout of flame, and immediately its warhead obliterated Schneller and his crew in a terrible roar of fire and smoke and stone.

I froze then with that vision, of helmets tumbling through the air, of shards of winter white anoraks with blackened frays, floating down like smoking goose down, the twisted red-hot barrel of a weapon spinning off to clang against a roof eave. And I thought this madness could not possibly be multiplied, yet with my feet rooted to the street I watched our command element fall upon the remaining Russians like an enraged pack of wolves. Behind me horses screamed with fresh punctures from the cross fire, and before me German muzzles barked so close to Russian flesh that sprays of bone and blood shot upward with the ricochets. I saw the shoulder of Lieutenant Gans's anorak punch up and out with the impacting Makarov bullet of one Russian survivor, and even as he twisted and fell, two of our own clutched their SS daggers in their fists and butchered that last defiant one.

A swooning dizziness came upon me then. The adrenaline coursing through my quivering limbs gripped my bowels, and I placed my hands upon my knees and bent over and a torrent of steaming bile stung my splayed lips. And as I watched the boiling ooze sink through the snow at my feet, I thought I heard my name.

"Brandt!"

I looked up. Himmel stood in the very center of the thoroughfare, his left fist cocked against his hip like a fencer, his right hand extended and his pistol barrel aimed at the cathedral window. Just beyond him, our troops kicked at the Russian corpses and shed them of their weapons. Near his feet, Lieutenant Gans lay writhing, rolling from his back onto his left shoulder, then back again as a medic bent over him and fought to thrust a bandage into his wound. From somewhere to the rear of the cathedral came an intense and continuous chatter of gunfire.

"Brandt!"

It was my master's voice, and I managed to straighten up and hobble to him in my profound weakness, and just as I neared him another antitank grenade poked from the window and Himmel fired five quick shots and the device clattered and slid away. The Colonel turned to me and calmly slid another of my grenades from my belt, popped the fuse, and I covered my ears and folded up like an infant as he waited, and waited, and finally spun the explosive into the window. Immediately after the incredible burst, I looked up at him to see him unmoved, his cheek split by a shard of something and a stream of blood dribbling over his collar.

From somewhere just within the cathedral doors, a high-pitched voice called out in Russian. Himmel turned to it, tucking his pistol into his belt and lifting the Schmeisser that hung from his neck. The urgent babbling grew louder, and then a man stepped out onto the cathedral steps. He was bald and quaking from his knees to his hands held high above his head. He was wearing a brown woolen monk's robe, tied at the waist with a heavy rope, and upon his feet were a pair of open galoshes. He glanced about and continued to entreat in a string of pleas and prayers, and all of our men lifted their heads to him and I thought this tableau of piety meeting perniciousness could not be real as Himmel grunted.

"*Hier sind keine Priester.* There are no priests here." He shot the father with a burst that flung him from the steps, though I did not see the priest fall, as my eyes were slammed shut. I clutched at a sob that made to escape my throat, knowing that here and forever ended all roads to salvation, with a deed that could never be prayed away.

"Noss!" Himmel called out. "Rope the doors and arm the satchels!"

Corporal Noss came on the run with his demolition team hauling the packs of explosives, while a thatch of men swung the church doors closed, muffling shouts from inside, and they bound the heavy latches with turns and knots of assault ropes.

"More magazines, Shtefan. From my pouch."

I moved to Himmel's back as I jammed my pistol into its holster, and I fumbled with his leather satchel buckles, managing to extract three Schmeisser magazines. He quickly loaded one and began to fire short controlled bursts into the shattered church window, as my cheeks and eyes flinched with each concussion. Someone trotted heavily past us, carrying a limp form across his shoulders.

"Where are the rest, Sir?" I managed to yell, little that I cared but more so to discover if I still had a voice.

"The rest of what?"

"Our men, Sir."

"They're behind the cathedral. Can't you hear them?"

Yes, of course I could hear them; they had been firing all along. And I realized that our element's purpose was to drive the balance of the Russians to the rear of the cathedral, where they were being slaughtered as they sought their last exit. Himmel began to walk backward now, firing at the window more intensely and in longer bursts, and I remained attached to his flank, more scuttling like a turtle than moving like a man. Urgent shouts rose up from within the building, and Himmel moved more quickly and he switched magazines and fired continuously now.

"Cover!" he yelled, and peripherally I saw our men hurry from before the cathedral's face. "Noss! Blow it!" he yelled again, and the corporal and his men rushed forward to the open window, their satchels already hissing with the sparks of rushing fuses. "Go!" Himmel slammed a palm into my chest, but its impact sent me sprawling onto my back. And then Friedrich had me by my arm and we were dashing away, past the cathedral doors, which bucked out now fruitlessly against our ropes as those within sensed their one and only chance of escape. And then the explosives detonated.

I did not know where I was. I did not know who I was. I lay facedown in the street, and I opened my stinging eyes to a cocoon of swirling, choking smoke. My helmet was gone, my gloves were gone, and as I regained the present, I was certain that the ringing gong within my head could be nothing other than the cathedral's bells. My spine ached as if it had been hammered, and as I gathered my elbows beneath me and raised my head from the sodden stones, the smoke drifted away and I saw Captain Friedrich. His face was close, a pair of bloody rivers running from his nostrils. His cheeks were bony white, and then his eyelids fluttered, just as I discerned a distant and repeated call, the order of which I'd been dreaming.

"To the plane!"

Yes! It was all I had wanted to hear, the only mission that could move me now, and the encroaching patter of more gunfire only spurred my final strength. I came to my knees and I reached out for Friedrich's battle harness, and then I squatted and groaned and with every twitching muscle I stood up and tried to run.

"Come on!" I screamed at the dead weight of Friedrich's form, yet his numbed arms hung loosely and his Schmeisser swung from his neck and struck me, and this obstacle to my survival only enraged me more as I shook him violently.

"Come on, damn you!" He jerked his white blond head up then and shook it, his helmet flying from its broken strap and clattering away, and he rose and turned and placed a hand upon my shoulder, and I charged blindly through the smoke, leading him like a cripple's dog.

My vision cleared and I reached out to brace against a stony wall, and then we were rounding a corner and all at once there was no smoke at all. The air was crisp and clear and virtually unsoiled, and as we stumbled into an open street, I realized with a slackened jaw that our disoriented state had taken us not back toward the plane at all, but past the cathedral and deeper into Chernovtsky. A squad of enraged Russians was racing toward us.

Friedrich pushed me violently away and fell to his knees and immediately began to fire his Schmeisser, and as I bounced beside a wall I heard a split of sonic cracks above my head. There was nowhere to go and nothing to save me, and cursing and grunting as I yanked my pistol from its pouch, I did not even feel the bullet whip through my trousers and pierce my thigh. My hands flew up above my head as I lay on my side and I fired madly at the rolling forms and flashing weapons beyond, and then my pistol went dry and I knew I had nothing left. I looked over at Friedrich, who was sitting there now fully on his rump, his legs splayed like a child as he gritted his teeth and ran out of ammunition, and I waited for him to be struck dead.

Himmel appeared then, rounding the corner, accompanied by Noss and two more men. They immediately crouched and released a murderous endless burst from their weapons, and then Himmel leaned forward and clutched at my battle harness, and I thought that he had gone completely insane, his face split with a grin so improbably gleeful.

"Have you both gone mad?!" he shouted. "I said to home!"

I needed no further encouragement, but in trying to rise, I collapsed over my wounded leg and someone slung my arm about his neck. I swooned then, and in half a faint I found myself between two SS, sprinting back along the main thoroughfare as if in a school yard three-legged race. I do not remember the final course of that hurried retreat to our airplane, except that I bounced along upon some giant's shoulders, and in the fog of semiconsciousness, I heard the constant echoes of gunfire close behind...

Somewhere high above Poland, I came to my senses. The rim of a water bottle was touching my lips, and the sting of its cold steel and icy liquid lifted my head from where I lay. Our medic capped the bottle and briefly touched the back of his hand to my forehead. Then he moved away along the fuselage, half crouching like a careful duck. I looked down at my right leg, which was bound at the thigh by a leather strap. The wound itself was numb, but with each beat of my heart a throb jolted from my heel to my groin. Beyond my boot toes, the unharmed men were stuffed like cartoned eggs against the fuselage wall, not one of them awake, their heads drooped and bobbing in a light turbulence. Beside them, the wounded lay in a line from stem to stern, and at the Junkers's rear I could dimly discern the dead, piled carefully like firewood, their boot soles inter-locked like the pieces of a puzzle.

I looked to my left. Captain Friedrich lay close, upon his back, yet between us in the steel troughs of the floor ran thick rivers of frozen blood, like flows of lava black-ened on a glacier. He turned his head and smiled weakly.

"In the future, Brandt," he said, "I'll thank you not to order me about."

I tried to smile at his quip, yet nothing in my face would function, and I looked away along the vibrating tunnel of carnage.

"Eight wounded, and five dead," I heard Friedrich say. "But we are all here."

I closed my eyes. No, we were not all here. *I* was not here. I had moved on into another of my worlds, where such notions as a light wound to impress a maiden were now foolish and selfish and blasphemous. There was no such thing as a light wound, for the nature of its making would never recede, the event could not be healed like su-tured flesh. I shivered, and I felt the squeeze of tears leave the corners of my eyes, freezing on my face before they reached my ears.

And I slept.

VIII

In April of 1944, I slept at heaven's gate.

For nearly two weeks I hovered in a semiconscious state, lingering at the precipice of my own mortality. The wound that had at first appeared to be merely a tunneling of my flesh, had in fact nicked a transverse branch of the femoral artery, and by the time the Junkers landed once more in France, my purpling thigh had ballooned to twice its size. The duration of the flight had allowed a sepsis to encroach, and the Wehrmacht surgeons declared that only the extreme cold had prevented me from bleeding out as well. My body temperature had soared, and I babbled feverish ramblings as the chloroformed mask was set upon my face, and thereupon I was sliced open nearly from knee to groin. The doctors extracted the Russian projectile, along with some chips of bone, then did their best to suture up the furrowed damages and left the rest to fate and meager medicines.

I dreamed of Vienna, for as my form lay fitful and battling its infectious demons, my mind sought refuge in my purest childhood, and I sailed into an ecstatic vortex, swaying to the strains of Strauss. The spires of the city reached into a robin eggshell sky, and I hung once more upon the caboose of a tram, my smile broad in the summer sun and my cap waving gleefully from my hand. Horse-drawn carriages clopped along the banks of the Danube, the sails of skiffs snapped in the breeze, my mother called to me from the balcony of our flat, laughing as she hung white bedsheets from a line, and I could feel the soft leathers of my lederhosen against my suntanned thighs. The tastes of her Schnitzel and Weisswürste lay upon my lips, the scent of her perfume in my nostrils, and my heart once more fluttered with gasping laughter as my father's coarse hands snatched me up and his fingers tickled me mercilessly. My eyes rose again in wonder at the secrets of the gargantuan museums, the grace of prancing horses in the Prater, the bunches of rainbow fruits and piles of sweets in the market, and I felt again the very first touch of my fingers to the slim waist of a schoolgirl with a shy smile and glossy hair as I danced my first waltz.

The purest streets of the districts then darkened with winter clouds, and a black rain swept the city into night, and hundreds upon hundreds of boots marched behind thumping snares. My neck ached in its arch as I looked up to watch a strange man haranguing thousands from a hotel veranda, and soon the fires began and they did not stop, and the thunder from the skies flashed close to me and I flinched as images flickered faster, and faster. A beautiful young woman kissed my eyebrows, her delicate fingers unbuttoned my shirt, and when her sweet mouth neared mine it turned blood red and widened like the maw of a fish. And then, an avalanche of murderous snow hurtled toward me, carrying upon its white tidal wave a tumble of steel helmets and amputated hands and rolling pirates' heads. And then, the blurred face of Friedrich hovered before my eyes as they streamed with helpless tears, and I knew he was dying even as he whispered comforts to me, and I could only grip his hand with all of my strength as I cried out to him, begging him not to leave me, and I sat up hard and with the force of all my soul I screamed.

Yet the face was not the captain's, and neither was the hand.

Both of them belonged to Gabrielle Belmont.

She stood directly beside me, her wavering image surrounded by a halo of darkness, her cheeks aglow with the lemon flicker of an oil lamp from somewhere and her full lips closed and calm. Her head was wrapped in a white woolen scarf from which some strands of her blond hair veiled a portion of her eyes, and her composure was in counterpoint to the panic of my waking. I did not know where I was, my heart still pounding and my lungs still gasping with the nightmare, and I dropped my gaze to find my white-knuckled fist gripping her small hand so that it most certainly was painful to her, yet there was no flinch in her expression. She slowly raised her other hand and covered mine, and with the warmth of her small fingers I slowly exhaled into a trust that I was indeed safe, and alive.

I lay back, finding my head upon a pillow, my body in

the canvas boat of an army cot, its wooden frame creaking beneath my weight. I squinted and turned my head from the lamp, for even its soft glow was too much for my eyes that had taken no light for a fortnight. I could see the damp walls of a large field tent, its sides rolled to the ground and buckling against a cold night wind. There seemed to be eight or perhaps ten other cots inside the tent, yet only three were occupied, all by men heavily swathed in bandages. The man to my immediate left appeared nearly mummified in strips of gauze that oozed with yellow antiseptic and watery blood serum, and between us, my master's gramophone sat upon an empty oil drum, softly crackling out the strains of "The Blue Danube."

I looked again at Gabrielle as she gently peeled my fist from her hand and laid it to my side, and she pulled up a layer of woolen blankets and tucked them about my neck. She was not looking directly at me, but appeared to be focusing on the precise maneuvering of the blankets, and I was not sure at all that she was really there until she softly spoke.

"Welcome back to your world, Shtefan Brandt."

I tried to swallow and speak, but it was as if a large dry ball was mired in a gullet of sand. Gabrielle reached for a water bottle, and she lifted my head and wet my lips, and the small cool stream felt wonderful in my throat. I flicked my eyes to the gramophone and back.

"The music doesn't disturb the others?" I whispered.

"I think not." Her eyes smiled a bit as they met mine. "They are in a deeper sleep than you have had."

"How long was it?"

"Two weeks. For a time, we thought it might be much longer."

It was then I remembered my wound and my leg, and not knowing what might have transpired while I was far away and deep in my dreams, I tried to raise my head and look.

"No." She laid a palm upon my brow and pressed it back to the pillow. "You still have your leg." For a moment, her hand remained on my forehead. "But you are fevered and must rest."

She moved away, and I lay there looking at the peaked ceiling of the tent, the oil lamp projecting her giant shadow there as she worked at something.

"Where are the others?" I asked.

"The others?"

"The wounded."

"Most of them are recovered and back to their work."

"Most of them."

"I am sorry, Shtefan Brandt. I do not know the names of your friends."

My friends. There was something in her tone, and the way in which she used my full name, and I realized with a sense of gloom that she was performing a task without care. If my recovery moved her, I would likely never know. She would not fret, perhaps over nothing and no one ever again. She had seen her parents murdered.

"I am the one who should apologize." My voice was a hoarse croak. "It seems late. You must be very tired."

"It is four o'clock in the morning." I thought I heard a smile in her voice, yet she placed a cold towel upon my brow, and I could not see her face, and I shivered. "Fatigue is a luxury long passed."

"Yes," I said, even as a profound exhaustion settled in my bones.

"Besides," she added. "We are young and vigorous, are we not?"

I tried to agree, but my voice had left me again. And yet, all that mattered at that moment was Gabrielle's admission of our link by youth, if by nothing else...

I awoke to a spring wind, emerging from the feathered edges of a dream I could not remember, except that it had something to do with a shimmering summer lake and a boat with a large sail. My eyes were heavy with encrusted sleep, and I raised a leaden hand and rubbed them, squinting up at the great canvas roof of the tent, which snapped and crackled with every whip of the breeze. The walls were still rolled to the ground, yet it seemed to be midday, for the heavy cloth nearly glowed with a mossy hue and thin shafts of light pierced the structure's errant holes and cracks. Outside, the wheels of caissons trundled across the muddy ruts, doctors shouted orders and the walking wounded murmured, and I could hear the labored breathing of my tent mates, though none of them stirred or moved.

Beneath the heavy blankets, I curled my toes against the coarse wool and was so pleased to find them functional that I tried to bend my knee. A blade of pain sliced up immediately from my thigh to my groin, and I exhaled a whispered hiss and returned my leg to its place, releasing my teeth from their clench. I turned my head to the right, and spotting a water bottle on a flimsy metal table there, I reached out for it and brought it to my lips. Yet as I raised my head to drink, I started and dropped the bottle in horror, for it appeared that a huge black spider was perched on my left breast.

I blinked, and then I blinked again. The object was not arachnid at all, but in fact the army's Iron Cross. I was wearing a heavy, long-sleeved undershirt, and the medal had been pinned to the sweat-stained garment, and in contrast to the drudgery of my hospital attire, it gleamed like an onyx jewel and its red, white and black ribbon was bright as freshly spilled paint.

The flap of the tent suddenly flew open, and the light was so bright that I covered my eyes with my hand. Squinting through my fingers, the figure that stormed through that rectangle of harsh sunlight seemed to be emerging from a blazing fire.

"Come come *come*, Brandt! You think you're going to sleep through the rest of the war?!"

It was Himmel, and he strode into the tent as if attending the surrender of General Eisenhower. It is difficult for me to describe how I felt upon his appearance. Yet I would dissemble if I denied the sense of joy, and I sat up on my left elbow and saluted him smartly, and I hardly noticed the complaint of my wound. The Colonel marched straight for my cot, followed closely by Captain Friedrich, whose appearance I interpreted as an exceptional compliment.

"You see, Herr Colonel?" Friedrich chimed. "He is a lazy boy, as I've always said." Yet the captain's words were accompanied by a wide grin.

Himmel stopped at my side, slipped a finger beneath my Iron Cross and flipped the medal once like a door knocker.

"Mmm. Very pretty." He frowned. "Do you think you deserve this?"

His expression was grim and gave nothing away, so modesty appeared to be my safest course.

"No, Herr Colonel."

"No?" Himmel placed his fists astride his hips. "*No?* So, you are telling me I did all of that paperwork for nothing?"

"No, Sir. I mean, I thank you very much for…"

Friedrich cut me off as he flanked the other side of the cot.

"And I suppose you think I don't deserve mine either, Brandt?" The captain snapped, even as he pointed to an identical medal on the left pocket of his tunic.

Their expressions were so serious, that I looked from one to the other at a loss, finally settling on Friedrich.

"Well…" I stammered. "Yours suits you."

And with that they both threw back their heads and laughed fully and with great pleasure.

After a moment, Himmel suddenly reached for the hem of my blankets and then snapped them off of my body with the flourish of a matador. We all looked at my leg. The entire thigh was swaddled in fresh white bandages, yet already a swath above the sutures was seeped through with an umber ooze. The flesh from knee to toes had a grayish pallor, like the belly of a lake fish, and Himmel crinkled up his nose.

"You stink, my young corporal," he said. He covered

me with another whip of the blankets. "Have the girl wash you."

Did he not realize that the "girl" of record was his own lover, Gabrielle? Yes, of course he realized it, but her exposure to my immodesty did not disturb him in the least. After all, his was the ultimate power in the land, he was king of the castle, and my filthy and half-crippled form was hardly an attractive sight to behold.

"Yes, Sir."

"And get up on your feet, Shtefan." He wagged a finger at my face. "A wound only begins to heal when you make it scream. Pain is the key, a message from the brain that the blood flows again into mending flesh, that your will shall conquer weakness. If you lie there and try to fight it, you'll simply rot. Believe me, I know." He gestured then at a spot on his abdomen, referring, I assumed, to the vivid memory of his own wounds.

"Yes, Sir."

"Besides, I need you back at quarters. My office is a shambles. Mutti's been typing for me."

Friedrich snorted and wagged his blond head. "He can't spell."

"Spell?" Himmel boomed. "He can't write, he's half-deaf, and he can't post a simple order. If he didn't cook so well I'd have him shot!"

Despite myself, I began to laugh. But it was not the bantering that so raised my spirits; it was the concept that I was in fact an integral part of Himmel's machine. My laughter was halted by the Colonel's slap of his gloves into his palm, and he became instantly stern again.

"I mean it, Brandt. I want you up and walking. By to-night."

"Are you taking over my command here, Herr Colonel?" It was another voice, and Himmel turned from the cot and I saw a Wehrmacht field surgeon standing in the tent opening. It was the very same officer whom I'd met upon first seeking the whereabouts of Gabrielle. Himmel lifted his palms up.

"I would not dream of superseding your medical exper-tise, Herr Doktor." He offered a short bow, which I recog-nized as utterly sarcastic. "I was simply offering my corporal some encouragement. His talents are required in my com-mand."

"Good." The doctor advanced, and in contrast to Himmel's rough inspection, he gently lifted the blanket hem and looked at my leg. "Because, as you well know, this young man's con-dition has been grave. The infection is only just receding. He was on the verge of death."

"Yes, well…" Himmel coughed, and immediately his con-ciliatory manner switched. "He's on the verge of life now, isn't he? Get him up."

The doctor blinked as he lowered the blanket.

"And all those needle pricks on his hip," Himmel contin-ued. "No more of that. No more opiates. He doesn't need them. I'll not have him addicted and staggering about until we have to slap him back to his senses."

The doctor had gone quite pale. "Are you issuing me orders, Herr Colonel?" His cheek quivered.

"Look at your rank." Himmel shrugged. "Then look at mine. Yes, I am that."

My master then turned to Friedrich, snapped his fingers

and gestured at the gramophone. Friedrich walked around the cot and picked it up from its oil-drum stand.

"I trust you don't mind if we have some music back." Himmel grinned at me. "We need the morale."

"Of course not, Sir. Thank you, Sir."

"Good. Now remember, Shtefan. Up, up, up!"

He turned and began to stride from the tent, with Friedrich and the gramophone close behind.

"Sir?" I called out to him. He turned and squinted his one eye at me.

"The men…" I began, but I could not find the words to ask after the dead. I did not need them.

"Heckler, Stolz, Von Tolberg and Hennig," Himmel recited. "Schneller you know about. And Rolf. He died here in this tent, four days ago." There was absolutely no emotion in his voice. "They shall be remembered. Is that all?"

"Yes, Sir."

He grinned and patted the gramophone as Friedrich held it.

"Have the girl sing to you. She has a magnificent voice."

And then they were gone, leaving the doctor at my side, muttering curses under his breath…

Gabrielle, of course, did not sing to me.

In fact, the gentle manner she had displayed upon my first waking seemed to quickly shift as my full recovery was evident. It was almost as if that, while I remained comatose, my fate uncertain, I hovered between Himmel's world and hers. Perhaps she viewed me then as an innocent creature, one enslaved in a sense like herself, with all the potential for escape and redemption, even if that meant my death. Yet as soon as I broke the bonds of my fevers and began to truly heal, Himmel had returned to reclaim me, and it was as if Satan had once again left his calling card, and she would have none of me.

When she first returned, on the afternoon of Himmel's visit, I attempted to make some conversation. Some spring warmth had risen with the bright sun, and Gabrielle wore a fir-green sweater over a gray woolen skirt, and over that her nurse's apron. She wore no cap, and although her hair was pulled into a tight ponytail, it could not make her features severe. I had then no power to still my own voice, for I so wanted to hear hers.

"The weather seems fine today."

"Yes."

"You must be tending your garden now. Planting fresh flowers."

"Yes."

I fell still as she changed my bandages, and I closed my eyes and blushed in silence as she stripped me and bathed me with a sponge. When she began to roll me to one side in order to slip a metal pan beneath me, I said, "Please. I would like to do this myself." She left the tent without a word.

In the evening, she summoned an orderly, and for the first time they helped me to my feet. With my arms slung about their shoulders, I curled my bare toes into the freezing mud of the tent floor, my right leg barely touching down like that of a hobbled dog. I wanted to scream out, but I would not, and I bit my lip nearly to bleeding as I made my first endless circle around the cot. At last, they laid me back upon it, my limbs quivering and the sweat beading my brow. Soon after, she brought me two apples, a small hunk of cheese and a fresh water bottle. Yet she did not stay to help me eat, as if assuming that my secretions and consumptions were equally private matters.

On the next day, the man to my left began to moan. The surgeon visited often, administering medicines and pain-killers to the poor soul, yet he fairly ignored me, as if I was the cause of his humiliation by an SS colonel. Gabrielle was also in attendance, and although she dressed my wound and again helped to exercise me, including the washing after-ward of my muddied feet, my attempts to elicit some humanity from her remained empty.

"Do you think he might recover?" I whispered, jutting my chin at the terribly wounded panzer crewman.

She merely shrugged.

"He is badly burned, isn't he?"

"Yes."

I began to despair then, experiencing waves of clashing emotions. I felt utterly and cruelly rejected, and unable to touch Gabrielle in even the most simple way, I swayed be-tween fury and self-pity. Lying there hour after hour, with-out conversation or a book or a distraction of any sort, my defenses began to crumble as I pondered my life. I thought so much of my mother then, of how she had cared for me when I was ill as a child, and I wondered where she was and how she suffered, and who if any might cool her own fevers now. I tried to summon the strength and righteous courage of my father, then fled from the horrible convic-

tion of what he might think of me now. The truths of what
I'd witnessed in Himmel's violent galaxy rose to the fore of
my brain, and I wept more than once, covering my mouth
with a tight palm so that no sob would emerge.

Sensing the approach of meal times or nurses' rounds, I
knew that Gabrielle would return. I would not allow her
to see a morsel of my distress, and I painted myself with
composure.

That evening, she sat me up upon my elbows and slipped
a shallow basin beneath my head. The water had been
warmed, and with a metal cup she sluiced it through my
encrusted scalp, then washed my hair with a bar of rough
soap. The touch of her small fingers massaging my ne-
glected skin was heaven, yet I poised there above the basin
with my eyes fully open as she worked, refusing to let her
witness my pleasure.

She rinsed my hair and toweled it, and then she produced
a comb from her apron and quickly parted and arranged it,
with all the warmth of a mortician. I lay back upon the pillow and looked at her. She wiped the comb on the towel,
and then pulling the end of her golden ponytail before her
face, she began to groom the thick strands. I watched her
for a long moment before I finally spoke.

"Do you judge me, Gabrielle Belmont?" I whispered.

She stopped in midmotion, frozen there as if I'd shot her
through with a steel arrow. She lowered her head as something came over her face, and her lips began to quiver, and
my heart filled with a pain as real as that in my thigh. She
reached down and took my hand, and she gripped it very
hard as she whispered.

"No." She slowly shook her head as a single tear coursed down her cheek. "No, Shtefan, I do not..."

And she dropped the comb and rushed from the tent.

A thing that was between us shattered on that night. Like a high thick wall of frosted glass, through which two people cannot gain a clear vision of each other, it crumbled to the ground to reveal a frightening truth. I know now that it was a barrier we had built, instantly constructed upon our first mutual glance. It was a veil of false disdain, of the type created by a pair of coworkers who may not touch, or married people who cannot betray their spouses, or even schoolchildren too young to confess their attraction. This was a fence we had made fast and well and strong, for without it, our very lives were in danger. Yet when it came down, Gabrielle and I began to slowly tumble toward each other, and gravity would not be denied.

Her visits to my bedside were no longer cursory, and she did not flee when the business of my caretaking was done. She appeared more frequently, and eschewing the aid of an orderly, she alone helped me with my exercise. Limping there in circles around my cot, I leaned my weight upon her, inebriated by her warmth and her strength and her scents, and the more I healed the more I denied my progress, and of course she quickly caught on and began to laugh. Yet the frequency of her visits could also not be disguised, the intervals between merely chasms of waiting, for we had begun to really talk.

"You are making fine progress," she said one day as we hobbled around our circuit.

"I am not. I believe it's getting worse."

"Don't be silly, Shtefan." She smiled as we walked, my arm draped over her shoulder, her hand gripping my wrist. "You cannot deny it."

"I shall. To the end. I'm having a relapse."

"Liar."

"I may have to be here another month."

"I would have to break your other leg to keep you here."

"Fetch a hammer."

She fed me slices of apples and cheese, and one day she somehow found a melon and we partook of its sweet fruit together. The Wehrmacht surgeon came upon us laughing over some sharing of childhood mishaps, yet although I instantly fell silent and falsely morose, Gabrielle would not disguise her new demeanor. He regarded her with an intense gaze of suspicion, which she returned with such defiance that he withdrew.

"He does not seem to like you," I ventured.

"His feelings do not concern me."

"Or perhaps he likes you too much?"

"Perhaps. I do have a talent for attracting obsessives."

We did not speak for a moment, both of us clearly thinking of our mutual master. On the previous night, she had not appeared at all, and another nurse had dressed my healing wound. I knew that Gabrielle had been with Himmel, yet even though her role as his consort had begun to fester in my heart, I was not the one who raised the issue.

"My body must be with him," she fairly whispered.

"I know."

"Yet my brain and my heart are elsewhere."

"I understand."

"You cannot understand this. Not really."

"I try."

"You are a slave only to your own actions. On any morning, you could run."

It was not so simple, but I let her go on.

"You are not violated. No children are held hostage for your constant surrender."

She had begun to tremble, her knuckles white around the fruit knife, and I took it from her and embraced her fingers with my own.

"Gabrielle, this is only one small part of your life," I said, trying to convince myself as well. "It will only be a memory one day. It will be replaced by so many better things."

She did not believe a word of it.

"What things, Shtefan?" She looked at me so intensely, her eyes glittering and hungry for hope. "I am so deep in my despair that I cannot imagine a happy morning."

"It will come. This war cannot last forever."

"Yes, I know. Of course it will end. The Allies will come and Germany will be done." She realized what she'd said, and then, "I am sorry…"

"No need. I know it. Even Himmel knows it."

She moved then, from the right side of my cot to the left, circling above my head, her hand never leaving mine. She glanced over her shoulder at the three still forms in their beds, as if any one of them might be a spy feigning his delirium. She leaned closer to me.

"He will never free me, Shtefan," she whispered.

"That is not so." I shook my head.

"It is. He is obsessed with me."

"No. He is a practical man."

"You do not understand. You do not hear him, how he speaks in…in those moments. He thinks of me as his possession, like some golden artifact he's found and will never relinquish. He wants to *marry* me, Shtefan."

A wave of heat rose from my chest then, and over my face. I could feel it burning in my scalp like a brush fire.

"He cannot marry you, Gabrielle. He is already married."

"I know that!" she exclaimed, and she squeezed my hand with both of hers until it hurt. "It does not matter to him, don't you understand? He thinks of himself as a being of godlike power, the power of life and death and fate. And he is right."

I lay silent for a moment, imagining the horror of a nuptial by bonfire, with Himmel grinning in his full dress uniform and Gabrielle attired in a soiled white dress, while the Commando made a canopy of sabers…

"You must go," I whispered. "You must escape."

"To where? To whom? Look at me, Shtefan." She pressed her palm hard to her chest. "Look at me."

And I did look at her, and I knew the curse of her appearance. She was immensely beautiful, a thing impossible to disguise. In a herd of fine and chestnut wild horses, she would still be the brilliant white mare, a thing instantly desired and brought to ground.

"How do you think a French Jewess survives this war?" she said as she thumped her chest. "By being coveted, by being wanted. I would not arrive at the very next village before another of your kind would take me."

"They are not my kind."

"Shall I shear my hair? Shall I bind my breasts and wear a woolen frock and wooden shoes like Jeanne d'Arc? Do you think it will make a difference?"

"No." I could not lie. Short of disfiguration, there would be no way to hide that face.

She nodded slowly, and satisfied that I no longer denied her predicament, she laced her fingers together as if in prayer and breathed a sigh.

"I will never be free." She squinted off into the darkness. "Unless he dies."

"Well, that is a real possibility. I have seen him in combat."

"And those children of Avignon." Her lip quivered a bit.

"You don't really think he would kill them if you ran."

"No. Not all of them. He has told me that if I left him, he would kill only one, and I could carry that soul with me for all my days."

Both of us believed it. Himmel was not a man of idle threats, but of tactics. She looked at me again.

"You are the one who should run," she said.

"I cannot. No more than you can."

"No. It is different. You are a man. You could make your way."

"I would not be just a deserter, Gabrielle. There is more."

She said nothing, awaiting my explanation. Until that moment, I had sworn to never tell a soul what only Himmel knew, and how he ignored my status and nurtured and protected me, even as he exposed me regularly to the jaws of death he viewed as no less than privilege. Yet no longer could I leave Gabrielle alone in her terror and conundrum, for her attentions to my health deserved no less than a returning of the debt, if only to provide her with a kindred spirit. And after all, I already loved her.

"I, too, survive only at the Colonel's whim," I said. "Perhaps it is charity, perhaps practicality. I do not really know. Yet he keeps this secret, and never reminds me of it."

She listened, saying nothing, and I went on.

"My father was a devout Catholic. He is gone now. And my mother, her devotion to the church did not matter. She is at Dachau, because her mother's mother…"

I reached for Gabrielle's apron, and I pulled her close and told her the truth in my simple French.

"Je suis partiellement Juif."

Her reaction was unexpected, no more than a small smile. She touched her fingers to my forehead and gently combed away some errant strands of my hair, and I realized that Himmel did indeed confide in her, in those moments…

"I know," she said. "I know." She bent over me then, and as she brushed her lips to my brow she whispered, "Welcome to my purgatory, Shtefan Brandt."

IX

In May of 1944, my master betrayed his true love.

Should my words mislead, I ask indulgence for the moment, as I realize that the images that come to the fore are perhaps implausible ones of Himmel spurning Gabrielle Belmont, of even casting her aside for some other of more perfect character and beauty. Yet it should be clear by now that such a deflection of Himmel's feelings for Gabrielle would not have been possible, for there existed no other creature of her ilk.

No, I speak not here of the waning of Himmel's romantic passion, nor of the diminution of his lust or longing for a woman. It was his purer love he began to cast away, the one most powerful and seemingly infrangible, the ardor for his rank and his uniform and his honor. And I was stunned to watch him as he planned to betray the army, and turn his back on Germany.

Having been at last released from the field hospital, I returned to the estate and the troop and Himmel with some deep trepidations, for I now carried with me the added burden of Gabrielle's touch. The horns of my dilemma were sharp and unyielding, for my feelings had to remain secret while I sought improbable resolutions. And so, delivered one bright morning by a rattling army ambulance, I climbed down and hobbled toward the mansion upon a makeshift cane, while my stomach churned and my mind raced like an auto engine with a snapped drive chain. Fruitless fantasies of escape once more surfaced in my mind, until a squad of the troop suddenly appeared from around one corner of the main house.

Friedrich led the welcome party, and while it certainly was no match for the pomp and ceremony once offered Himmel by firelight, my joy at this reception certainly dissolved my quandaries for the moment. The men marched and clapped in unison, singing an SS choir of battle, and despite the early hour they upheld a single, large, foaming tankard of beer. In the midst of this unruly throng was Blitzkrieg, coaxed gently along by Corporal Noss, and his neck was garlanded by a string of wild daisies and his empty saddle held a scabbard and a cavalry blade. When my stallion saw me again, he lifted his head in some wild nods, whinnied loudly and surged forward, and when he butted my forehead with his wet nostrils, the men roared and passed the stein around and pounded me hard enough on the back that my leg nearly collapsed.

Himmel emerged from the house then. He was wearing boots and his uniform trousers and snapping his braces over a long-sleeved undershirt. A cigar was already clamped in his mouth, and he grinned widely when he saw me.

"Brandt!" he yelled. "Thanks be to God!"

The squad turned to him and fell somewhat silent, awaiting some order or remonstration. But the Colonel only jabbed a finger in my direction and boomed, "Five minutes to drink. Then get in here and *type*."

He withdrew and slammed the door then, and indeed I enjoyed the time allotted, parrying the lurid jokes of my comrades and their disdainful finger pokes at my Iron Cross. That dreadful night in Russia, though fermented now by a month's time, was fresh enough to not be spoken of. No one mentioned the faces of the lost that still hovered in the air, but when at last I asked the men how they were faring, there was a moment of silence before Noss finally grinned.

"Well, it's spring, Brandt," he said as he clapped my shoulder. "We all need a really good fuck!"

With a laugh at that, I nuzzled Blitzkrieg, and the men led him away and returned to their tasks, and I to mine. I inhaled a dollop of the morning air, the scent of infant flowers and fresh cool rains, and I limped into the house. Mutti was clearing the Colonel's breakfast plates, and when he saw me he intoned "At last!" as he blew me a grateful kiss with both hands and raised his clenched fists into the air. Edward, who was attempting to decipher and arrange a pile of maps and papers, dropped them on the map table and came straight for me, taking me in a bear hug that stole my breath and surprised me with its genuine warmth. Himmel then strode in from his bedroom, rubbing his hands together like the gleeful witch of some fairy tale.

"Get out, you bumblers," he called to the cook and driver. "My prince has come!"

I smiled as the two men gratefully withdrew, though I hardly felt the dutiful son of any righteous king, but more the Hamlet to my uncle. I was not then aware of any changes in my master, while my own were at the very forefront of my mind. I had as yet no burgeoning plan, no concept of the future, no idea of what the morrow might bring. It had always been so in Himmel's service, for I was subject to the whims of war and my master's missions. I only knew that now I was in love with Gabrielle, and to keep my grasp on that fragile and flowering blossom I would have to betray this man. Already it roiled within me, and although back in the comfort of this house, it was no longer home.

"To arms, to arms." Himmel was waving at my work desk, upon which a pile of unfinished reports and requisitions looked as massive as the entire inventory of a paper mill. "We've only a week or so to finish all this and get ready."

I smiled a bit and limped toward the desk, slipping into the wooden armchair and sliding my makeshift cane beneath. It was an oak branch that had been carefully whittled by a wounded Luftwaffe gunner, who had suddenly died from an infection.

"Ready for what, if I might ask, Herr Colonel?"

"For Paris." Himmel strode into the kitchen and poured

himself a steel mug of coffee. "We shall be moving up. The Allies are coming."

"Are they?" I had begun to check the ribbon in my typewriter, but his words stilled my hands. I had heard no news of an invasion, although such was certainly inevitable.

"Of course they are. They'll be hitting the northern coasts any week now." My master sipped from the mug and pulled a face. *"Scheiss Dreck!"* he spit, as apparently Mutti's cooking skills were also faltering.

"Is there intelligence?" I asked.

Himmel looked at me above the mug, then threw his head back and laughed once and with great disdain.

"Intelligence? From the General Staff? Those fools think the Americans are going to wait until August, until after we've thawed out from Russia and have had a nice comfortable summer gorging ourselves on cunts and fresh fruit!" He placed the cup on my desk and leaned into me, as if at last enjoying again a proper and attentive audience. "But *I* know they're going to come now. Right now." He slapped the desktop. "As soon as the weather can sustain a channel crossing. And Rommel knows it too. He's been trying to get Hitler to give him command of all panzer divisions in Europe, but our illustrious Führer has taken that task upon himself personally. So, Rommel will be sitting on his ass while the Allies storm the beachheads, and then he'll come to the party after the cake's already on fire." Himmel turned away and sucked on his cigar, and as he swung the coffee mug, I could see its black waves sloshing over the sides. "But thank God we're not tankers, Brandt. Thank God we're SS, where every colonel's a king."

"Yes, Sir," I agreed, though I was not pleased to be reminded that I was an indentured servant to a crown. "Paris, then," I whispered. The thought crossed my mind that a move to the French capital might indeed free Gabrielle from her bonds, for surely Himmel would not bring her there, especially on the brink of a final battle.

"Yes, Paris. So, get to typing." He stabbed a finger in my direction. "We need requisitions, with deliveries to be made en route. What we've ordered up in the past for missions and training, double it all. No, *triple* it. Ammunition, grenades, demolitions, everything. Also, I want every man's file up to date. Edward bollixed up all the citation forms, so do them again. Got that?"

"Yes, Sir."

"And get me the precise train routes for all of northern France. Even if some of the rails are out, I want a detail of all tracks remaining intact and functioning, civilian and military. Mark them out for me on the large-scale map, right?"

I was furiously making notes with a pencil, and I failed to notice that Himmel had circled around behind me.

"And Brandt." I winced as the Colonel clapped me on the back. His face bent and drew near to my ear, and my body tensed as I immediately suspected that some accusation regarding myself and Gabrielle would surely be hissed. "How's that leg?"

"Fine, Sir," I managed without stuttering.

"Good. Exercise it well. You'll need to be able to move as you did before. All of Germany's going to soon be on the run from the Allies. But first, we're going to do some running *at* them." He gripped my shoulder and snorted. "You're good at that. Maybe we'll add some oak leaves to that Iron Cross."

With that, he fetched his tunic and went off to the day's training, and I began to type.

I welcomed the work, for at last I was no longer imprisoned upon a hospital cot and left idle for hours to contemplate the future. I had often heard it said that hope was the most subversive foe of the combat soldier, for such speculations could snatch a man's reflexes when he might need every instinct and synapse. My weeks of rest had indeed sapped the warrior spirit I had endeavored so long to construct, and even the appearances of Gabrielle had brought equal measures of delight and despair. And so, I embraced the opportunity to drown myself in a tidal wave of *Papier Krieg*—paper war.

Edward had indeed made a shambles of the men's files, and although I might have made corrections and prettied them up, I chose instead to begin at the beginning. Sheet after sheet of *Schutzstaffel* letterhead flew through my machine, and it hammered away like a light machine gun, and its bell rang like a fire wagon's gong as I rewrote the recent history of every man in the troop. By Himmel's written order, everyone who had participated in Russia deserved some sort of citation, and I executed each request to perfection, crimping each completed page with a watermark, smacking it with an ink stamp, and assembling a neat pile for the Colonel's signature. And then, it was on to the requisitions. Heinz's armory was vastly depleted, and I ordered up crates of small-arms ammunition, hand grenades, *Panzer-*

faust missiles, satchel charges, mortar bombs and spare parts for every weapon in the pot. I pounded every urgent order with a brace of bold *Achtung!*'s, and it was not until nearly 4:00 p.m. that I suddenly swooned with dizziness, realizing that I had not taken food or drink for the entire day. Yet it was a blessing, for I had thought of nothing but the work.

I was done at last, exhausted though sated with accomplishment, yet when I made to go into the kitchen to fetch some nourishment, I could not rise. My leg, ignored and folded beneath my chair for so many hours, had stiffened like a shank of meat left in a freeze box. I massaged it for some minutes, wincing as the blood tingled through my healing wound, yet even with my palms planted on the chair arms I could not rise. And suddenly I felt a hand beneath my right armpit, and another beneath my left, and I was gracefully lifted to my feet.

I stood there trembling, my hands braced upon my desk, and I looked sheepishly up at Edward as he wagged a finger in my face. And then I turned, expecting Mutti, but finding instead Gabrielle.

Her hand withdrew from my arm, and taking in her freshly washed hair and her soft and billowy teal summer smock, I instantly realized that she was not here in attendance to my health. She was here for Himmel, Edward had fetched her, and all was as it had been before my wounding, and I felt my facial expression turn instantly from its momentary glee and come crashing down like a shattered windowpane. Gabrielle's own expression was as frozen as arctic granite, for to reveal a connection between us more personal than professional could mean instant disaster. Even so, I made to speak, but something in the glitter of her eyes stopped me.

"*Ach, mein Schatz!*"

The three of us turned to the boom of Himmel's greeting. He came pounding in through the rear door of the mansion, his boots encrusted with mud and his face smudged with powder residue, and with him he carried the wafting, sweet stench of explosives. He slipped from his leather battle harness and hurled it, along with his machine pistol, onto the very same divan upon which I had once seen him fornicating Gabrielle, and with arms outstretched and the warm grin of a Christmas elf, he made straight for her and gripped her shoulders, kissing her hard upon her right temple. She glanced up at him and smiled.

"*Bonsoir*, Erich." It was nearly a whisper.

"Ach, but I must *stink*." Himmel stepped back from her, looking down at his soiled uniform. "Someone should draw me a bath."

This had always been my task, and although still wobbly, I bent to fetch my cane.

"Not you." Edward gripped my elbow and turned to Himmel. "I shall do it, Herr Colonel. Brandt's all in." He cocked his chin at my neat pile of completed labors. "Look, Sir."

Himmel stepped up to my desk, his one eye widening as he thumbed through the orders and requisitions.

"Today? You did all of this *today*, Shtefan?"

At some other time, I might have blushed and nodded proudly. Yet here in Gabrielle's presence I felt nothing but shame for my subservient position.

"Corporal Brandt should rest, Erich," Gabrielle stated flatly in her detached nurse's tone. "He is not nearly healed."

"You mean *Sergeant* Brandt, I should think," Himmel boomed. "Look at this work!"

I regarded my master, and he would have winked at me had he possessed two good eyes.

"You would like to finish up this war as a sergeant, wouldn't you, Brandt?"

I hesitated, and then I said, "I would be happy to simply finish it up alive, Herr Colonel."

"Ha!" Himmel laughed, then raised an instructional finger. "At some point, life must end, my young adjutant. But glory goes on forever." I merely smiled as the Colonel gestured at his driver. "Yes, let's send him off to rest, Edward. You can fetch Mutti and have him prepare something special for our dinner." He moved to Gabrielle, interpreting her slight smile as he wished, and he grazed the backs of his fingers across her cheek. "And after that, do draw me a bath," he ordered over his shoulder. "Nothing coarse and unclean should touch purity such as this."

That was all I could endure, and I bowed crisply to his back and gripped my cane, hobbling away and out of the mansion as quickly as my leg would carry me. The grass behind the house was wet and the earth soft as pudding, making for clumsy going, but I swallowed great gulps of the early-evening air, praying it might wash my brain of those images of Himmel and Gabrielle that crawled through my mind like black jungle asps. As I made for the carriage house, Edward caught up and gripped my bicep, helping me along and looking straight ahead as he intoned a warning.

"Whatever is between the two of you," he muttered, "it shows too much."

I felt the blood immediately rise in my face. "I don't know what you mean."

"You and the girl."

"We have done nothing."

"Maybe not. But if I can see it, then others will as well. She asked too many things about you, in the car."

"That is beyond my control," I protested.

He yanked me to a dead stop and looked at me hard. "Kill it, Shtefan," he hissed. "Before it kills you." And he released me to my own struggles and hurried on to fetch the cook...

The evening shadows fell gracefully, quilting the estate in darkness, though I failed to notice the passage of the hours, as to me each minute was an agonizing eon. I sat at the rough dining table in the carriage house, my eyes fixed upon a bowl of rabbit stew and the rough rolls with which I slowly sopped its gravy and brought it to my mouth, tasting nothing. By the flickers of a pair of oil lanterns, Edward sat on the other side, muttering as a deck of cards repeatedly trounced him in solitaire. And Mutti, his uniform armpits stained with sweat, hurried back and forth between our quarters and the mansion, delivering fresh courses to our master and his mistress.

At one point, the cook halted long enough to take half a cigarette as he stirred a cold plum soup.

"I've never seen him eat so fast," he complained to himself. "The way he's looking at her, I half expect to find him fucking her on the table before dessert."

He picked up the glass bowl and made his way back to the mansion, and I dared not look up at Edward, for my ears burned with what was surely a deep crimson hue. Edward's tin of cigarettes lay upon the table, and I stopped eating and reached out for one and ordered my hand to be still as I lit it and inhaled.

"Would you do something for me, Edward?" I asked.

He lowered his hand of cards to the table. "What is it?"

"Would you go to the barn, and have a private fetch me Blitzkrieg?"

He did not ask why I might not go myself. Edward may have been a simple man, but his emotional instincts were very fine. He knew that in my present mood, I did not wish to face the banter of the troop.

"You should not ride with that leg, Shtefan."

"Would you go?" I inhaled a long stream of bitter smoke and oxygen. "Please, Edward."

He rose from the table, touching my shoulder as he left.

I had never before, nor have I since, felt physical pain such as on that night. The initial shock of a bullet wound often cues the body to shut down, roadblocking the messages between shorn nerve endings and the brain, which is why soldiers are commonly unaware of their own wounds until a battle stills. And in my case, shortly afterward my veins had already inhaled their measures of morphia, and so it was throughout my surgery and hospital healing. But now, splayed upon the rough leather of Blitzkrieg's saddle, my heavy sutures were bitten by the weight of my own body smashing down upon my leg, and my inner thigh felt as if the naked flesh was mounted on a slab of iron thorns.

I do not know how long I rode that night, at first attempting to ease my pain with pressure in the stirrups, trying to prevent all contact with the saddle. Yet I quickly realized that simply using my leg muscles caused the sweat to bead upon my face and set my teeth gnashing, and no degree of care would ease the affliction. Just the rhythm of Blitzkrieg's easy walk was excruciating, a light gallop even more so, and he sensed my imbalance and discomfort and turned his head and snorted at my grunts, as if to say, *If it all hurts you so, we might as well run.* And so we did.

We galloped, Blitzkrieg and I, he with the joy of freedom at last, and I with the rage of a tortured heart. We raced across grasses frothy with rain and we sailed over fences jagged with upturned splinters, and the wind raised his black mane like the standard of a pirate's galleon and it swept my tears into the runnels of sweat upon my cheeks. The moon flashed between purple and silver fists of clouds, and as we thundered over meadows and crests and splashed across sparkling streams, the pounding of his hooves was matched by distant crumps of midnight bombs, flashing like earthbound storms in the distance. And I leaned forward as far as I could, and I gripped Blitzkrieg's reins up close and slipped my fingers in to clutch his hair, and as the steam of his heated snorts coursed back over my face there was nothing I could do to keep my thigh from slamming upon the leathers, and it seemed that no matter the speed I could not outrace the images of Gabrielle upon my master's dining table, and as the blood began to run in rivulets into my boot I screamed, and I kicked him harder, hoping to churn us both into oblivion...

On the next morning, I overslept, which was generally not a forgivable lapse in the German army. Yet apparently Himmel was so pleased with my previous day's work that he had ordered that I be left to rest. I awoke at last sometime after nine, and I remained cocooned beneath my rough woolen blanket, listening to the murmurs of Edward and Mutti, my ears open wide to catch any hint of indiscretion from the driver. Yet he did not mention his suspicions regarding Gabrielle and myself, and I was grateful.

My leg throbbed in waves right up to my neck, for upon my return from our midnight gallop, I had inspected it to find three sutures soundly torn apart. I had washed the rent in freezing pump water that sprang tears to my eyes, and then fetched a roll of gauze from the stores and bound it well, after first sprinkling a healthy dose of sulfonamide powder into the wound. By the time I had toweled Blitzkrieg's flanks and returned him to the barn, I was barely able to crawl into my bed, where my tortured mind at last succumbed to sleep.

Now, I so fervently wished to remain where I was, protected from a new day's truths by this imaginary shelter. Yet all at once I realized that such uncharacteristic behavior might sound some sort of alarm in my master's mind, and I suddenly struggled up, fetched my cane and limped off to shave and make ready, leaving Edward and Mutti to blink at me as I stalked away.

I steeled myself before making my appearance in Himmel's

quarters, resolving to retreat to those days during which I had been able to engage Gabrielle with utter formality. Thankfully, only the Colonel was present in the salon. He was drinking coffee, and he absently returned my salute as I made my way to my desk. I sat there patiently, watching him as he paced, one hand in his trouser pocket, the other holding his steel mug. He seemed preoccupied, and at last he docked at my desk flank, though he stared outside through a mansion window.

"Women," he muttered. "Who understands them?"

"Not I, Sir," I replied. "I assure you."

The Colonel did not smile.

"What a horrid night." He slowly shook his head. "She would have none of me."

I said nothing. I stared at my typewriter, wishing I could rudely slip a sheet of paper through the spindle and begin hammering away. I did not want to hear this, and I wanted to hear every word.

"She cried and fussed." He slipped his hand from his pocket and whipped his fingers in the air. "She claimed she was having her monthly visitor. She mourned for her mother and father. She was like a little child, utterly impossible."

I strove for a reply, but I was mute.

"I could have taken her anyway, of course." He turned to me, then raised his shoulders in a comical shrug. "But what fun is that? With those kinds of tears?"

"None at all." I finally managed something. "I should think."

The door to the bedroom opened, and we both turned our heads. And there she stood, wearing the same dress in which she had arrived, her hair in a single loose braid and her eyes dark and rimmed.

"There you are, *mein Schatz*," said Himmel.

I nodded at her brusquely and immediately made to sifting through my piles of documentation, and I did not look up again as their conversation continued.

"Some breakfast, then?" Himmel offered.

"No, thank you." Her voice was small and hoarse.

"I can have Mutti fix up something you like."

"I will take some coffee. I am not hungry."

I heard her make her way into the kitchen. I imagined her hands as the liquid was poured.

"There are crowds of flowers in the yard," Himmel observed with exaggerated brightness. "Perhaps you'd like to pick some, before Edward takes you home."

There was a moment's contemplation. "Yes. That would be nice."

I heard the Colonel march off toward the rear entrance, and I heard the light clip of Gabrielle's shoes approach my desk. My heart began to pound as she moved around in front of me, and I wanted to scream at her, *Get away from me, for God's sake!*

"How is your leg, Shtefan Brandt?" she asked.

"Fine, thank you." I glanced up at her for merely a second, cracking the briefest of false smiles while my eyes blazed a warning, and I immediately looked back at my work.

"Edward!" Himmel boomed into the backyard. "Go fetch the car."

"You should be careful with it," Gabrielle said. "Or you shall wind up back in hospital."

She was so bold that it absolutely horrified me. "Yes," I said into my typewriter. "I shall be."

And thankfully she plucked at her dress and stepped away, taking a basket from the kitchen and making off to pick some flowers. I heard Himmel mutter some words and kiss her cheek as she departed, and then he closed the kitchen door and returned to the salon.

For some time, my master did not speak. He moved through the rooms of the mansion, and I heard the doors of wardrobes opening and closing, the latches of window locks snapping home. His activity reminded me of the superstitious inspections of a child, checking for ghosts and goblins before retiring to bed, until at last he appeared again and moved to the front door of the house, and that, too, he fixed and locked. I had by then fetched a recent Abwehr intelligence report on railway schedules in northern France, including which lines had been pounced upon by Allied fighters and those quickly repaired by Wehrmacht engineers, and I had begun summarizing the details pursuant to Himmel's request. Yet his silence unnerved me, and even as I sat and worked the tiny hairs at the nape of my neck prickled in the charged atmosphere.

"We must talk, Shtefan," Himmel said at last.

I stopped typing. Had I wanted to, I could not have continued at any rate, for my hands had begun to quake uncontrollably. I looked at my fingers, the tips fluttering like the helpless limbs of a pinned insect, and I laced them together and folded them upon my desk. With a wretched and silent bitterness I cursed Gabrielle and all of her false spiritual valor, for certainly she had spurned my master's advances and somehow revealed her feelings for me, making me the cause and culprit of his unrequited lust. Perhaps she had fallen into an ambush of Himmel's design, slipping out a revelatory expression at his mention of me, or perhaps she had murmured my name in her sleep. But what right did she have to invoke me? What right did she have to risk my life?! I felt the fury and fear rise within me as a single helpless scream, as I waited for the hammer to fall.

"Did you hear me, Brandt?"

"Yes, Sir." I sat there, still as a marble statue.

The Colonel came from behind my chair and walked to the plotting table. He leaned back against it, crossed his boots and came up with a fresh cigar. He lit the tobacco and inhaled deeply, blowing a perfect ring into the air.

"This war is going to end," he said.

"Yes, Sir," I agreed in a hoarse whisper.

"Soon, Shtefan. It is going to end soon." He turned his head and his single eye bored into me, and he jutted the glowing cigar in my direction. "What we are about to say shall not pass from this room. Are we clear?"

My brow creased. "Of course, Herr Colonel." Whatever was afoot, it was not what I had expected.

"Good." Himmel folded his arms, squinting off through the smoke that rose from his gesticulating hand. "I have always been a patriot, Brandt. In order to be a truly effective soldier, one must believe in one's country, is that not so?"

I nodded, although it struck me that I was in fact this man's polar opposite—a boy without a country.

"However," he said, as he rose and began to pace, one fist on his hip, "a professional soldier must also be a realist. There is a time to attack, and a time to retreat. There is a time to press for victory, and a time to accept its impossibility. Only fools and tyrants deny the inevitable."

I watched him, my hands still clasped together, yet no longer quaking as I understood that this soliloquy had absolutely nothing to do with myself or Gabrielle.

"The Allies are going to conquer us." The Colonel turned to me. "Do you accept that, Brandt?"

I swallowed, searching quickly for the proper response. "I respect your assessment of such things, Sir."

"Of course," he said, though he was unsatisfied with my obsequious reply. "Why do you think there are weight classes in boxing, Brandt?"

I prepared a guess, but the Colonel marched onward.

"Because it is a fact of nature that two animals of equal fighting skills are mismatched when of unequal stature. Our soldiers are as skilled as theirs, our equipment a match for theirs or better, yet it is a fact that we shall be overpowered by numbers and economics."

I had rarely heard my master digress so into complex analysis. It struck me that he had the makings of a university lecturer.

"Germany simply does not have the resources." He ground one fist into a palm, as if frustrated by his inability to shift the course of events. "We lack oil, steel, synthetic manufacturing capabilities. We have no remaining venues to harvest these necessities, while America is a vast field of factories and wealth and manpower. Respective to our size, we may be fine of form and in perfect shape, but in the end, she is the bigger boxer. She is a heavyweight, while we shall remain the bantam."

"I see, Sir," I said.

Himmel stood still then, and he smiled at me. "No, my young adjutant. You do not see." He gestured at his own face. "But I will be your eye." He moved to the plotting table again, pulled a chair from it and sat very close, and he leaned into me, which caused my posture to stiffen even further.

"I do not mind the fate of being killed in action," he said. "But I shall not be taken prisoner. I shall not be shackled and bound and humiliated and tried for crimes, which has been the fate of the vanquished throughout history. I intend to live. I am a warrior, and I shall survive to fight another day."

"How will you do that, Sir?" My voice sounded very small to me.

"The Allies shall storm these beaches, Shtefan." He swept his arm across an imaginary shore. "There will be hundreds of thousands of them, and they shall swarm over Germany like a horde of cockroaches, like the plague of the ancients that is told of in your great-grandmother's Bible."

I merely sat, striving to prevent my eyes from bugging like a child's.

"They shall come with their machines and their weapons and their endless supplies." He raised his trigger finger. "And yes, they shall also come with their paymasters, for patriot or not, no soldier will fight for very long without his monthly stipend." He paused for a moment, allowing me to keep apace of his logic. "And this troop shall fight them where we must. We shall take some of their lives, yes. But we shall also take a substantial sum of their American dollars. And then, my young adjutant, we shall depart for sunnier climates."

Himmel looked at me closely, as if inspecting my expression for any hint of shock or rejection. I have absolutely no idea what my face might have revealed just then, for I could not believe what I was hearing. Yet apparently, my blank visage offered enough for my master to continue.

"So, Shtefan Brandt. Can you surmise the nature of my next question?"

I felt my chin wag imperceptibly.

"You are a noncommissioned officer of the Waffen SS. Soon, you shall be a war criminal. Do you prefer the prison camp, or freedom? Do you prefer the hangman's noose, or a living fate with Erich Himmel?"

If anything in my life had ever been clear to me, it was that my master was not offering me a choice. He was extending two closed fists, yet each of them held the very same card. And I believe to this very day, that had I hesitated for a moment, or foolishly refused him, my skull would have hosted a pistol bullet on that very morn.

I raised my right arm in a crisp salute. Himmel grinned and extended his hand, and I shook it with the strength of one redeemed from the gallows...

X

IN LATE MAY of 1944, I was shackled to my master's secret madness.

Through the waning days of that long month, I limped into a reluctant summer, as the seasons seemed to war no less than the millions of men under arms. Each dawn the sun would rise to take the fields of France, steaming the dew from the early flowers and drying the feathers of thawing songbirds. And then, often before noon, an assault of purple nimbus clouds would sweep our brilliant star from its battlement, pummeling us with winds and rains indiscernible from those of early March. It seemed that nature herself was gripped in a struggle with her very own soul, unable to clearly choose this side or that, and my own thoughts were in concert with her maelstrom.

The activities of the Commando proceeded apace, without indication that this process of decamping for Paris might be different from so many relocations that had come before.

The men repaired and prepared their equipment, crated up belongings that would not serve any immediate emergency, and stole some intervals to pen letters to homes which they could not be certain had survived the Allied bombings. These hardened combat veterans undertook their warrior tasks with somber professionalism, yet the unscarred portions of their hearts were still very young. Their missives to their mothers were never scribbled, for during that era the artistry of simple penmanship was instilled in every schoolboy, and even the lowest private from Bavaria was something of a calligrapher. I share with you my still-crisp image of the wiry Corporal Noss, sitting on a tree stump and carefully preening the blood rut of his commando blade, while nearby the giant Sergeant Meyer so carefully sketched a rose as letterhead to his sister.

When the sun shone, the men often chased a soccer ball before the call to a formation, engaged in spontaneous and silly grappling contests, and even practiced forgotten waltz steps to the accompaniment of their own a cappella hums. Once or twice, after long days of training, they captured young Frenchwomen from the town and engaged gleefully in their tradition of fornication for barter, a practice that no longer shocked me, yet engendered my pity for the stain upon their souls. Mutti plucked my sutures out with forceps boiled in his pot, and Captain Friedrich managed to acquire a camera and film from somewhere, and I was included in the practice of memento poses to be frozen forever in cracked emulsions of black and white, printed by a chemist in Avignon. For all the years since then, I have kept a small packet of these photographs, sealed in an envelope and taped behind the toilet tank of every dwelling I inhabited. And to this very hour, I have shown them to not a single soul.

Throughout these swirling days, the secrets I now kept in the caves of my heart roiled like a coil of serpents, threatening to overcome me and escape from my clenched mouth. I pitied myself, for I knew too much, and I so wanted to be a simpleton without the curses of love and conscience and betrayal. My master had kept the secret of my birthright, and I in turn now kept the secret of his planned treachery, and both of us loved the same woman, who slept with him while wanting at the very least my hand in her own. With each passing hour, my spirit curdled with the dread of a hopeless future, yet even in this accursed state there was a blessing. The constant activity and dedication to my assignments served as a welcome distraction, lifting me into a high pitch of physical motion, and without my even realizing it my leg healed quickly.

Contrary to my own emotional vortex, my master's spirits seemed to lift and soar, and although he was ever the realist, I suspect him now of indulging then in a fantasy catalyzed by a suspicion of doom. While most of my assignments consisted of the comparatively mundane preparations for combat, there were other strange tasks he bade me undertake.

I compiled the detailed railroad reports for all of northern France, accompanied by aerial photographs from Luftwaffe reconnaissance flights. Then, like a fledgling stockbroker, I was made to delve into the values of all currencies presently in use on the European continent, and curiously,

South America as well. The ranges and cargo capabilities of certain aircraft were added to the list, as well as the dimensions and volumes of various fuel containers. Much of this was gleaned in standard requests to the Abwehr, under the guise of mission preparations, and Himmel took great care in posing his questions beneath a camouflaging skein of apparently urgent demands. He summoned up numerous transcripts of the Gestapo interrogations of Allied aircrews, and I confess a cringe of nausea as I read them, imagining the methods of coaxing used to elicit the guttural responses from these pitiable British and Americans. For Himmel, I underlined only the mundane facts of methods and amounts of conscript payments, for it was only I who knew what he was really getting at.

At one point I noted that American pilots based in Britain were remunerated not in American dollars, but in British pounds sterling. With this Himmel simply smiled and declared, "A pound is a pound."

My master spoke often to me during these few days, perhaps more so than he had ever done before. His new practice of sealing us both together in his quarters became a strange ritual smacking of paranoia, albeit justified, and as I worked he would perambulate about the house and muse upon the subjects of patriotism, loyalty, morality and practicality. He offered up the certain conviction, without specific proof, that many officers of the Nazi hierarchy were like-minded in their postwar preparations. He whispered tales of plundered gold stores, collections of Jewish art, small factories of counterfeiters and even safe houses packed with conquered jewelry. He had no doubt that whatever the fate of postwar Europe, much of its wealth would be spirited away in the pockets of a few clever survivors. Yet he declared himself above such practices. He was not a thief, and he regarded our final mission as no more than a climactic commando raid, to be executed just once for the good of those who would risk it.

On the last day of the month, we received an official notice from SS headquarters for the address of our relocation. It was to be a château on the western outskirts of Paris. Immediately Himmel dictated a telegraphic form to be sent to the SS transportation element. He was summoning his wife to the château, and she should leave the children with their aunt near Munich.

As I typed up this new order, my brain twisted in confusion. My master was absolutely unpredictable, a trait that confounded his enemies as well as his troops. Why in heaven's name was he summoning his wife at this juncture? I assumed now that he planned to bring Gabrielle to Paris, so did he dream of some erotic *ménage* with his wife and his new lover? He was planning an escape from this war, but did he intend to spirit *both* his favorite women to his new hideaway? And what of his poor children? Were they to be abandoned to relations, while he expected his wife to comply? And what role was I doomed to play in this seemingly endless tango of frustration and longing?

There was no way for me to ask my master of his intent. I was clearly nothing more than another passenger in his lifeboat, and he regarded me as lucky to be so.

Gabrielle made her appearance again on two evenings, each time fetched from her home by Edward. On the first of these nights, Edward sought me out in the carriage house before making for our Kübelwagen. I was sitting by the lamplight in trousers and braces, repairing a boot, and he leaned close and took my elbow.

"How is the leg?"

I looked up. "Very strong. I hardly need the cane."

"Good. You should ride Blitzkrieg tonight."

I furrowed my brow. "Why?"

"I am going to fetch the girl."

"I told you, Edward…"

"Never mind what you've told me. Be gone, and save yourself from your own dour face in the Colonel's presence."

I nodded, having begun to appreciate the corporal's wisdom. And I understood as well that he was entreating me for his own sake. My emotions, if unchecked, risked not only my own well-being, but that of everyone associated with me. And so, I rode that night, though modestly and in a controlled rhythm, so as not to damage myself once again. And although Blitzkrieg was pleased to be out on the meadows, I could feel his impatience with me. It was as if, like Edward, my steed chastised me for foolishness of heart.

On the next day, Himmel was of a foul mood, muttering his complaints about incomprehensible women. And I, assuming that Gabrielle had once more rejected his sexual advances, was both relieved and frightened by her boldness. I so wanted her to shun his touch, yet I knew so well that she should not dare it. As the afternoon approached, Himmel brightened somewhat, anticipating another go at his French beauty. And again, with evening, Edward bade me ride, and he crossed his fingers in the hope that the Colonel would have a better night of it. But it was not to be, and on the next day my master was full of fury.

When I entered his quarters just after breakfast, the mansion was rife with silence and tension. Gabrielle was not to be seen, and Himmel sat at his table, his shoulders bunched and his one eye burrowing into his metal coffee cup, as if fishing in that black swirl for the solution to his frustration. At last, the door to his chamber swung open, and Gabrielle emerged. She said nothing, but swept quickly to the kitchen door, and I winced with the anticipation that she might slam it home. Yet she let herself out, without so much as a blown kiss for the Colonel, and she closed it so carefully one might have thought her exiting a wake.

"What the hell do I need her for if she doesn't fuck!" Himmel hurled his empty cup across the salon, where it banged and bounced upon the slate floor of the kitchen. "Am I some lovesick schoolboy?" He thrust his splayed fingers high into the air. "Was I made to endure the pathetic rejections of some reborn virgin?!"

He exploded from his chair, marching about the rooms, snapping his braces like rifle shots as he whipped himself into his tunic.

"Tell me, Brandt!" he spit. "You tell me! She's much closer to your age than mine. Does her world turn upside down on a wave of teenage hormones? She's as frigid as a fucking nun these nights. What the hell am I supposed to do?"

My own typing table trembled with the thunder of his

howling. I sat very still for a moment, listening to my master snorting as fiercely as a wild bull.

"Flowers, Sir?" I finally proposed in a half whisper.

He looked at me for a moment, and then he threw his head back and laughed so hard that it caused the windowpanes to vibrate.

"Flowers?" He nearly choked with it, holding his hard belly and letting his shoulders roll in waves of bitter mirth. "Flowers?! I've given the little bitch food and sweets and gifts and everything else no damned French whore could even dream of in this place! And you know what else, Brandt?"

I sat still, looking at him, waiting while he swung his arms wide like a deranged orchestral maestro.

"I've given her power! *Yes.* Something no other man on this continent can give her. She comes and goes as she pleases, she works when she likes, and she can tell any Wehrmacht officer at that damned hospital to go screw, because they all know that she's the chosen one of an SS colonel!"

He moved toward me then, facing me directly and gripping the edges of my table, and I glanced down at his white knuckles and then quickly back to his face, for I could not react as a cowed puppy. He was not scolding me, but confiding in me, and to act in any way responsible for his misery would not do. I do not know from where I summoned the strength to regard him with apathy and commiseration, but I held that blazing eye with both of my own, even though I thought he might lift my table and hurl it through a window.

"I've given her life, Brandt!" It came out as a roaring air-burst, and knowing too well the frustration of not being able to have Gabrielle, I actually pitied my master. "Yes. Life." He banged my table legs once on the wooden floor. "And if she thinks that merely the presence of her beauty is enough to satisfy me, she's making a fatal mistake. I can take that life away from her, yes, with the snap of my fingers."

My heart began to flutter as Himmel slapped my desktop once, then turned away from my table. Almost instantly, he spun back on me, jabbing a finger.

"You, Brandt!"

I swallowed, frozen as an army deserter in a Gestapo lineup.

"Yes, you." He stabbed the finger repeatedly. "You'll go and fetch her tonight. You'll talk some sense into her. Maybe she can be made to understand my limits, if the other side of my character is painted by someone like yourself."

I did not move, but only squeezed my fingers into my palms, which began to immediately sweat like Blitzkrieg's flanks in the heat of a gallop. Himmel's face eased into a smile as he tucked his thumbs into his belt and regarded me with a raised eyebrow.

"You remember Salzburg, Shtefan?" he asked. "When I forced you to lose your virginity?"

"Yes, Sir."

"Well, tonight, your assignment is to make sure I enjoy a similar ecstasy."

And with that, he laughed with the conviction that I would execute this order as perfectly as any other, and he made off to inspect a formation of the men. And I was left, as he had been only moments before, gripping the sides of my table and barely managing to stop myself hurling it through a windowpane...

My evening ride upon Blitzkrieg to the house of Gabrielle Belmont was a misery veined with hungry anticipation. I brimmed with anger and slaughtered pride, having been turned into the messenger whose purpose I despised. And yet, the very image of her appearance growing near set the strains of my love for her echoing in my ears. Halfway to the town, I realized that my choice of the horse, rather than the car, spoke volumes of my subliminal intentions. I had been ordered to fetch her and bring her to his bed, yet I'd chosen no anonymous or comfortable way to do so. If she was to accompany me en route to another betrayal of what we felt for each other, then she would do so pressed up behind me on the saddle, forced to embrace me, at the very least like this.

The early moon threw sharp shadows from the steeple of the broken church, and the bomb in Gabrielle's garden had become twined with soft vines from the earth she somehow found the time to turn. I reined Blitzkrieg to the splintered fence post, and he looked at me from those huge black eyes and shook his head just once, as if to warn me off it all. I was fully in uniform, my tunic buttoned to my throat, my cap set straight and with purpose on my blond scalp. My pistol nestled in its holster, loaded and the leather flap unlatched. There were partisans in the town and invasion in the air, and any SS corpse would somewhat quench a thirst for revenge.

My heart was fluttering and my palms damp as I approached her threshold. I still limped a bit, but I had discarded my cane. I wiped my hands as I smoothed the rough wool of my tunic, and I knocked.

"*Entrez-vous.*"

Her voice was small, fatigued, and I opened the door and stepped inside the house and removed my cap. I stood in a small foyer. All about were dark, rough wooden beams, and a floor of polished planking seemed to lead from my boots and into distant chambers of a treasure I coveted. A single room was visible straight away and beyond, encompassing a kitchen corner, a dining area and a salon. High windows of white slatting were thrown open to the early-summer breezes, and the flames of two oil lamps flickered from the counters, and it all seemed so very small, like the house of a melancholy fairy tale.

There was a thick wooden table in the center of the room. At its distant head, a single, stiff and high-backed chair addressed the table, and I thought its posture mimicked that of Gabrielle's spine. She stood beside the table, slowly cutting carrots into slices. She wore a long, cream-colored dress of burry cotton, and her hair was loose about her shoulders. The sound of the knife's slicing stopped as she turned and looked at me.

"Good evening," I said. Looking at her, I felt that my lips were trembling.

She placed the knife on the table and wiped her hands on a cloth. She turned fully toward me, and I watched her take in a long breath.

"Hello, Shtefan Brandt." There was so much in her tone,

so much that I could not discern, for I did not really know her. She tilted her head, peering behind me. "Where is Edward?"

"He's not coming." I stepped forward a few paces, shifting my cap from one hand to the other. "I've been sent for you."

Her chin lifted a bit, and her expression darkened. She turned back to the table and picked up the knife and resumed her cutting.

"I am not going anywhere."

I moved closer, placing my hands behind my back. "You must, I'm afraid," I said as gently as I could.

"Hmf." It emerged as a small snort from her nostrils.

"You must, Gabrielle. He wants you."

Her shoulders stiffened. I watched her knuckles whitening around the knife hilt.

"He wants me," she barely whispered.

"Yes."

"And you want him to have me."

I felt my cheeks burning, my scalp simmering beneath my hair. I moved toward the table and barely touched the wood with my fingertips, for I could not touch her.

"No."

"He wants me." She sliced a thick chunk of carrot. "And he sends *you* to bring me to him."

"Gabrielle," I stuttered. "It cannot...you cannot go on like this with him. He is angry. It is driving him mad."

"Yes." She nodded slowly as she sliced. "I am his whore, and you are his pimp."

I said nothing, but only blushed even more deeply with my shame.

"What a *hero* you are, Shtefan Brandt," she hissed. "But of course, you are only following orders."

My heart sank, falling into an endless chasm somewhere below my rasping lungs. Whatever wonderful thing we had had together as I lay in hospital was surely gone. The realities of our lives had returned to both of us, the wall that had fallen away risen up again and impenetrable. There was absolutely no way for me to be with her. But at the very least, I could save her.

"Listen to me, Gabrielle." I reached out for her elbow, and she half turned to me and looked down at her arm, as if my fingers were a scorpion. "I hate this," I said. "I despise every minute of it. But you must do as he wants. You must be with him again. You are nothing to him if you are not his. Don't you understand that?"

She spun on me then, tearing her arm from my fingers and slamming the knife onto the tabletop. Her blue eyes were wide and afire and shone with the flickering lamp flames, and her cheeks were pink with anger and her full mouth bared from her white teeth. She smelled of wildflowers.

"Do *I* understand?" she snapped. "Do *I* understand?!"

"Gabrielle…"

"Here in this house," she said, snapping out one small hand in a wave. "Here, in this house of the Belmonts of Le Pontet, who were murdered by *them*. Here, where only I remain to remember my father and mother, where I have my only peace, and alone here in this place I think at least there is *one* who cares. There is one among them who lives a lie, lives it as I do, who will not surrender me." She was nearly shouting now, her fists clenched and her neck roping. "And you come here to this place to take me again to be soiled like a pig, so that you can survive your meaningless life!"

"Gabrielle." I raised my voice, trying to snap her tirade. "Stop it. You must stop this and…"

"Do you even know what I've been thinking?" Her voice cracked as she shouted, and she stabbed a trembling finger up at me. "Do you know why I've not been sleeping with him?" Tears welled from her eyes and coursed down her cheeks, and I felt my own throat choking with pity. "Because of you! Because of you, Shtefan! And your love is as pathetic as your courage!"

She slapped me. She slapped me very hard across my cheek. I did not move, my neck stiff and my face stinging with the lash of her fingers, and I watched her as she curled her hands into fists and pressed them together against her chest, and she looked down and sobbed as she shook her head.

I reached out with both hands, and I grasped the sides of her head and I kissed her.

She started and tried to pull away, yet I would not release her, and as firmly as I held her head was as softly as I kissed her. Her lips were like the petals of a burning rose, and I covered them with my own, feeling her hot and tear-glossed cheeks against my face and her breath warm and laced with her sobbing. She sank her fingertips into my shoulders and tried to push me away, yet I would not

retreat, and with my heart pounding up into my throat
and my legs trembling like the stalks of a newborn doe, I
breathed my love for her into her mouth until at last her
fury turned.

She sighed, and her hands rose to the back of my neck,
and she opened her mouth and kissed me in return. She
kissed me deeply, and I felt her small tongue twining with
my own, and she covered my face and my eyes with quick
presses of her lips, and then she suddenly pulled away and
looked at me. I will never forget her eyes, as they looked
on that night, as they still appear to me now.

She grasped my face in her small hands and kissed me
with an urgency that weakened my thighs and sent a thunder of blood into my stomach, and the intense hunger for
her that I'd suppressed for so long coursed so quickly into
me that I thought my body would alarm her. Yet it did not,
and as she felt my urgency pressed against her she fumbled
for my tunic clasps and began to tear them apart. She kissed
my neck and my throat, and in a moment my uniform was
yanked from my arms, and she pulled my braces from my
shoulders and gripped the flesh of my waist as her mouth
crushed against my chest.

It was a struggle, a battle over who would taste and who
would kiss. When I reached down for her dress, she stood
erect and pulled it over her head. And when I saw the
half-moons of her breasts heaving from her cotton bodice,
I kissed her glistening skin and she curled her fingers into
my hair and groaned. I lifted her onto the tabletop, and I
turned to stand between her legs and glanced down at her
loose white bloomers. She placed one hand upon the table,

and with the other she pulled my head into her chest, and as I kissed her there again she pulled her bodice down and arched her back. The sight of her swelling breasts made me swoon, her nipples so pink and pebbled hard, and as I kissed them she muttered, *"Oui, Shtefan…. Oh, oui."*

She reached out for my trousers, fumbling with the buttons. And as she dragged them from my hips, my hands slid up to her waist and I pulled her panties down and off of her and flung them away somewhere. Her eyes widened and her mouth opened as she took me in her hand, and I lifted my head and moaned as I felt her pulling me toward her.

She lifted her legs, high and wide, and she slipped her other hand behind my neck and pushed her forehead against mine and peered into my eyes. Her breathing was so ragged, and mine, I could not hear it for my heart. I dared not look down as she guided me toward her, closer, and nearer still. And when at last I felt her soft and urgent wetness, it seemed that my entire body was plunging into fire as we both yelled out, in phrases neither understood.

We clutched at each other, our mouths feasting on each other's lips, my hands caressing her warm breasts and her fingertips digging into my buttocks. We both moaned deeply as our hips pounded together wildly, over and over again. I could not see. I was blinded by her scent and her tongue and her thrashing hair and her hot flesh sucking at my own, and as my body surged over the precipice of any control, hers did the same, and I was calling her name into her mouth and she into mine as we gripped each other's faces and cried out something that I hear to this very day.

For many, many minutes, we remained motionless, but

for our ragged breathing. We held each other so tightly, our noses warming each other's flushed necks. Our skins were slick and fevered, our temples thundering.

When at last I managed to look at her, I searched quickly for sorrow. Yet I only found relief, and certain joy, and our eyes were mirrors, each to each.

"I will not come back with you tonight," Gabrielle at last managed to whisper.

"No." I did not want it. I did not give a damn for the consequences.

"What shall you tell him?" she asked. She was not frightened.

"That you were ill."

"Yes."

She kissed me, long and deeply.

"I love you, Shtefan Brandt," she said.

"And I…"

She placed a finger over my lips.

"And you shall tell him," she added, "that I promise him that when we get to Paris, I shall give him a night he will never forget."

XI

IN JUNE OF 1944, I accepted the likelihood of my death, while secretly praying for my life.

If hope was the enemy of every good combatant, then I most certainly warred with that scourge courageously, while succumbing to its onslaught with every thought of Gabrielle. One must always remember, even in the twilight of one's life, those precious and powerful gems of one's first true love. For there is nothing quite comparable, no joy born of success or adventure or the climax of a quixotic quest, that returns to us throughout our lives and approaches that first virginal sting of passion. I was faint with it, I breathed it with every breath, it tortured my soul even as it lifted it up to soar in the cool blue heavens of dreams that could not be.

I had been frightened to death to face my master with empty hands, the very same hands that still twitched with the memory of Gabrielle's skin. I shuddered at the thought of returning to his lair, offering lies from a mouth that yet tasted of her lips. I imagined with horror his tempestuous expression, as he would surely see through my deception, his nostrils flaring with her scent wafting from my uniform. As Blitzkrieg and I thundered over the pastures and streams and broken roads en route to the mansion, I strove to strike the glorious and fresh images of our lovemaking from my fevered brain. Yet the more I tried to slash my lover from my mind's eye, the more her trembling body appeared before me, and even the pummeling of the saddle below could not prevent the libidinous reflex that pounded upward from my loins into my heart.

It was well into the night when at last we trotted onto the expanse of soaking grass behind the house, and taking in the scene before me, I looked briefly heavenward to thank my dubious deity. In the fierce and flickering glow of a brace of torches, the entire troop had abandoned the barn. All of their equipment lay in growing rows of metal and canvas humps upon the pasture, and the noise of clanking steel and hurrying boots was a welcome symphony to drown out my labored breaths of fear. The transport trucks had appeared and huddled close, their drivers fiddling with and tuning their engines, adding to the cacophony of hasty preparations. Captain Friedrich marched about the ranks, his fists on hips as he issued orders, and the men moved with rapid jerks in the flashing lights of the flames, their expressions somewhat gleeful in anticipation of a change of scenery.

I struggled down from Blitzkrieg, roped him to the water pump and hauled on the handle, providing him with a drink from the trough. And as he slurped the cold liquid over his snout, I joined him and sluiced palmfuls over my face, hoping to dissolve the scented veils of Gabrielle that certainly still clung to my cheeks. I dried my face on my sleeves, finger-combed my hair, straightened my uniform and marched into the house.

The mansion blazed with light. Every lamp had been lit, as if the rooms encompassed a crime scene and such illumination would aid the detectives in their search for clues. In fact, the purpose of such an atmosphere was similar, for Himmel was packing up, and he no doubt wanted to be sure that no wayward belonging might be abandoned in a shadowed corner. A large number of empty wooden ammunition crates were set out on the floors and tabletops, while Edward and Mutti hurried to pack them up with Himmel's uniforms, his weapons, equipment and personal effects. Two of the crates were apparently designated for the Colonel's favorite dining implements, such as his coffee mugs and silver cutlery. But as my master stood in the center of the salon, his hands on his hips and a frown curling his lips, he found it necessary to orchestrate each of these selections.

"*Mutti, du blöder Hund,*" he snapped, pointing at a large iron pot the cook was struggling to squeeze into a crate. "Leave that! We're relocating to a château. Don't you think the Parisians cook?"

"*Jawohl, mein Standartenführer.*" Mutti blushed and surrendered the pot, searching for smaller and rarer implements. Edward was the luckier of the two, having to make no decisions as he was packing up Himmel's personal gear, none of which could be left behind.

The Colonel spotted me in the kitchen doorway, snapped his fingers and summoned me with a wave.

"Come, Brandt! I've left you all the files and orders and maps." He gestured at three empty mortar shell crates. "No one knows this rubbish like you do, so order it as you will."

"Yes, Sir." I marched straight into the room and immediately began to sort the paperwork that remained untouched upon my desktop.

"We leave tonight," said Himmel with certain satisfaction.

"So I gathered, Sir." I began to sort the materials according to purpose, and as I packed the crates I recorded the contents with a wax marker on the rough wooden tops. I started as Himmel dropped a large steel ammunition box at my feet.

"In here, you'll place the plans for our next mission."

I looked up at him. Having only one eye, he could not effectively wink, but the brief flash of his single lid divulged his intent.

"I understand, Sir."

"Good. You shall keep it with you at all times. Clear?"

"Yes, Sir."

For a few moments, there was no sound save the rustle of papers and equipment and cookware as we three of his staff worked quickly. I knew the question was coming, and I braced myself for it.

"So?" Himmel said at last. "Where is she?"

I straightened up, offering an apologetic frown and an arching shrug.

"She was ill, Sir."

Himmel's expression began to slowly turn. I watched his one eye squint and his mouth turn down from the energy of action to the vexation of an insult.

"She was *ill*?"

"So she said, Sir." I suddenly saw her mouth before mine, her lips open and wet and her eyes blazing as we slammed our bodies against each other. I quickly returned my focus to my work, and I heard the Colonel's boots clipping the wooden floor as he began to pace. A long moment passed, and then another as his paces quickened and suddenly stopped.

"To *hell* with her, then!" he roared, and something flew across the salon. "Dammit to *hell* with her!"

I flicked my eyes at him. His face was crimson, and he was waving a clenched fist. I felt Edward's eyes upon me, but I dared not look at the corporal.

"She can stay behind, the foolish little bitch! If that's what she wants, it's fine with me. She can stay in this godforsaken pigsty of a town and starve to death with all of her precious brethren. I'm not good enough for her? Then she can have them all, all the rest, the Wehrmacht rejects and the skulking deserters. She can be worked to death and find her reward in the rapes of a hundred infantry. We'll leave her to the support troops, the stinking *Ausländer* bringing up the rear. If that's what she prefers, so be it!"

The Colonel's helmet had been sitting upon the dining table, and with this last exclamation he swept it off and it clanged on the floor as he stormed off into his sleeping quarters.

I slowly raised my head, as if a volley of machine-gun fire

had just died away. Edward and Mutti were frozen in mid-task, staring after our departed master. Their eyes swung to mine simultaneously, their glares of accusation all too clear. I raised an upturned palm, about to attempt some excuse or explanation, yet they both shook their heads and returned to their labors.

I was in the grip of a complete panic. My God, I had to think quickly. Did I *want* Gabrielle to remain behind? Himmel's fury was rife with horrible speculations, but in fact would remaining in Le Pontet be better for her? Who knew what sort of creatures might take our place here? She was clever, resourceful; she could certainly make her way. Yet she was beautiful, magnificent, cursed with her own attributes. At least, away from Himmel, she could not be his; she would not be defiled by him. And yet, she would not be protected by his power. And what of us? If I let it be, if I did not attempt to have him reconsider...

I might never see Gabrielle again.

I dropped my work, and I went to him. He was in his quarters, thrusting photographs of his family into a map case. I stood in the open doorway.

"Herr Standartenführer," I said.

"Finish your work, Brandt," he snapped without turning.

"Yes, Sir. But I did not complete my report."

Himmel said nothing.

"Gabrielle had a message for you, Sir."

"I know. She is under the weather..."

"Not that, Sir."

"...well, she shall soon be under the *earth*."

"She said to tell you, that she promises that when we get to Paris, she will give you a night you shall never forget."

Himmel stopped packing. He raised his head and he turned to me.

"She said that?"

"Yes, Sir. I'm sure she did not realize that we would be leaving so soon. After all, I did not realize it either, or I would have insisted that she pack and return here with me at once."

"Mmm." The Colonel rubbed his jaw.

"Shall I fetch her again, Sir?" I strove to avoid summoning the images of another frantic adventure with her.

"No. I need you here."

The Colonel strode past me, his heavy shoulder brushing mine so that I felt his curled strength in the way I'd felt threats on the soccer pitch.

"Edward!" he called out to his driver. "Stop what you're doing, and go and fetch the girl."

I stood there, feeling suddenly faint, a long silent sigh hissing from my lips.

"Yes, Sir," Edward replied.

"And if she makes you any excuses," Himmel added, "feel free to shoot her."

We worked in silence, my master and I. He with his thoughts, and I with mine. Edward had departed in the Kübelwagen for the town, and Mutti had retreated to the carriage house to assemble his personal effects for our departure. From behind the mansion, the murmured chorus of the troop at work gave some relief to the atmosphere of tension within, and I was grateful that occasionally a junior officer would appear to consult with the Colonel on some matter of order and transport. Yet between those brief respites, my master was sullen and within himself, and I sensed his embarrassment for his recent outburst of emotion. I pitied him his uncontrollable divulgence, for I understood too well the nature of his obsession now. Heretofore, he had been a man who truly loved only his uniform, his men, and his mission. Now, he was lost in an unfamiliar wilderness, stumbling through a labyrinth of his soul he had never imagined to enter.

For many minutes, Himmel's eye would not meet mine. I remembered the first and only time that my father had openly wept before me. His mother, my paternal grandmother, had died, and he had gripped the mantel of the fireplace as his shoulders shuddered and the tears coursed down his cheeks. It had frightened me, and surged pity from within me, but I could not touch him or comfort him, and we had both been mortified by it.

Perhaps only thirty minutes had passed since Edward's departure, and I prayed that Gabrielle would be found by him and respond quickly and affirmatively to his appearance. I had completed my tasks and was sealing up the mortar and ammunition crates when Himmel suddenly appeared behind me, his hand on my shoulder.

"Your horse, Shtefan," he said.

I straightened up, turning to him. "Yes, Colonel?"

"Blitzkrieg, correct?" He smiled thinly.

"Yes, Sir."

"There is no way to take him with us, you know."

It struck me like a hammer blow. My God, in all the rush of preparations and my fevered plotting and images of Gabrielle, I had completely forgotten about Blitzkrieg. I know that my face fell, my expression crashing, and I could feel the tears well in my eyes and Himmel's head cocked a bit with sympathy. My mind raced for a solution, but Himmel sadly shook his head.

"No, you cannot ride him. You could not keep up with the trucks. He's a fine animal, but he cannot gallop from here to Paris."

My lips trembled, and I covered my mouth with my hand as I desperately searched for a way. Himmel's fingers squeezed my shoulder, and he looked off toward the rear of the mansion and out into the meadows and the barn.

"It is also not fair to leave him here alone, Shtefan."

I could not believe that my master, a man whom I wished so desperately to find satanic, was thinking of my adoration for an animal at this juncture. I had to hold myself in check with every muscle of my heart, so that I would not sob.

"He might survive for a while, yes," said Himmel. "But you know, as this war goes on, he will be more appealing to the French peasants as food than as a fine runner."

My shoulders slumped. I knew that my master was right. I could not expect him to allow me to ride Blitzkrieg from the south of the country to the north. It would take days upon days. And we had no facility, no boarding truck in which my horse could be moved like a racing steed.

"You should take him out to the meadows," Himmel suggested in a sympathetic murmur. "You should finish him, rather than leave him to his fate. He would be miserable at any rate, without you."

My guilt crashed upon me like a tidal wave. This man, who had taken me in and ignored my past and treated me like a son, this man whom I had betrayed this very night, was concerned for my affections for a simple beast. I could hardly bear it.

"Is there some other way, Colonel Himmel?" I croaked through a throat thick with liquid.

Himmel moved away from me, staring out the kitchen window at the troop working over their equipment. After a moment he turned, glanced at the watch on his wrist and looked at me.

"Your work is completed here?"

"Yes, Sir."

"And your personal gear?"

"I have little. It would take me moments to prepare it."

"Fine. I'll give you one hour. Take your horse and find someone who will care for him."

I leaped for my cap and strapped my pistol belt about my waist. Himmel moved closer, pointing a finger at me.

"One hour, Shtefan," he warned. "We must move well before first light."

"Yes, Sir!" I saluted him smartly, clicking my heels, and he suppressed a laugh as I snatched out for his hand and shook it very hard, and I was off…

Somewhere between the mansion and the wounded church of Le Pontet, it began to rain. The sky turned starless and black, with a thick mist enshrouding those few homes that still had lanterns lit at this late hour, and both Blitzkrieg and I stretched our necks far forward, our eyes squinted to focus on the meadows and our teeth bared as the thick, cold drops pelted our cheeks. He was unhappy with me, my tolerant steed. A single jaunt in an evening was a pleasure, but twice in one night, especially in this storm, was a trial. He had whinnied in protest when I pulled him again from the barn. And once, halfway to the town, as a gnarled hand of lightning struck the horizon and a wide sheet of rain thundered down a lane, Blitzkrieg halted hard and reared back, and I was forced to heel him in until he began to run again. I whispered apologies he could not understand, for behaving like a cruel master, for taking him I knew not where, for repaying his loyalty with abandonment.

We pulled up before the house of Gabrielle, and I vaulted from the saddle and strapped Blitzkrieg quickly to the fence post. The Kübelwagen was parked at a strange angle to the garden, as if Edward was reluctant to take on Himmel's task. I was soaked to the skin as I pushed through the gate, and there was the corporal, standing on the walk before the open front door. Just inside the foyer stood Gabrielle, and silhouetted by the kitchen lanterns I could see her dressed in her long coat, her hair pulled up beneath a woolen cap. By each of her small feet rested a meager valise, and as I approached in the utter darkness, I could hear Edward's entreating voice.

"Be wise, young woman! No harm will come to you if you do as I say."

She saw me then, as I loomed from the darkness, and she

flew from the house and nearly toppled Edward as she ran to me. She threw her small arms about my neck and held me so tightly that I could not breathe, and she kissed both sides of my face and muttered something I could not hear for the pelting of the rain. I saw Edward spin from us in disgust, hurling a cigarette into a puddle on the walk and stomping upon its hiss.

"*Gott im Himmel*, you're both mad!" he spit. "Absolutely mad!"

"He is trying to get me to *stay* here." Gabrielle leaned back from me, holding my face in her hands and searching my eyes.

"What?" I had been certain that he'd been coaxing her into the Kübelwagen, insisting that her resistance might indeed bring about a pistol shot.

"Yes. He says I shall be safer here."

I looked over at the driver. He refused to face us, his back hunched and his fists conducting an invisible choir as he nodded and called out.

"Yes! You should stay here, young foolish woman!"

"Edward?" I could not believe what I heard.

"You are both fools! Damned fools. You have no idea what might befall her if she comes to Paris."

"But your orders, Edward. Himmel's orders…"

"To hell with my orders, you little idiot!" He tried to remain in his position, as if refusing to witness our embrace might save him from a fate akin to that of Lot's wife. Yet his fury twisted his body around and his eyes were ablaze as he struck out with a finger. "If she stays here, in her home, in this town, it is far more likely that she'll survive this war and perhaps even flourish. But if she comes with us, Shtefan. If she comes with us, she is right back in the cauldron. She's with Himmel, and you together, nothing but a keg of powder awaiting a match flame, and you will be taking her to the shores of a front where the war is about to drown us all. You are playing Russian roulette with her life!"

I was stunned. I looked at Gabrielle. Her small fingers were covering her mouth, and she looked up at me, and both of our hearts melted with pity for this poor man. We slowly walked to him as one, and the three of us stood beneath the hammering sky, the puddles bouncing up around our feet. I reached out my hand and touched his sleeve, but he merely looked down at the encroaching mud.

"She is not a child, Edward," I said.

"That is correct," Gabrielle agreed, yet warmly. "I am responsible for myself."

"You are *both* children." Edward shook his head angrily. "You have no idea what you are doing."

"I think we do," I said.

"You will die from this," he whispered, as if we had both contracted some horrible affliction. He lifted his head, and jewels of rainwater fell from his mustache. "I have seen this before, and I know you cannot help yourselves. I am trying to save you, but my warning is all I have to offer, Shtefan."

Neither of us answered him. He closed his coat around his neck and looked away as he sighed. "I will wait for you in the car. Be quick." He marched off along the path. I turned to Gabrielle.

"My horse," I said.

"Yes?" She looked over my shoulder, squinting off toward Blitzkrieg.

"I cannot take him, but if I leave him at the barn, no doubt someone will make a meal of him. Himmel has given me one hour to find another way. Half of that hour is gone."

Gabrielle looked at me. She kissed me lightly. Then she brushed my soaking hair from my brow. She raised a finger and said, "Wait here."

She lifted her coat and ran quickly into the house. I looked off toward the garden fence, where Blitzkrieg was rooting his snout in some dripping weeds, and Edward sat sullenly in the car, the flicker of a cigarette flashing against the rivulets coursing down the vehicle's flat windows.

Gabrielle emerged from the house carrying a small leather packet, but she did not come to me. She ran quickly toward the side of the garden, and I was surprised to see her deftly vault the fence. She disappeared into the darkness, and after some moments, I saw the lamps flicker in a nearby house. I stood there in the rain, wondering, then made myself useful by carrying her valises to the car. Edward said nothing to me as I set them upon the rear seat, and as I closed the car door, I saw her again, leading a small figure along the cobbled road. She stopped beside Blitzkrieg, petting his snout as he quickly snatched a carrot from her hand. A small old man appeared at her side, and I walked to them.

"Shtefan, this is Monsieur Almont."

"Avec plaisir," I said.

The Frenchman nodded.

"Where are we going, Shtefan?" she asked.

"Pardon me?" My brow furrowed. The old man was stroking Blitzkrieg's shining flank.

"In Paris, Shtefan." Gabrielle pulled at my tunic. "Where are we going in Paris?"

"A château. It's called Montre Temps, just west of the city."

The old man nodded, offering a small smile for Gabrielle.

"Monsieur Almont shall care for Blitzkrieg. And he shall bring him to Paris."

I opened my mouth, but I could not speak.

"Yes." Gabrielle touched my cheek. "He is a farmer and he has such a vehicle, for the transport of animals. Yet he does not know when this shall be. Soon, he hopes."

I stepped to the old man, taking his gnarled hand in my own and pressing his wet flesh and pumping his arm.

"Merci, mon ami," I whispered hoarsely. *"Merci!"*

I took Blitzkrieg's head in my hands, stroking his long snout and looking into his black eyes. His elegant lashes blinked once, as if to assure me that he trusted my judgment. I kissed him once alongside his nose, and I unstrapped his reins from the fence and handed them to Almont.

"Bonne chance," said the old man. He was looking at Gabrielle, and with a trembling hand he stroked her cheek. Then he walked away, leading my horse behind him.

Gabrielle took my waist, turning me away and leading me to the Kübelwagen. I stopped her at the door of the car.

"What did you say to him?" I asked. "Why is he doing this?"

She looked away, into her garden, at the sunken bomb whose skin had become soft with vines. She looked at the home of the Belmonts, the kitchen lamps still glowing behind the windows, beyond the door that I had closed for her.

"I gave him the deed to this house," she said as she opened the door of the car. "I doubt that we shall live to return to it."

XII

ON THE SIXTH of June in 1944, the Commando roared for Paris.

We swept away to the north, abandoning our relative comforts for an uncertain future, and without a hint of the events already transpiring in Normandy. Le Pontet, quaint and pale beneath the clearing dawn sun, receded from our trundling convoy, its tiny windowpanes flashing farewell glints of the unfolding light. With spirits rising in anticipation of the French capital, we hurried from these quiet pastures toward fields of fire, unaware that the skirts of distant beaches were being licked by waves of briny blood.

Our staff car led the procession, its canvas roof folded away, an MG-42 machine gun mounted on its center post to stave off Allied fighters. Edward drove as always, with Gabrielle beside him and Himmel in the rear. Yet I was gratefully not present, as upon seeing the Kübelwagen over-burdened with the Colonel's effects, I had quickly found an excuse to volunteer to ride with the troop. And so, should some Mustang or Spitfire choose to pounce, my master would have to work the *Maschinengewehr* alone, though in such a contest I had no doubt who would get the better of whom.

I sat upon a slat bench at the rear of the first of the canvas-covered lorries, gripping the wood with both hands as the bench creaked and bounced on its hinges, lifting my rump and then slamming me down, over and over again. The big wheels raced over unrepaired holes and ruts, and the tattered canvas flap whipped in the wind, revealing glimpses of our other vehicles straining to keep apace. The steel truck bed was piled high with ammunition crates and equipment bags, while the men were squeezed into the benches along the flanks.

Captain Friedrich sat across the way, with dark-eyed Lieutenant Gans, now well recovered from his Russian shoulder wound, beside him. To my right flank was Corporal Noss, and next to him the huge and baby-faced Sergeant Meyer, and Private Donau was there as well, and Heinz, the armorer. Nearest to the truck's opening, Mutti hunched over a large washbasin full of raw potatoes and carrots, and somehow despite the tumultuous ride he peeled them one by one with a flick knife and tossed them to the troops, a treat which fueled their jolly moods and raucous jokes. They chewed and smoked and passed some gas, along with a bottle of *Apfelkorn*, and Gans called out to me above the din.

"So, Brandt. Have you been demoted?"

I squinted at him, cupping one ear with a palm.

"I said," he shouted, "has the Colonel busted you, Brandt?"

I shook my head, wondering at the question. I also realized that ever since Russia, no one had again referred to me as "Fish."

Noss leaned toward me, his green eyes mischievous. "He wants to know why you're riding with us."

"Ahhhh." I understood, and I called to Gans, "No room in the Kübel."

"Ja," someone remarked. "The Colonel needs that whole back seat."

"Ach, Jaaaa," someone else chimed in. "The wind in his hair…a French mouth on his cock…"

I smiled as much as I could manage, while the laughter echoed.

"So, this isn't punishment for you?" Gans prodded.

"The pleasure of your company is a reward, Lieutenant." I saluted him and he grinned.

"I heard you're making sergeant," said Meyer over Noss's head.

"Just a rumor," I replied. "And I'm still stuck where I am."

"That's too bad." Private Donau feigned dismay. Our boyish similarities could well have made us brothers. "I wanted your job."

"Careful, all of you," Friedrich warned. "He's the Colonel's spy, and he can outrank all of us with the flick of a pen." He winked at me.

A spy. No, I was something worse than that. I was a betrayer to all and everyone around me, and the smile I forced then trembled at its corners. I knew of Gabrielle's true virtue, yet I would not defend her. I knew of my master's obsessive love for her, yet I had slaughtered that bond. And here and now was the very worst of it, sitting there before my eyes, merry and hopeful and ignorant. The Colonel planned to betray these men, to lead them into crimes against their own convictions, these courageous souls who placed their beings and trust in his hands. And they had become my friends and comrades, yet I could not tell them, I would not save them.

I looked at them, and searching within my own character for its compass, found nothing about myself that was left for me to love.

Our convoy rumbled on, through Orange to Montélimar, toward Valence and Lyon. For one entire day and night, we drove astride the Rhone, its rushing waters always on the right, swollen by spring melts from the towering peaks of the Ardèche, always on the left. This route to Paris was indirect, yet it was as if Himmel had chosen the road for a final taste of peace, sheltered in the lee of fir-green peaks ablossom with spring flowers. He had made that decision, as he made all of them, on the basis of his instincts, on the scents of war winds inhaled by his commando pores. He could not have known then what we learned soon after.

As the Allies hurled themselves against the thorns of Normandy, the entire German army turned its ear to that distant thunder. The SS divisions, as always, were first to strain at their leashes. In Belgium, the Leibstandarte Division barked to be set free, yet Hitler had ordered that they not be released without his express permission, and on that day he simply forgot them, finding himself somewhat preoccupied. In Dreux, between Paris and Caen, the Hitlerjugend Division was not so shackled, and was the first to go into action. Technically, our Commando was an element, albeit detached and independent, of the Das Reich Division, all of which was stationed in Toulouse in anticipation of southern landings which never developed. And so, on that morning, Das Reich began a long march to Normandy, encountering heavy Maquis resistance with every step. The French captured and executed forty German troops and a high-ranking SS officer. Das Reich held summary hangings in Tulle, and slaughtered the entire town of Oradour-sur-Glane.

Somehow, Himmel spared us all of it, as if he smelled the blood of frenzy in the west, and so chose east.

We traveled day and into night, with scant respite, the flesh of our rumps bruised and sore, shifting from cheek to cheek as we groaned and cursed. Our spines compressed and we gnashed our teeth with each rutted hole in the road, and our bobbing heads bunched the muscles of our necks into fisted knots. Our early banter born of a change in venue turned to mumbling rails of complaint, interspersed with long stretches of silence and broken snores. When we slept, we did so fitfully, our heads upon each other's shoulders, like virgin schoolgirls on an outing, unafraid to be close.

When at last we stopped, the convoy gathered on the road's shoulder, in the lee of the mountains. The commandos, their muscles paralyzed and stiff, helped each other to the muddy roadside. The men shivered as they groaned and urinated in the dark, some limping off to relieve themselves further among scrawny bushes. With Himmel's permission, Mutti quickly made a fuel fire and propped his steel basin above the flames. He deftly flooded his mix of carrots and potatoes with water from an *Einheitskanister*, or jerrycan, and even mixed in strips of boar meat he'd cooked up prior to our trip. The spirits of the men rose as they stood in line for the soup, scooping it into their metal mess tins and smoking to disguise the primitive and petrol-laced taste as they slurped.

Himmel strode along the ranks, from truck to truck. I waited near the tailgate of my lorry, sipping Mutti's concoction with a spoon kept always in my trouser pocket. I watched as my master approached each cluster of men, and I could see his teeth flashing with his commander's grin, and the postures of the troop straighten as they gratefully absorbed his encouragements. I did not turn to look for the Kübelwagen, though I longed to meet Gabrielle's eyes, even as much as I feared the accusatory gaze of Edward. When I heard her voice in the dark, a hollow whisper from somewhere near, my heart raced with fear and joy.

"Are you all right, Shtefan?" She was standing near the cab of the truck, in the deep shadows of the moon. No one else was near, but I did not turn to look at her.

"I am," I muttered through clenched teeth. "Are you?"

"Yes."

"You should return to the car. We will be able to talk in Paris."

I heard her small feet shuffle, and a long sigh.

"The invasion has begun, Shtefan," she whispered urgently. "In Normandy. The Germans are saying nothing, but he listens to the radio and the Maquis are speaking of it, almost openly."

"Go back to the car, Gabrielle."

I heard her steps recede. I imagined her head lowered, her eyes filled with tears, and my heart was pounding and torn...

We drove on, and upon the break of dawn it grew cold and our teeth chattered, and we huddled against one another beneath coats and cloths of any kind. Every one of us smoked, as if that foul cloud might somehow trap the meager warmth emitted by our quaking limbs. Mutti, whose saving graces should well have earned him an Iron Cross he would never see, somehow fashioned a small cup warmer right there in the bed of the truck. He had filled an empty vegetable tin with dirt from the roadside, mixed it with cooking oil and strips of weapon cleaning cloth and set it alight. With fingerless gloves he poised a steel mess mug above the wavering flame, until a brutal mix of raw coffee and water and half an eggshell could be boiled enough to be sipped by all. It is a taste I shall never forget, and no gourmet caffeine shall ever surpass it.

As we neared Lyon, the road began to slowly fill. I squinted through the drawn flap of canvas, and it was as if the ghosts of France and all her conquerors had begun to filter from the trees. Country peasants, with their woolen caps and frayed long coats, led donkeys laden with beaten leather cases, blankets and stalks of bound hay. German infantry, a myriad of mixed battalions and uniforms unmatching, marched along with rifles slung, their tunic throats unbuttoned to release the heat their efforts made. Motorcycles coughed and sidecars bounced and rattled, and there were more than a few horses hauling caissons and snorting steam into the morning air. I thought of Blitzkrieg, then struck him from my mind, the certain knowledge that I would not see him again too painful to consider.

I heard a voice, a thin cry above the wind of our forward motion, and I pushed the canvas flap aside. From the cab of the truck behind ours, the driver was leaning far outside his window, and when he saw the pale orb of my face, he gestured wildly with a thumb toward the vehicle following his own.

"*Brennstoff!* Fuel!" he shouted, and then drew his fingertips to and fro across his throat.

The trucks had traveled far, and one of them was apparently choking on its final fumes. I waved at the driver, then quickly nudged Corporal Noss, who passed the message forward. Soon, I discerned our own driver calling out to Colonel Himmel, but we pressed on, passing a Tiger tank, its mottled fuselage bristling with panzer infantry slopped across its enormous hulk. We trundled by another monster, and another, and then there was a fuel truck with many drums laid end to end, and our convoy rolled to a halt.

I thrust my head from the rear and looked forward. Edward had pulled the Kübelwagen directly across the path of the lead Tiger of this panzer company. My jaw fell, as the steel treads of the tank had halted just a meter from the car, and perhaps its commander had only reined it in upon the sight of Gabrielle's shimmering hair. Himmel was standing in the road, fists to hips, along the flank of the giant machine, looking up at the officer poking from its hatch. The man was a general, and I squinted hard, as if that might increase my ability to hear the harsh exchange between them.

"We're dry," Himmel growled. "And you have plenty, *Herr General.*"

"I also have a mission, *Standartenführer.*" The general smacked his hatch ring with a leather glove.

"These pigs will be on the road for days." Himmel waved a dismissive hand at the general's convoy of tanks. "My men and I can be in Paris by nightfall."

"You can go to hell!"

"I intend to. And I am under the Führer's direct orders to be there forthwith." And with that, my master drew his pistol from its holster and calmly pulled back the slide. Yet he held the weapon astride his thigh, and called out with measured calm as I winced and waited. "The decision is yours, *Herr General.* However, I should think you might choose comradely generosity, over execution."

The Panzer general stared at Himmel, bug-eyed, and then he suddenly dropped inside his tank, reached up for the hatch cover and closed it with a bounce and resounding bang. I was certain he intended to simply roll forward, smashing the Kübelwagen, and I nearly leaped from the truck. But apparently the officer had issued orders into his command radio, and soon the crew of the fuel truck were scrambling to disengage some drums.

I sank back into the truck, realizing that Friedrich and

Gans and Noss had also thrust their heads outside to witness the exchange. Friedrich snatched up Mutti's cup, shivering as he sipped the foul brew and shook his head.

"My Colonel, my Colonel," he muttered. "He'd shoot his own mother for the sake of the mission."

If only you knew the nature of the mission, I thought, and we trundled on...

The Arc de Triomphe presented itself in the distance, no larger than a gritty staple thrust into a maze of gray sugar cubes. By then, we had endured a frightening strafing which left us untouched beneath a copse of trees, but slaughtered half a platoon of infantry ahead. We had raced throughout the daylight, bypassing Dijon and praying for the night across the open plains that swept us toward the capital. It was as if where German boots had gathered here in numbers, there was a pox upon the land, for bomb craters blossomed and every Wehrmacht tent was set aflame. Dispatch riders lay in twisted death beside their motorcycles, where Maquis snipers had found them from the trees, and untethered horses, their harnesses set free by their masters' deaths, ran wild over fields of char.

We did not enter Paris, but skirted her for Aubergenville, and in the deepness of night, we at last came upon the château.

It was a thing of beauty, that final castle of my youth. It rose from a sprawling meadow of unmanicured grass, its rough walls hued like pale mustard, its beams and window shutters creamy white. It climbed upon itself in steps of ever elegant squares, each climaxing in those sloping French roofs the shape of nuns' hats, and with the clearing of the clouds, a spray of stars set the black tiles glistening beneath fresh rainwater. The château was ringed by a large horseshoe of stone fencing, its feet presenting an open gate to a drive of pebbles, and within those walls a garden of ancient trees dipped their heads in the wind, and their leaves whispered as if to welcome.

Our convoy halted outside the gate, still many meters from the château's doors. Slowly, unfolding tortured arms and legs, we dismounted from the trucks, and it was as if the atmosphere of elegance demanded speech in mannered tones. The officers walked among the men and issued murmured orders, and equipment was lowered to the earth with care, and we behaved inexplicably like urchin boys invited to lodge with the generous family of some compatriot, embarrassed by our own appearance.

I stood in the road, within the deeper darkness beneath a large tree, carefully assembling a pyramid of ammunition boxes as they were passed along by a train of the men. I glanced forward as I worked, seeing that the Kübelwagen had also halted shy of the gate. In the distance, the château was the size of an upturned hand, yet I could see the flickering light as its doorway opened beneath a portico. A figure appeared in the frame, and by the diminutive posture and prim blond hair, I knew it was Himmel's wife. Her small fists poked into her hips as she watched him stride, alone, his arms outstretched and his voice booming and carried on the breeze.

"Mein Schatz!"

The Kübelwagen suddenly backed away from the gate, its tires spinning up gravel as it swung around, its headlights blinding me. Edward cruised the car carefully between the men, and I knew he only stopped beside me because Gabrielle's small hand was firmly clenching the crook of his elbow. Her side of the car was close, but the men were dangerously near to me as well. I set down a crate and stood erect and proper, as if that scant formality might still disguise familiarity. Edward was staring straight ahead, his jaw clenched. Gabrielle looked at me, her eyes wide with confusion and fear.

"He is sending me away, Shtefan," she whispered.

Edward gunned the engine, hoping to drown our voices and our foolishness.

"What?" I was instantly alarmed, knowing full well that my master's plans could never be outguessed.

"Yes," Gabrielle hissed. "He does not want me here! I am to be shut away, like some royal concubine." Tears glistened in her eyes, though I knew they were not sprung for separation from her captor, but of humiliation and shame and desperate uncertainty.

I looked at Edward.

"Brandt!" someone called out. "Are you still working? Or are you retiring from the SS?"

I raised a hand to still the voice, as I stared at Edward.

"To where?" I demanded.

"To the convent at Meulan," he snapped, as he put the car in gear.

Gabrielle put her hand to her mouth, as if to hide the trembling there, and Edward stomped the gas pedal.

"I cannot seem to reason with *you*, Brandt," he hissed as he drove off. "But maybe a priest can put the fear of God and Himmel into *her*."

XIII

ON THE EIGHTH of June in 1944, there were tears in the sea and steel in the wind.

The invasion, although still many kilometers away, was nearly a palpable thing. It hunched like a gargantuan bear, just there beyond the edge of a darkened wood, and we could sense its heat and hear the snorting of its compressed rage. The skies were thick and purpled, roiling with the hums of iron swarms, and the turgid summer earth trembled with thunders not of heaven's design.

The Château of Montre Temps, which had appeared to me so elegant and perfect from afar, revealed the pains of its ordeals within its arching rooms and spiral staircases. Its interior was no less impressive than its face, although the scars of passing battles had taken telltale tolls. The grand salon was magnificent, with an arching apse to equal any small cathedral, from which dangled a chandelier of many silver arms. At the center of the room, the polished claws of a splendid dining table curled into the nap of a huge Algerian carpet, and in one corner a grand piano of moorish hues raised its upper jaw toward towering windows of gleaming leaden panes. Above and all around, a curving walk with ship-like balustrades led off to freshly abandoned bedchambers.

Yet so many of the chandelier's three hundred crystals had succumbed to rude reverberations, falling from their perches to shatter on the dining table, whose skin had already been marred by the feet of German typewriters. The boots of Wehrmacht officers had turned too often on the carpet, its gentle coat now scuffed and matted down. And those once carefully preened windowpanes had spidered here and there, and the photos of some French gentry, once ordered carefully upon the piano, had collapsed and lay this way and that in a film of dust from the high plaster ceiling. But it mattered not that the chandelier was broken, for its energy had long since ceased to flow, and the storm lanterns lit by us seemed more appropriate to what I regarded as a tomb.

I see those lanterns flickering now, in the late gray gloom of that day, hurling shadows of antique slat-back chairs upon the high cream walls. The silhouette of Colonel Himmel paces to and fro between those waving bars, while urgent German voices stammer from a large field radio, their orders issued and rescinded in the confusion of shifting battles. A huge mahogany desk, which I and others had dragged in from a study, sits with its flank to the dining table's head, forming a conference "T" that would surely have no attendees. The desk is piled high with orders and communications, and as Himmel stalks and smokes and flips through every missive, I know that most of them are meaningless to him, for he has other plans. And there beyond him, her blond hair tight and gleaming upon her skull, Frau Himmel glories in the surviving fineries of a vast kitchen, humming as she turns her stew, the stench of pig and simmering entrails wafting toward me as I sit at the table, hammering my typewriter as if the machine has stubbornly refused to sprout wings and spirit me away.

The gramophone now hunches upon the piano, a platter spinning out the slowly building urgencies of "Vienna Blood," and Himmel suddenly stops midmotion, looking ceilingward as the thrum of heavy bombers nears. The half-denuded chandelier shivers, and beyond the kitchen archway, Frau Himmel turns, a wooden spatula clutched in her small white fist, and as her eyes widen in alarm, my master glides to her and snatches her up. And they waltz, clumsily at first, his spine erect and arm outstretched in fine form, while she resists, frowning up at his impish grin. Yet he cannot be dissuaded, my master, and somehow, together, they recover the graces of their young courtship, and they begin to spin. Faster and faster they waltz, from the kitchen to the salon, around the massive dining table, prancing out more perfect pirouettes as the airplane engines roar above and the ordnance thunders near, and at last Frau Himmel's coiffure tumbles loose and in unison they roar with laughter as I type, and type, and type.

To me, it all resembled a collection of grotesque Russian nesting dolls, one hell trapped within another, for I could think of nothing but Gabrielle. And although a single day had hardly elapsed, I longed to see her, or at the very least to know of how she fared. Yet I would be privy to no such information, for Himmel had broken with tradition and this time billeted me close, in one of the spacious chambers above the salon. It was as if he wished me to witness this ruse as he played it out with his poor wife, and I concluded that he wrapped me closer in conspiracy, to ensure against my treachery.

The conversations of the couple, full of her questions and his lies, relaxed Frau Himmel into an agitated state of optimism. Their children were safe, sent off to reside with a spinster aunt in the mountains south of Munich, and after this brief nostalgic honeymoon, their mother would be securely escorted there, to wait out the war and the return of her hero to a quiet life in Bavaria. Meanwhile, in counterpoint to my witness of this happy subterfuge, Edward and Mutti and the commandos camped beyond the comfortable château walls. Yet there was no barn or carriage house, for these had been burned to the ground, and the men huddled in leaky infantry tents. I shuttled back and forth, bringing them whatever comforts I managed to sneak from the country kitchen, and no one needed gaze upon me jealously to elicit my sense of shame.

After one such excursion, Edward followed me halfway back to the château, gripping my elbow and turning me.

"She's all right, you foolish boy," he said, knowing too well my pensive expressions at this point. "She's in a nunnery, a convent. Where could she be safer than in a church?"

"Monte Casino was a church," I said, reminding him of

the Italian cathedral that had been bombed to rubble, and he waved me off in disgust.

I had indeed become pathetic. What was required of me now was action, yet a paralysis had crept upon me. Should I seize the staff car by night and race off for Meulan to rescue my love? I could dispose of the vehicle by the roadside, abandon my uniform and join her in the convent, disguising myself as a monk. Yet I knew that Himmel would appear there forthwith, and the mere anticipation of his reaction curdled my fantasy. Perhaps we could run, from the arms of the blessed sisters and on toward Allied lines, yet I knew too well the nature of combat, and that rape and execution were barely the afterthoughts of battlefield adrenaline. For some brief moments, I entertained the thought of murder, for my master's death would certainly terminate our unspoken struggle for Gabrielle's soul. Yet I shook this option off, reasoning that my trigger pull would end my life as well, though secretly aware that I was incapable of the act. You see, to me he wore an impenetrable shroud of power, a cloak of protection he had often folded me within, and I failed to muster enough reason to betray him with a bullet.

I would have to ride with him, wherever that might take us. I would have to watch, and wait for opportunity's blessing, and then plot quickly and execute a plan that would not deprive me of sleep for the rest of my nights. Could I somehow snatch both Gabrielle and part of Himmel's coming treasure, leaving him alive, and us to still survive?

The next three days were unbearable, the pressure slowly swelling like a boil that will not burst, my every nerve stretched thin as catgut on a violin. The invasion roiled to the northwest, taking shape, rising like an inevitable tide, and as with all such terrible battles, rumors coiled together with truth, making information fleeting and worthless. American and British paratroopers were everywhere, pushing quickly east. No, there were only a few of them, harassing German positions here and there. Canadian tanks were on the road from Lisieux, moving like lightning and unstoppable. No, they had been halted north of Caen, and a Hitlerjugend *Kampfgruppe* under Kurt Meyer had decimated them. With strident confidence the broadcasts from Berlin insisted how the Luftwaffe swarmed above the battlefields, yet I could hear the urgent contradictions spitting from the field radios. German infantry commanders begged for air cover, but none was to be had, and Allied fighters roamed as free as wild eagles, sinking their quick talons into every scurrying Wehrmacht mouse. And we were only spared the pummeling of heavy bombers because of our proximity to Paris, its glories guarded by the entreaties of Charles de Gaulle in London.

Meanwhile, in the garden of Montre Temps, the Commando built a house of twigs. With cigarettes and captured British bayonets, Friedrich bartered for camouflage netting from a panzer crew, and it was strung from the trees and woven with a thousand leaves to hide our tents. From the vantage point of a streaking cockpit, it surely appeared no different than the crown of woodland nearby, while beneath the men squatted, and smoked, and preened their weapons, and waited. They were restless with inaction, yet patient in the knowledge action soon would come, and they watched the tanks and lorries passing on the road beside, nodding their farewells, squinting at compatriots riding off to graveyards.

And within the château walls, Colonel Himmel marked his time, carefully perusing some intelligence reports, willfully ignoring others. He made urgent telephone calls on a landline that still functioned, while waving off many that came through to me as I covered the mouthpiece and whispered the interloper's name. He often strode to the road, inviting officers returning from the front for brief respite, and they further crushed the carpet with their dusty boots and sipped Frau Himmel's coffee with their soot-lined faces. Yet every conversation had its purpose, and I watched my master glean and sift their information, then send them off with a cigar and a grin and a pat on the back. And whenever his wife faltered, losing interest in her cooking hobby and unable to accomplish knitting for her jangling nerves, he would suddenly sweep her to a bedroom up above. Sometime later, the Colonel would emerge, rebuttoning his tunic and throwing me a wink. And later still, his wife would follow, appearing to be slightly dizzy, yet the corners of her mouth upturned.

On the evening of the third day, I could bear the château no longer. Frau Himmel had taken to ordering me about like a servant, and preoccupied with his conspiracies, my master seemed not to hear.

Shtefan, clear the dining table.

Shtefan, help me polish the silver.

Shtefan, set the things quite nicely, as if for members of the Reichstag.

She had dressed in evening wear, a long black gown and gleaming pearls, the dinner no doubt a farewell repast before some driver would fetch her for her trip to Munich.

And when at last she proudly lit a brace of candles, Himmel realized his role and took his seat, and as she waved me off the Colonel smirked and shrugged a silent apology, yet I was happy to escape this Transylvanian nightmare.

A light rain pattered in the garden as I hurried toward the tents of the Commando, desperate to take in the purer exhalations of their warrior breaths. Above the tents the spring leaves rustled in the camouflage net, and beyond the copse of trees the horizon flashed with dim artillery bursts that teased the clouds. The center tent was open, its flaps rolled up and roped, and within the men sat upon ammunition crates, smoking and playing cards by the glow of a hurricane lantern. Edward was with them, and Mutti was scooping the last of a stew into mess kits gripped by grateful hands. Captain Friedrich saw me first, as I nearly tumbled in and found a spot beside Corporal Noss, shoving his rump aside as I snatched a cigarette from his mouth. Pale faces leaned expectantly toward mine.

"What the hell's going on, Brandt?"

"Damned if I know."

"You do. You always know."

"The Himmels are having a dinner party," I scoffed.

"What the hell are they celebrating?"

"Fornication," someone snorted.

"She's leaving soon, thank God," I said. "She thinks I'm her butler."

"And the Colonel thinks you're his maid."

"Where is his 'maid,' by the way?"

"She's become a nun," Edward murmured.

"And it's the servants who know everything anyway, Brandt. So, spit it out!"

"*Ja*, where are we going? When are we getting into this fight?"

"I don't *know*," I insisted. "Maybe he doesn't know yet either, or at least he's keeping it from me. Deal the fucking cards."

For two hours we sat, and it was fine for me and refreshing as cool, clear water. It was as if with the commandos I could remember who I was, a young man like them, with hopes and dreams and foolish optimism floating in calamity. In Himmel's private world, I was sapped of strength, a mere ghost of his will, while within the Commando's cocoon I stretched the aching muscles of my cramped individuality. It had been days since I had laughed, and with their raucous jokes I expelled the dour poisons from my lungs.

A motorcycle pulled into the drive, a dispatch type with a sidecar, and in the distance we could see a black-frocked figure heading for the château doors.

"Go spy!" Friedrich shoved his hand against my shoulder. "Find out what's afoot!"

I obeyed reluctantly, wanting desperately to maintain this comradely alliance I'd just rejuvenated, and I returned to the château, entering very quietly. I halted just before the arch to the salon, my hands folded behind my back, not hiding my appearance, yet making no announcement. The dinner had been cleared, and I could hear Frau Himmel banging pots in the kitchen, to which she had clearly been banished. Himmel stood before a small man wearing a long leather coat and peaked cap, his gold-rimmed spectacles gleaming in the candlelight. The two were very close, they spoke quietly, and I recall their cryptic murmurs went like this.

"You are certain of this, Klaus?" The Colonel held a grin at his lips.

"Yes. We still have loyal French in Epron and St. Contest."

"And it's a single freight car?"

"Guarded front and back."

"Tomorrow night? You are sure?"

"Yes, Erich. From Cabourg toward Caen, on the old line. But it will be forced to slow, and certainly hold up, before their front and ours."

Himmel gripped the small man's leather sleeve, leaning closer.

"It is the paymaster's train, you are certain."

"Yes, but its precise contents and sums can only be discovered in the taking."

"Your best guess, then. American notes?"

"I think not, as they won't be useful here in France. But certainly some other continental currency, sterlings or francs."

Himmel smiled fully now. "As long as it all exchanges well."

"It shall, almost anywhere on earth, I should assume." The small man smiled back.

And with that, Himmel placed both his hands on the man's cheeks, and bent and kissed him on the forehead.

"You are going to *love* South America," he whispered.

At this juncture my brows were knotted in a cleft. Who

was this man? And who was he to Himmel? Two Wehrmacht officers, embraces, a kiss, and a conversation that
churned my stomach. But I could not turn and run. There
was nowhere for me to go. I clicked my heels and cleared
my throat, and both men turned to me at once. The visitor
stepped quickly back from Himmel, his expression showing
alarm, but my master only waved a beckoning hand to me.

"Come, Brandt! Come, come, come!"

I stepped into the room, saluting as I moved.

"I want you to meet my brother, Klaus. He is a captain
in the Abwehr."

I bowed, as Himmel clapped me on the shoulder.

"Brandt is my right-hand man," he said to his brother.
"You can trust him as you would a priest."

Klaus Himmel made a small smirk as he nodded in my
direction. "I never trusted *our* priest, Erich."

"True. I'm sure he was buggering half the boys' choir."

The two men grinned at each other.

"Well, I must go," said Klaus Himmel. They shook hands
firmly.

"I will see you in forty-eight hours," said my master.
"You don't still get airsick, do you?"

"I'll live through it," the smaller man replied, and he
was gone.

The Colonel paced for a while, rubbing his hands together as he thought, stopped moving, touched his eye
patch and continued. I stood there stiffly, waiting, still
stunned at the appearance of this sibling, and somehow
offended at having been denied the knowledge of his ex-

istence. And I wondered further that Klaus Himmel had not bothered to bid his brother's wife farewell.

"Fetch the file, Shtefan." Himmel's order snapped me from my thoughts. "Spread the large-scale map of the coast, and all the aerials that pertain. And summon the officers."

As I worked, laying the map out upon the dining table and the reconnaissance photos in order, I realized why I had not been privy to his brother's existence. He was an Abwehr officer, an intelligence agent. So many of the reports I'd used to glean facts pertinent to my master's plan had come not from some anonymous source, but directly from his brother. Klaus was Himmel's coconspirator, and if an aircraft was to be engaged, no doubt there were more.

Himmel sent his wife upstairs to pack her things, while I ran to fetch Captain Friedrich and Lieutenant Gans, and with them came Sergeant Meyer and Heinz the armorer, who always had to be kept in the know. My teeth were clenched in stubborn silence as we returned to the château, and the panic rose within me, knowing that with each step toward Himmel's plot so grew my distance from Gabrielle. What was to become of her? Had Himmel's growing fervor for his scheme expunged her from his plans? Yet I hadn't time to ruminate, as soon we surrounded the dining table and the work began.

The Colonel made his brief, announcing the target, a French locomotive and a single Allied freight car. The small train would be moving on the rail line between Cabourg and Caen. He tapped at the map with the tip of a sheathed bayonet, emphasizing route details, obstacles and points of rendezvous.

"Our front line is established north of Caen," he clipped. "From here to here, through Epron, St. Contest, Buron and all the way to Rots." He dragged an arc above the city. "Here, the Canadian 3rd Infantry and British 50th are attempting to break through, but 22nd SS *Panzergrenadier* is holding them."

My brain was addled as I listened to these details. Its warring vortices focused partly on the tactics of the mission, then skidded to my master's lips disguising its intent, and dissolved into my imagined images of Gabrielle, alone and weeping in her abandonment.

"We shall move first to Troarn, holding east of our own lines, and then northwest to Merville." He raised the bayonet. "We shall be deep behind enemy lines at that point, but we shall wait, and take the Allied train tomorrow after midnight, as it slows up before the front. The freight is guarded, but I expect our lightning ambush will eliminate the problem." I watched the blade again, as he slowly drew it down and stabbed a point quite distant from the rail line. "And then, we shall withdraw with the prize, toward the airfield here, at Carpiquet."

I held my breath as Friedrich inquired after the nature of the mission, and the "prize" to which our commander had referred.

"All in good time, my Captain." Himmel frowned at Friedrich, which was enough to stifle curiosity. "It's quite a long way from here to Merville, and any one of us might be captured en route. Not that I suspect you might crack, mind you."

There were sharp nods and clicks of heels all around.

"Make the men ready, Captain," Himmel ordered. "Full combat gear, but leave the rest behind. We're off before first light."

Friedrich and the rest spun on their heels, and as I watched them hurry from the château, I could feel their blood stirring. My master had played them well, suppressing a secret that would only goad them on, making them murmur and wonder speculations, enhancing their will to charge.

"Pack up the car, Shtefan."

I turned to him, a question in my eyes, while his single orb held a mischievous glint.

"With nothing," he added. "Nothing, that is, but what you hold most dear."

What I held most dear was somewhere near, in a convent, but I dared not voice the question that choked my throat. I could not even casually ask after her, for I knew my face would crack and it would all come tumbling out.

"And your things, Colonel?" I whispered.

"By now you know what is important to me, do you not?"

"Yes, Sir."

It would require but a small satchel to contain my master's dearly held effects. It would hold his medals, some bloodied souvenirs of combat, the few memento photographs I'd taken with trembling hands. There would be citations from the Führer, perhaps some letters to and from the Colonel's family, in all merely a kilogram or two of the man's essentials.

And my own satchel, it would indeed contain nearly nothing. I had no letters from my mother, for none had ever come. There were some photographs, and I would take them, without imagining to ever really sit in peace somewhere and marvel at this past. But in the end, I had grown the instincts of a soldier, and my pack would harbor mostly ammunition, underwear and socks.

I began to work quickly, while Himmel loped up the stairway to the chambers above. I heard his pacing boots and the throaty murmur of his assurances, interlaced with the nervous patter of Frau Himmel's feet and the higher whine of her interrogations. Their muted conversation turned a corner, rising to a higher pitch of hissing accusations and counterthrusting shouts. And then I thought I heard the neighing of a horse, yet dismissed it as a wish, until Mutti's growl called to me from the garden, and my arms were full of my effects and my expression of annoyance as I stepped outside and froze.

The men were there in ranks, as always before a mission, laying out the tools of impending combat. Mutti and Edward, shoulder to shoulder, stood grinning wide and pointing like a pair of vaudevillians. And there stood Blitzkrieg, snorting and pawing at the earth, and next to him the old man of Avignon, removing his cap.

I walked to my horse, thinking I must be hallucinating, until he raised his head and nodded fiercely, and I dropped my things at my feet and threw my arms about his muzzle.

"Mon Dieu!" I stammered to the old man. "I cannot believe it!"

"And well you should not, young one," said Monsieur Almont. "Nearly every soldier on the way wanted him, and not a few brigands tried to take him from me."

I stroked the glossy flanks of my horse, as only my touch could assure me that he was real. Yet just as quickly my joy dissolved. His deliverance was not a gift to be relished, for we were leaving, and once again I could not take him with me.

"Where is Gabrielle?" the old man asked. "I would like to see her once more."

And then I knew what I should do, for it was the only hope.

"And so you shall," I said, and I fumbled in my pocket for every Vichy franc I still possessed. I grasped his hand and stuffed them into his palm. "She is nearby, at the convent of Meulan. Please, take him to her there."

"I cannot," he protested, shaking his matted white hair. "We barely survived this trip without his being thieved from me."

"Tell anyone who troubles you, that this horse is the private property of Colonel Erich Himmel of the Waffen SS." I squeezed the money in his fist. "I beg of you, *mon aîné.*"

The old man considered this, and shaking his head sadly, he stuffed my francs into his pocket. "As you wish." He shrugged, and Blitzkrieg turned and looked at me with blazing accusations in his eyes, as he was led away again into the darkness.

It was not long before the Commando was ready. Himmel strode from the château and formed them up, yet I heard none of his battlefield encouragements. My eyes sought out my horse, gone to where I longed to go, and then the men were on the trucks and Himmel ordered Friedrich to hold them up at Thiberville and wait for our arrival. The lorries rolled away, leaving only a cloud of diesel smoke drifting through the empty tents. And then, only Edward and I were left, and the Colonel instructed us to load the Kübelwagen and keep it running in the drive, and to wait with it there.

We sat together in the car, side by side in silence. The engine warmed our feet as the chill of rising dawn turned the night to foggy gray, and the birds in the trees chirped urgently before the certain rumbles of artillery would silence them. It seemed an hour passed, though certainly much less, and I knew my love for Gabrielle had bricked up a wall between the corporal and myself. Edward had no more fear of death than any man, yet this secret threatened him in ways far worse than that, and I was not sure if his silence stemmed from rage, or from regret. We smoked, and a light rain hunched our shoulders, and Edward sighed as his gloved fingers tapped the steering wheel.

"You think you love her, Shtefan," he whispered at last.

I looked at him. "I know I do."

He nodded. "Then forget her, for now."

"I cannot."

"It is a selfish thing, this love. Like his for her."

The comparison jabbed me deeply.

"This coming battle will be hard," he continued. "Unlike any other. Survive it first, then think of her. Not tomorrow, but in a year perhaps." He turned and looked at me fully. "Our Colonel's lust for her will fade. He is a man of conquest, not maintenance."

I knew that he was right, yet I could not bear the logic of patience, and I was certain that his reasoning was born of ignorance.

"Edward, you have no idea what he is planning."

"Oh yes, I do." His smile was a grimace. "Our Colonel is a professional, remember. He never trusts his plans to only one."

I settled in my seat, my bones aching, my spirit exhausted by it all.

"He cannot pull this off, Edward," I said.

"Really?" Edward scoffed and drew a long draft from his cigarette. "Have you ever seen him fail?"

It was then I heard the music. The château was distant now, there well beyond the broken stone gate, yet the sound was unmistakable. The vibrant tones of Himmel's favorite waltz once more crackled from his gramophone, shivering the château windows and wafting across the garden. Edward's eyes met mine, our squints questioning beneath our furrowed brows, and then we heard the gunshot.

I sat straight up and stiff and flicked my head around, and I felt Edward's hand grip my forearm. My heart thundered as I wondered. No escort had in fact arrived to take Frau Himmel home, and had she somehow gleaned my master's plot and purpose? Had she in her panic and her fury done him in? I pulled away and leaped from the car and sprinted for the château, ignoring Edward's warning snap of *"No!"*

My boot soles pounded the driveway as I ran, sending sprays of pebbles up as the château grew and trembled in my bouncing vision. The strains of Himmel's waltz swelled, and the lantern light flickered in the windows as I stumbled up the entrance stairs and gripped the handles of the double doors. But they were locked, and I stamped back and stared at them in shock, and when just about to pound the heavy wood with both my fists, I suddenly retreated and looked about. There was a servants' entrance around one corner of the house, providing a slim dark stairway to the second floor and bedchambers above, and more than once I'd silently escaped this way from the château's gloom for breaths of summer air. Crouching low, I hurried to the building's flank. The door was open.

The stairway was in deepest shadow, and I felt my way along its wall as I rose on tiptoes, breathing hoarsely, my hand fumbling to unlatch my pistol holster, though I had no precise motive for my weapon. My ears were pricked up and sweat beaded on my brow beneath my cap as the music ballooned and echoed, and at last I reached the polished wooden catwalk high above the salon, and I crawled on hands and knees to the balustrade and gripped the upright rails with trembling fingers.

My breath caught in my chest, my pupils soaking in the scene below. Some windows had been thrown open, their soiled curtains waving in the breeze like the pale arms of ballerinas. The lantern flames upon the dining table bowed and fluttered in the air, and upon my master's desk sat every document and map and missive I had so carefully compiled since the day of my arrival to his charge. The piles skewed this way and that, overflowing down onto the carpet, and from there my eyes flicked to the dining table's top. A bottle of burgundy lay on its side, its contents seeping out a flood onto the wood, and there it ran in rivulets, dripping from the edge onto a pair of shoeless feet below. I could not see Frau Himmel's corpse, for most of her lay underneath the table, yet beside her crisscrossed heels, a single bullet casing gleamed atop the carpet's fur.

The waltz was deafening now, the platter spinning on the gramophone below, its brass arm gently undulating up and down with the warping of the wax. I hunched down low as Colonel Himmel came into my view, appearing from the kitchen, a cigar clenched firmly in his mouth, its ember glowing fiercely. I could see that he was humming, his shoulders slowly spinning within the music's rhythm, his knee-high jackboots scraping leather as he danced. And cradled in his arms as gently as the loveliest of partners was a ten-liter jerrycan of petrol, its contents spurting and spilling from the spout. It spit onto the mounds of papers on his desk, and then the polished face of the dining table, and even onto the black and white piano keys as he passed. My master's movements were interrupted only once with each full orbit of the salon, as he encountered Frau Himmel's gunshot-stiffened legs. Yet this seemed not to disturb the Colonel, as he simply added a small leap to his waltz to negotiate the corpse. Oh yes, he was very graceful, my master.

I scuttled in reverse, the nausea boiling in my gullet, and in the dark I missed a stairwell step and tumbled out to fall into the yard. I staggered quickly to the car and fell into my seat, but I could not speak to Edward. He stared at me and gripped my tunic, wanting desperately to know, yet I managed but to shake my head, and all my efforts went to breathing and fighting a rising swoon.

I trembled in my seat as boot heels clicked upon the driveway pebbles. The Kübelwagen's door flew open and Himmel piled in behind us, while our eyes stayed straight ahead and locked into the morning sky. The fire burst to life and roared then, the sound of cracking windows clear, as tongues of flame leaped out to eat the house. Yet I only clenched my teeth and wished that I were deaf. I saw the Colonel's hand clamp down upon Edward's shoulder.

"To the convent at Meulan," he ordered, his voice betraying nothing but resolve for new adventures. "And be quick," he added. "I would hate to be late for my own wedding."

XIV

ON THE ELEVENTH of June in 1944, there were no more cruelties left for me to fear.

The Colonel's car raced quickly over fields just breathing morning fog, their rolling grasses smashed and scabbed by the crisscross tracks of tanks. Some trees we passed seemed whole and healthy, while others looked no more than leg bones shattered at the thigh. There were untouched country houses on the plains, and just as many broiled black and flat. The sun was rising in the east, beyond the distant roofs of Paris that rose and dipped behind the knolls, but the sky was blistered still with rain clouds, tossing steaming drizzle on our engine hood.

I sat there in that rumbling vehicle, my slackened jaw just bobbing with each bounce, my mind and body paralyzed as if by serpent's venom. I could not fathom how I'd come here, to be the man I was, a servant to a murderer, a conspirator in carnage. And still this whirlpool twisted ever quick, taking me to deeper levels of calamity, for soon the only thing I loved would be branded like a calf.

His, forever.

Mine, never.

My vision blurred with slowly blinding rage, as within my brain I saw the truth so clearly. He knew me very well, my master. He understood the weak and wanting fiber of my being. He toyed with me, as would a boy with a soldier puppet, loving and abusing it, wondering at its breaking points. He had taken me through fire, to see how much I'd singe, and he had dangled a bauble before my eyes, to watch me swallow my own drool. I was certain now that he knew I loved her, and that to him such suffering was but another test. He forged my metal in fires of his own concoction, and wondered when I would finally turn, to become him.

I wanted so to turn just then, to draw my pistol and shoot him more than once. Yet I had in fact learned much from Colonel Himmel, and such an impulsive unplanned deed would fail his trials, and no doubt be deflected by some parry. Oh, yes, I certainly would shoot him, but only after he had signed for every crime. I'd grit my teeth and witness this foul wedding, and I would help him steal his fortune. And only then would I make my Gabrielle a widow, and snatch our future from the rigored fist of this thief of hearts and honor.

The convent soon appeared upon a gentle hilltop, its modest stone church like a brown nipple on a wide and muddy breast of gnarled grapevines. Behind the church, the wooden convent squatted, more like a soldiers' barracks than the quarters of the holy. A rutted road snaked left and right directly to the apse, and already in the vineyard female figures bent to trim the stems, their cloaks and hoods disguising any features but their weather-beaten hands. Edward drove the Kübelwagen quickly up the road, as if he too wanted to be done with this and gone, and the engine's roar made starlings flutter from the bushes, but no sister turned her face to acknowledge our intrusion.

We stopped before the church's steps and Himmel vaulted to the ground, slapping the grit from his uniform with his gloves. From somewhere I heard the neighing of a horse, the snap of bridle leather as he strained against some hitch, and I was glad I could not see him as his nostrils flared with my scent upon the wind. The Colonel, hands behind his back, strode for the church's wooden door as Edward elbowed me, snapping me from my stupor. I exited the car, my knees trembling, my breaths coming shallow and quick.

The door opened and a priest emerged. He wore a rough farmer's trousers and a heavy brown jacket, his high white collar tight beneath his dangling neck folds. Upon his head sat a wide straw hat, with tufts of silver hair curling from the band, and from his neck hung a black bead rosary and an olive wood cross, which he slowly fingered, as if greeting a vampire.

"*Bonjour, mon père.*" Himmel nodded.

"*Bonjour, mon Colonel,*" said the priest. He waited, knowing that an SS officer would soon reveal the reason for his visit.

"We are here for the wedding," said Himmel.

"Really?" The father raised a bushy eyebrow. "And might I ask whose wedding that would be?"

"Mine," said Himmel. He bounded up the stairs and strode into the church, and I felt Edward's hand against my back, and we followed.

As with all churches, this one seemed much larger from within. Its nave was high and braced with stout black beams, like the ribs of an ancient sailing vessel, and its floor was polished plank with rows of waxed slat pews, embracing a single aisle. The walls of its clerestory were of cold stone, within which stained-glass windows rose, barely broader than archers' slits. There were no lanterns here, but morning light lanced down in perfect blades upon a simple podium, behind which a wooden Christ hung his thorned head from a bone-white crucifix upon the farthest wall.

"Perfect," Himmel said, and his comment echoed as he stood there at the center, looking up at a god who no doubt he had rejected as a child. The priest had followed us inside, and Himmel turned to him with a gentle smile.

"Please fetch the girl called Gabrielle."

The priest had removed his hat, his white hair askew in wispy tufts. He shrugged and pursed his lips in apology.

"I am afraid I do not know..."

"The new one," said Himmel. "Blonde and beautiful, from the south."

The priest stepped forward, his light eyes crinkling in innocence as he raised his hands to the sides.

"My Colonel, you know I cannot marry you to a sister of this order."

And quick as lightning, Himmel's pistol was out and

cocked, its cold blue barrel pressed against the father's forehead. I was standing now just behind my master's left shoulder, and my hand sought out and gripped the back of a pew to steady myself. Edward was behind the priest, and he deftly moved aside. We had both previously witnessed Himmel's respect for the clergy.

"Do you have a mother superior here?" Himmel asked.

"Yes." The priest's legs were trembling.

"Then if you cannot perform the rite, I am quite certain she can manage it."

The priest swallowed.

"Fetch the girl, if you please." Himmel's pistol barrel stretched the father's skin. The priest sighed, stepped back, and turned for the door, and the Colonel called after him. "And Father, I suggest you urge her to comply, rather than run. Your convent looks like firewood, to me."

The door closed quietly, and my master laughed a bit and shook his head. He strode among the pews, chose one and sat, crossing his jackboots upon the one in front. He pulled a fresh cigar from his tunic pocket, looked at it and put it back, apparently deciding there were limits to his sacrilege.

"You might like to take this opportunity to pray, gentlemen," he called out.

I looked at Edward, and he at me, and we retreated to some deeper pews and sat, though not together. He rolled his eyes and I closed mine, dropping my head into darkness. Yet I could not pray, for I no longer believed in any helping hand from heaven. Surely a million souls had prayed with all their might these years, their entreaties unanswered even at the precipice of death pits. I knew these nuptials were meaningless, this wedding of a Nazi atheist to a Jewess in the house of Christ, yet the looming ceremony screamed at me to stop it. And still, a showing of my courage now would have but one result, the choosing of my grave here in this convent, perhaps a tomb where Gabrielle and I would at last hold hands once more, in death. My teeth ached as I ground them in anguish, and then indeed I prayed to the imagined spirits of my Catholic father and Jewish great-grandmother, who might somehow hear me here and haul me through these minutes.

Another door creaked open, and from a darkened corner of the church's front the priest returned. He was dressed now in sacramental robes, white cotton flowing to his feet. Behind him Gabrielle came next, followed by twelve sisters of the order, all cloaked in black, their snowy chapeaus raised like feathered wingtips.

Himmel jumped up from his pew, his boot heels snapping on the wooden floor.

"Ahhh!" he exclaimed. "And a righteous audience, to boot!"

He marched straight for Gabrielle, who stood there stiff and rooted to the spot. She was wearing an umber mourning cloak, and as he reached out and swept her hood away, her blond hair flowed upon her shoulders. My heart hammered in my throat as I saw her, and the priest and nuns turned their heads away as Himmel kissed her on both flushed cheeks.

"Erich," she stammered, and her wide eyes flicked to me quickly, and back to him. "What are you doing?"

"I am making you an honest woman." He chuckled. "Only one of us can be an eternal sinner."

He took her by the wrist and walked her to the podium. The sisters filed past and sat into the pews, kneeling on their benches, clutching rosaries and bowing their heads. The priest shuffled up to Christ and whispered to him, his back turned to this blasphemy.

"No, Erich." Gabrielle twisted her wrist within Himmel's powerful grip. "Not like this."

He snaked an arm around her waist and pulled her to him hard. "Nothing could be more perfect than this, my love."

She shook her head. She looked around in utter panic. Her eyes met mine, yet I only closed them tight against the tears that threatened. I tried to will my brain to scream to her in silence, *Just do it! It means nothing!* Yet I heard her cry out thinly.

"Why here? Why *now?*"

"You may begin, Father," Himmel ordered the priest, though now his voice held no further patience.

"*Non, mon père!*" Gabrielle pleaded to the father, and then again to Himmel. "Why can't we wait?"

He ignored her, and then he knelt, pulling her down to her knees beside him.

"*Aber deine Frau!* But your wife!" she whispered urgently in German, yet some sisters raised their heads, understanding all too well.

"It's all right." He smiled at her. "I am a widower now." And he took her face in his hands and kissed her roughly, and I knew that this was it. She would explode, she would run, she would scream for help from me and it would all end right here in this place with rage and gunfire. I snapped my head to Edward, but he was already rushing past me up the aisle. My hand fumbled for my holster, my palm dripping slippery sweat across the leather as Edward touched his fingers to the Colonel's shoulder.

"Excuse me, Sir," he said.

Himmel looked up at him, his one eye squinting in displeasure. Edward clicked his heels with formality.

"Might I have the honor of escorting the mademoiselle down the aisle?" the corporal asked as gently as he could. "After all, she has no father. And it is properly done so, in a church, with prayer."

Gabrielle looked up at Edward, seeing something, sensing something. She placed a hand on Himmel's sleeve. "Yes, Erich. Please. At least that."

The Colonel shrugged and came to his feet. Edward offered Gabrielle his elbow, and she rose, taking it. He covered her hand tightly with his own, and they walked a mournful shuffle to the rear of the church. I kept my head bowed as she passed me there, but I clearly heard my corporal quickly murmuring to her, and her frightened whispers in return.

"You must do this, Gabrielle, in grace and silence."

"No. *Never.*"

"Yes. *Now.*"

"But I would rather die."

"And so you shall, and all of us as well if you don't comply."

"I hate him."

"Do this thing, child! It means nothing. He becomes

reckless and he will not survive for long, but if you do not stop this foolish struggle, if you show one gram of what is in your heart, you'll kill our Shtefan as surely as with a bullet!"

There was silence after that, as she protested no more. I knelt inside my pew, staring straight ahead, my hand retreating from my holster, my quaking fingers interlacing, knuckles white upon the wood. I heard them turn behind me. Ahead, Himmel stood, erect and proud, waiting. The priest said something and the nuns rose. They began to sing a dirge in French, and Edward and Gabrielle passed me by in solemn ceremony, as Himmel lifted his head, calling out to me.

"Come, Brandt. After all, you are my best man."

I do not recall the nuptials, for they were like an auto accident, a flash of images occurring between cognizance and wounding. The priest's words were in Latin, a language I had failed to grasp in school. Yet I remember well my waking, as Himmel slipped a ring onto her finger, and I recognized the diamond that had flashed from Frau Himmel's hand as she made her final château meals.

My eyes sought out my boot tips as my master growled gleefully, *"Mann und Frau!"* I heard his kiss, and then his gentler tone as he explained to Gabrielle, "My apologies, my beauty, that we cannot consummate this bliss. Brandt and I must be off to a small venture. But we'll be reunited tomorrow night, so be prepared to travel."

I could not believe that he actually thought that Gabrielle would wait for him. Had the frenzies of his fantasies turned his brain to madness? Had he failed to read in her eyes what was so plain and clear to all? Yet apparently, he had not, for he turned to Edward.

"Stay with her. It would be a shame for her to wander off before the honeymoon."

"Yes, Sir." Edward clicked his heels, and Himmel cocked his chin at me, and we strode together for the door.

"Off to battle, Brandt." He clapped me on the shoulder. "It's a shame we have to hurry. I would have loved to fuck her in that habit."

XV

ON THE TWELFTH of June in 1944, my master's race be-came his only war.

He drove the Kübelwagen now, his black gloves tight about the steering wheel, his jackboot flattening the pedal to the floor. The roaring wind whipped summer dust about his cap and set his tunic's epaulets aflutter, and the sun had risen sharp and hard, its burnished face reflected in his buttons and his eye. A fresh cigar was clamped between his easy snarl, and his squint revealed a focus only on the future, as the road between this place and that was fraught with obstacles to be dismissed. And I rode there beside him, hunkered down and helmeted, his only passenger.

My breaths came shallow in my chest, my stomach sore as if bruised from within, for I had swallowed all too much this passing year. It was a task to summon recollections of how I'd once felt safety in his presence, and even charging into gunfire I had seen him as a shield. Once, between each of such frightening events, his mere shadow had assured me of protection. Yet somehow there along the way, he had grafted me into his decaying soul, and mortal danger hovered now, wherever he was present.

Yet even now, I did not hate my master, no, despite the things I'd witnessed while enfolded in his cloak. The simplicity of that emotional excuse had left me, for both our childhoods had swept us to this road, he with his convictions firm, and mine just forming at his feet. At every turn he'd shown me another side of life, and left me to acceptance or rejection of its right, and what I had learned was simple: that choices were the only things a man could truly own. He had warned me once of destinies, and as I trembled there in silence for the bloody night to follow this bright day, I heard his echo in my head.

In the end, your kind will find my kind. Yes, you will.

That road rushed west toward Normandy, our tires flicking up its dust. The distant thunders of the night had turned to steady cannon rumble, and I recalled my father's readings from the Bible, for the far horizons indeed held pillars of fire. Troops marched quickly on one shoulder for the front, while the other dribbled wounded stragglers returning in its ruts, and on my side of the car I did not comprehend why some who passed raised stiff-armed salutes directly at me. My master laughed at my confused expression.

"They think that if a colonel's driving the car," he called above the engine noise, "then you must be a *general*, Brandt."

I looked at him, checking his expression from beneath my iron turtle shell, and as he shifted gears and glanced at me he laughed again at the absurdity. A smile crept into my lips, it seemed the first I could remember, and suddenly again it was just us two, together in nostalgic conspiracy. There were no women here, no bright blue eyes to capture, no heart to cause a war of our affections. We were once more the simple warrior comrades, separated only by rank, intrepid and carefree upon one last crusade, and for that moment I pretended she had never come to soil my subservience, or his paternity.

An infantry lieutenant hobbled toward us down the road, his left arm in a tattered sling, and as we neared, he snapped his healthy hand toward me in perfect Nazi Party fashion. I flopped my palm up in return, an imitation of Hitlerian dismissal, and Himmel banged the steering wheel and laughed so hard the tears streamed from his eye.

My mood was lighter for some time, as I released the burdens of the past. It would do no good to occupy my mind with Gabrielle, when soon just living through the night would summon every reflex. And certainly my master knew this marriage was a sham, merely one more conquest etched into his score book, without forethought to playing through.

"She will tire of me," he suddenly said.

I started as he clearly probed into my mind, but thought he lacked perception here, for she had tired of his kind before she ever met him.

"Yes, Sir," I agreed without emphasis, and I knew my bold response was due to the proximity of death.

He smiled. The engine's roar had kept our conversation to a minimum till now, yet he had things to say.

"If we survive this thing tonight, and make our way to

South America," he stated with a nod, "she'll wake up one day in the sun and see me. These spring and autumn things don't work for long, you know."

I wondered if just once since Montre Temps, he had thought again of his wife, or of his abandoned daughters. I nearly closed my eyes and shook my head, but instead performed those gestures in my mind. Himmel shrugged and shifted gears again, pushing the car along as quickly as he could.

"But in the meantime." He grinned. "We'll have some fun."

I knew by now what such a concept meant to him. He was not picturing some frothy palms waving over sunlit beaches, or tangos in the moonlight to the strains of soft guitars. He was thinking of a gunfight, that precipice upon which his spirit soared, and even true love was but a drink to quench the thirst after one such bloody sprint, and prior to the next.

We drove on fast, and as we did, the countryside grew thicker with steel carcasses. Strafed and burning lorries had been pushed aside by Tiger tanks, and sometimes in the fields astride the road, shirtless troops dug shallow graves for comrades stricken from the air. The stench of petrol mixed with rotting flesh blew past our faces, and the troops we passed, riding upon half-tracks or hurrying on foot, lifted their sweat-streaked faces up whenever distant engines droned.

We wound our way through heavy clusters of equipment, perhaps near Brionne, but all the road signs had been axed to foil Allied navigation. Yet my master seemed to always know his route, as if he'd battled here before in other incarnations. We reached a major crossroads, where panzer grenadiers waved traffic on with quick and jerky gestures, like policemen working in a thunderstorm. And then, the road was straight and nearly clear except for battle sundries dropped in haste. No vehicles moved on it, and those that had lay on their sides, their slowly spinning tires smoking.

But for our Kübelwagen, nothing seemed to stir. No starlings flew, no hungry field dogs wandered. We raced along the broken tarmac, and Himmel bent a bit into the windscreen and touched his cap to set it firm. I looked at him as his eye glanced up and flicked from left to right.

"Fighters," he said.

And sure enough, a dot appeared before us in the hazy sky. It skewed in from a northern field, and as it turned and showed its wings and settled on its course, my master shifted gears again and stamped down twice upon the pedal. The shape took form out there ahead, its wingtips forming sharp and clear as bayonets, its propeller spinning sunlight, and I felt myself grow smaller in my seat. I gripped the door ledge tightly and my other hand squeezed seat leather, and Himmel only pushed the car, faster and faster, throwing down his gauntlet.

The plane sank low, perhaps to just ten meters there above the road, its wingtips nearly scraping treetops, and I bit my lip and clenched my teeth as its engine screamed and its guns began to flash and spit. A line of spewing clots and chunks sprang up as heavy bullets carved a churning furrow in the macadam, and Himmel raced straight at that raking death, and I opened my mouth and yelled as he suddenly spun the wheel.

The horizon blurred as we careened to the right and bounced hard over the shoulder, skidding in the soggy field, our tires throwing mud and stone. I fell halfway against him, yet just as quickly he reined the car back to his will and I smashed the other way against my door. We bounced once more, screeching back onto the road, and he resumed his drive.

I twisted around in my seat, my lungs gasping for air, my helmet half-askew. The fighter droned away behind us, banking for some other prey and leaving a double track of smoking scars. Himmel merely raised one gloved finger to his forehead and stroked away a bead of sweat. He kept his gaze ahead and grinned.

"The trick," he said, "is knowing when to turn."

The day grew dim that afternoon. As we raced west a growing pall of combat smoke mixed with swelling clouds and drizzle, and I was grateful to inhale that noxious mix, for above it engines droned yet pilots found it hard to spot their prey. The trees were thicker here along the road, and panzers rested in the camouflage like napping elephants, their crews crawling over their thick hides. A mix of vehicles came our way, strange contraptions I had never seen before, some small tracked things and even some with hulls like boats, and many army ambulances. All of them held wounded on their litters, but they rumbled without haste, as if knowing they would soon be simply hearses.

It was nearly night when we reached Thiberville, noth-

ing more now than a cluster of abandoned village buildings at a crossroads. A pair of privates from the Commando
had no doubt stood their watch for hours, and although
grateful at our arrival, their salutes were weary. Without
a word they mounted dented French bicycles, and we followed them along a slim and twisting lane until the houses
faded and we reached a small and darkened field embraced
by a half circle of trees.

Himmel stopped the car and sat, displeased with what
he saw and clearly reassessing. There was but a single truck
among the trees, its canvas pocked with bullet holes. Where
forty men should have been saddling up their gear and
ready, no more than twelve stood helmetless and hunched.
Between them Heinz the armorer and Private Donau stood
knee-deep in a short and shallow trench, stabbing at the
earth with spades and making a black mound of sodden soil.

Captain Friedrich walked toward us from the men, and
as my eyes followed him I saw a heavy double line of bullet
punctures in the field. The furrows made off straight from
left to right, into an open area, and ending with a form
lying prone beneath a rain cape. Close to that sat Mutti's
cooking basin, resting on a triangle of broken logs, some
twigs beneath still wisping smoke. Just then a thunderous crack made me nearly grip my chest, a battery of 88s
opening up from somewhere near. The reverberations sent
leaves spinning from the trees, and for a second the flashing muzzles lit the scene like lightning, but Himmel did
not flinch, nor Friedrich, who stopped and saluted, his jaw
muscles clenched.

"Where are the rest?" Himmel asked, his manner quiet in anticipation of bad news.

"Division Hitlerjugend took them, Sir." Friedrich's voice was hoarse, and I knew his day had been a nightmare. "For Caen."

"On whose authority?"

"A general, Sir."

Himmel nodded. He looked at the line of punctures in the field and raised his chin off toward the distant corpse.

"I told him not to do it, Sir." Friedrich sighed. His bright blue eyes looked pewter dull and glistened. "But you know him. One last meal, he said. He made the fire small, but a Mustang smelled it and came in and killed him, just before dinner."

I got out of the car and walked. Yes, many men had died this year, and I had seen some flutter with their final breaths. But Mutti, he was nothing of a soldier to me, and I had always thought of him, like Edward, as an observer, here to watch and help and bind the wounds of others who deserved a combat fate. Not him.

His body lay beneath the rain cape; the sudden end of life had finally stilled the ooze from wounds I could not see. But his face was there, his eyes closed by some gentle fingers, the drizzle bouncing from his forehead and beading in his beard. I knelt beside him, the blood and water soaking through my knees, and I would have said a prayer had I been able to recall the words in any language. Nearby his cooking basin sat half-full, its nourishment gone cold and lifeless as his form. And as my trembling hand pulled on the cape to cover up his face, I saw that in his fist he clutched his wooden spoon.

I could not rise, until some of the men appeared to lift him from the ground. And then I staggered after them, looking at his boot soles, while soft rain dripped from my helmet rim and blended with my silent tears. And as they laid him carefully into his hasty grave, a thin vision from my childhood appeared, some distant memory of the funeral of my mother's mother. I knew nothing of tradition, yet the ritual seemed right to me.

I eased the spade from Donau's blistered hands, heeled it into the mound of black earth and let the soil spill on Mutti's chest. And then I passed the task to Heinz, and he to Corporal Noss, and he to Lieutenant Gans, and so it went as the artillery boomed nearby and flashed the treetops white, until at last the grave was nearly done and Himmel tossed the final shovelful.

He slowly knelt near Mutti's buried head, and as the cook had carried neither rifle nor bayonet, the Colonel plunged the wooden spoon to half its hilt and hung his servant's sodden cap upon the ladle. He rose then, and looked about at all the men, their hatless heads hung low, their chins brooding on their chests. And then he looked once more at what was gone.

"Leider, ist die Küche geschlossen," he whispered without irony. "Alas, the kitchen is closed."

No one spoke, nor dared a sob, although I know those words and tears were choking in our throats, young wild wolves who'd lost our only semblance of a mother. But Himmel always knew the precise allowance for emotion he

should spare, before things turned to gloom, and he nodded sharply at the roaring 88s and barked, "Gentlemen,
this war's not over yet!"

The Commando split and snatched their gear and vaulted
quickly then into the battered truck. And I think now, if
one could view that scene again, it might appear that vengeance stirred their haste and flushed their muscles with
some itching for a fight. But I knew clearly it was time
and the proximity of death that made them hurry, for with
every passing minute our numbers dwindled, and no mission could be carried out with fewer men than this. In half
a minute, I sat beside my master in the Kübelwagen, with
Sergeant Meyer now manning the machine gun in the rear,
and we roared off for the road again with the lorry straining to keep up.

The night was thick and black above now, its clots of interwoven clouds spilling waves of rain and offering a fine
protection, putting the absent Luftwaffe to shame. German
vehicles and men warily poked their snouts from clumps of
trees and came into the road, moving west as we did, headlights doused and shoulders tense. Yet Himmel drove as if
his single eye had been inherited from a bat, skirting obstacles and slower tanks and transports, on through Lisieux and
following the roadway as it thinned and twisted, his only
guide the nearby flashes of artillery and combat flares that
streaked up between dueling clumps of infantry in nearby
fields. Only once, after an hour, did he ask to see the map.
I held it up for him, beneath the crimson glow of a night
lamp, and he glanced at it and nodded and drove on.

At the turnoff for Troarn, an entire platoon of infan

try lay prone beside a high hedgerow. Their mortarmen hunched beside their heavy tubes, sticking fingers in their ears and bowing away like Moslems do to prayer rugs, with every cough and flash. Himmel slowed and stopped the car as a captain waved him down and saluted.

"Past here it isn't safe, Colonel," the young officer warned.

Himmel smirked. "You mean, here it *is* safe?"

"Not exactly, Sir." The captain smiled, yet I could see that his uniform was soaked through with rain and his collar stained with sweat, and he trembled.

"How's the way to Troarn?" Himmel asked as he pointed to the turnoff.

"Lots of British and Canadians about. It's not ours."

"Not yet," said Himmel, and he gunned the engine as the captain skipped aside, and the infantry looked at us as if we were mad as we raced by.

Turning north, the road became a winding lane, protected by a cave of shredded trees and hedgerows thick as sheep's wool on both sides. Yet I was not heartened by the illusion of cocoon, for I had been in no-man's-lands before and smelled it here again. From the east the spitting of light arms flickered through the brush, and to the west the broken building clusters that were Caen echoed with the batteries of our own artillery. The Channel was no longer far away, and somewhere out there ships rolled as their turrets boomed, their heavy shells whining overhead to stutter up and down along the line.

The hems of Troarn were nothing more than rubble. A pair of artillery spotters lay atop the highest pile, peering through their field glasses and whispering hoarsely into radios, and they did not glance at us as we picked our way through chunks of fallen facades. Then Himmel found a hedgerow gap and turned the Kübelwagen, and our shrunken convoy rolled on for a kilometer and down into a small valley. It was perhaps a hundred meters wide, with gentle ridges bracketing it north and south and a slim stream drifting through the middle. He parked the car before a single tree, and as the troop truck rolled up next to us, I saw that it was finished, its forward tires going flat, no doubt from some stray bullets.

The tailgate dropped and Friedrich leaped to the ground, followed by the men, who saw the stream and began to open up their water bottles.

"No." Himmel wagged a warning finger at them. "It's no doubt full of blood and sepsis. Drink the rain."

The men nodded, lifting their mouths to the sky instead, and Himmel strode across the stream and climbed the small hill as he snapped open his compass. The commandos checked their battle gear and slung their weapons at the ready, and despite the warmth I donned my gloves, knowing that my pistol grip would otherwise be slippery with my sweat. The Colonel raised his fist and we sloshed across the shallow water, and I knew that from now on I would be running.

And I remembered Russia, that freezing night upon a plain of crunching snow, that winter black that made bones brittle and stilled my sweat to ice. And here we were once more, sprinting over foreign lands, yet even with the summer air and rain just cool enough to ease the heat of fear, my teeth began to chatter. I tucked myself up once more behind my master, my weaker leg ignored, matching him step for step as the men spread out behind and to our flanks, gripping their weapons so that their snaps and buckles would clank less, their necks garlanded with machine-gun belts like hellish sacramental priests. Their breaths matched mine, like voiceless horses snorting with their gallop, and we loped on like hunting steeds after a fox, leaping over rows of brush and splashing over fields that had been flooded to drown unsuspecting paratroops.

It was not long before the steel railroad tracks gleamed in the distance. They emerged from behind a pair of northern hills, curving down from Cabourg on the coast and straightening before us right to left on a long and narrow berm that disappeared en route to Caen. On the far side of this stretch of track, a modest ridge was covered with a grove of silent trees, and seeing that, Himmel slowed and raised his nose, sniffing for an ambush.

He flattened out his palm above the ground and quickly knelt, yet like a practiced dance partner I had learned not to impact with his back. I came down to his right, with Friedrich at his left, and the Commando nestled flat behind us. He watched, and waited. The guns had fallen distant now, yet the quiet was unwelcome. My master clasped the back of Friedrich's neck and whispered in his ear.

The captain turned and waved his hand in signals. Corporal Noss and Private Donau sprinted forward and some distance to the right with their heavy satchels, and knelt beside the tracks, working holes beneath the ties with hands and spades. Lieutenant Gans sent two light machine gunners across the way to set up halfway up the hill and somewhat left, so that their cross fire would not kill us, and then he set the rest up on our side and well concealed in cover. Himmel looked at his watch. It was just after midnight, and he plucked at my shoulder with his fingers, and I followed him to hunker down behind a thick tree.

I do not know how long we waited there, perhaps ten minutes, perhaps an hour. The rains returned to mist and then were swept away by wind, and the clouds above were broken and revealed some teasing stars. And in that time I labored to keep every hopeful image brief that sprang into my mind. My father, if he still lived, might feel some shame if he could witness this. But I decided he would understand survival, and know that someday I would make this right. My mother, if she still lived, would cheer each instinct I could summon to keep myself alive until tomorrow. Like every mother, she'd judge her children only by their smiles. And my thoughts of Gabrielle, well, they were crippling here, so she was banished.

And the train came.

It was moving cautiously, emerging there between the distant hills. Its black locomotive had a face of driver's slits above a huge and rounded nose cap, while its stack steamed heavy puffs into the air, though no one blew its whistle. And just as Himmel's brother had reported, the heavy locomotive pulled a single car of slat wood, its guards perched on its rooftop, boots dangling and Tommy helmets gleaming. I held my breath, thinking of the American Old West, when wagon trains had raced through perilous valleys, hoping speed would save them from those lusting for their scalps. The train straightened on the track and picked up speed a bit, and next to my face Himmel raised his hand and snapped it into a fist, not of signal, but of victory.

Noss's charges erupted then, just before the engine reached the spot. The light came first, and then the soaked earth rumbled in a wave as the steel rails lifted and curled back like butterfly tongues. The driver had no time to brake, and nothing screeched or squealed there as the spinning wheels left tracks and ties and the train's cowcatcher funneled up a plume of dirt as it listed over and plowed into the hill, its fat form trembling the earth like some fallen prehistoric beast.

The railcar was untouched. Its coupling had been shorn away, and it simply smacked into the curled-up length of track, bounced back three meters or so and stopped. I bit my lip and squinted, waiting for the gunfire to begin, yet nothing happened, and I realized that Himmel had stridden out there into the open. He gripped the spine of his Schmeisser in his left hand, yet his right was extended wide, and I quickly followed him as no one fired. Two guards had fallen to the track bed from the car, helmetless and bruised and shocked. Two more were coming to their feet upon the rooftop. They were British or Canadians, I think, and as they looked around and saw our Commando emerging from their cover, they all leaped away and staggered off into the night, and no one stopped them.

The locomotive lay upon its side, snorting like a crippled horse. Its driver never showed himself. Himmel paced, issuing clipped orders in a heavy whisper, and Gans brought in his ambush team and set up the machine guns to cover down the tracks, while Friedrich placed the rest into a semicircle facing out. The cargo car had a single sliding door and heavy lock, but Sergeant Meyer used his giant shoulders and Noss his tools to split it from its rails until it fell.

Inside, the car was piled halfway up with metal foot-lockers. They each had pairs of rope handles, their green skins marked with nothing more than serial numbers, their catches bolted with single padlocks. Himmel stood there nodding, his fists upon his hips. He touched his cap and clapped his gloves together, and Noss joined me and we hauled one to the ground. It was very heavy, and I felt my master's hand upon my shoulder.

"Hurry, Brandt. A mission's like a woman."

I knew what he was thinking, and of course I'd heard it all before.

"Too easy, and it's wise to be suspicious," I panted.

"Exactly."

Noss climbed inside the car and squeezed behind another box. He lifted as I leaned into the door and pulled, and as he grunted hard and hissed, "These better be the Queen's own jewels inside," a bullet pierced the far side of the car and killed him.

It was not a single sniper, but a full-blown British ambush. Who knows if they had waited on that hill for us, or just arrived? It did not matter, for they unleashed all the fury of their pent-up wait in England for this chance. Their bullets spit into the railroad car and churned its walls to chunks of flying splinters, they rang like fingers hammering piano keys across the tracks and sparked from all the wheels, and as I slammed into the ground I saw someone spinning like a top, stitched with rents across his belly. Himmel dived behind a railroad wheel and shouted something as his Schmeisser set to chattering, while Gans's gunners tried to bring their MG-42s to bear. It was Stadler, I think, the belt feeder who gripped his face and screamed, while Weitz came to his feet and fired the machine gun from the hip until a hand grenade blew him end over end. I saw bullets chunking at the earth where Friedrich stood, hurling his potato mashers high above the car into the night, and all the rest who had survived crawled up close to the shattered car and fired madly up and into flashes that were far more numerous than ours.

Meyer leaned inside the open doorway, loosing careful bursts right through the wooden walls that had been mostly shredded. Himmel came to him and gripped his arm and yelled something, and the giant sergeant blinked at his commander but obeyed. He bent and hauled one of the lockers onto his shoulders, and he began to run.

"Withdraw!" Himmel screamed as he slashed his arm from side to side. It was an order I had never thought to hear again from him, and certainly not in answer to an enemy assault, yet I would outright lie to pretend it was not a breath of life. One by one the men sprang after Meyer, while others fired even more and longer bursts to cover. Someone hoisted Noss's corpse upon his shoulders and made off, while Private Donau limped straight at me and bent for one handle of the locker that was near. I gripped the other, and we freed our screams as we began to sprint, while bullets chipped off leaves and tree limbs all around us, and we fled.

★ ★ ★

The British did not follow us into the valley. I do not know why, but sometimes even now I hear their cockney taunts of victory behind us as we ran. Perhaps, like schoolboys trumpeting their triumph in a fight, they preferred to relish in our losses, while they still had none. They well deserved their joy, I think, for who knows if and when their turn came later in that war.

The bowl of grass with its slim stream was relatively quiet as we staggered there, but for the sounds of distant shells and something closer, like the spitting of some roaring hearth. The rushing water glowed bright yellow, for the Kübelwagen had suffered a direct hit from some missile of artillery. Its twisted body had gone a charcoal black, and the compartment where I'd sat and thought and learned so much was broiled up with crackling flames. The mounted machine gun jutted up like a dying arm reaching from a witch's cauldron, and its ammunition popped and sputtered, singing off into the night.

Sergeant Meyer sat upon his captured locker, breathing hard and cradling his Schmeisser as Donau and I fell beside the stream with ours. I tore off my helmet, and Donau his cap, and both of us ignored our Colonel's earlier warning as we splashed our faces with the water and sputtered it out in gasps. Donau groaned and turned and sat down on the muddy bank, looking at his calf, which had been pierced right through by something hot and jagged.

They came in slowly. First Gans, and then three boys who'd replaced those killed in Russia, and whose names I had not learned as yet. Heinz the armorer appeared, barely able to walk, and I realized that I had forgotten he was even with us on this night. Friedrich crested next, and it was he who carried Corporal Noss, and by the burning fuel light I could see the tears that tracked his cheeks and dripped from furrows near his straining mouth. And finally, my master trotted into view.

No one was untouched. Every uniform was torn, some by shrapnel splinters, others creased with holes of English calibers, though none appeared to be in mortal danger, except for Noss. I felt the blood that slowly welled from a slit beneath my eye, but let it dribble as it would, and watched as Captain Friedrich knelt beneath the shadow of a tree and let the corporal's limp form slip to earth.

The Colonel walked up to the stream and squatted. He removed his gloves and cap and smeared some water through his brushy hair, and as he straightened his eye patch and stood, I gathered myself and walked away, no longer able to be close to him. I neared the Kübelwagen and stood there, breathing in its dying warmth. *Ten of us are left*, I thought. *And Noss is dead, for what?*

"For what, Sir?"

But it was Friedrich's voice, not mine, full of liquid and remorse, and I turned to watch as Himmel looked at him and cocked his head.

"I would like to know, Colonel," the captain continued. "What is this prize we've fought and died for?" He flicked a finger at the lockers, while Meyer rose from his and moved away, as if knowledge was none of his business.

Himmel nodded, and placing one boot on the nearest

locker, he donned his gloves, put his fists to his hips and raised his chin and smiled.

"Your future, Captain."

A small crease formed between the captain's brows, yet he did not move or speak, but only waited. His Schmeisser hung from his neck, his wrists resting on its furniture beside the straps, and the nap of his sodden tunic gleamed with streaks of Noss's blood.

"Yes, that's right." Himmel laced his hands behind his back, his own machine pistol dangling in front. "You have no future here, and nor do I, and nothing waits for us in Germany but prison or the hangman, once this war is done." He pointed at the locker, but kept his eyes on Friedrich. "It is money, my Captain. Your mortal enemy's treasury notes. Two million is my guess." He smiled with utter arrogance. "If not for fate we'd have a larger prize, but this will do for all of us here. And what waits for us at Carpiquet is an airplane to take us not east, but west, to a place where we can live well and spend it wisely."

And I shall never forget the expression that unfolded on the captain's face. It was as if all that I already knew had come to him at once. And so it had, and it rose into his cheeks as a slowly raging flush suffused with mottled white.

"Money?" Friedrich whispered.

Except for mine, the jaws of all the men had opened, their eyes confused and darting. Himmel placed his fingers to his hips.

"Yes. Money. I trust you don't object to being well paid at last, for your efforts?"

"Money?" Friedrich said again in disbelief. He looked at

Noss's corpse beneath the tree, and then around, as if seeing every fallen comrade from now or from before. His jaw
slid forward as he squinted at his commander, and his lips
trembled. "Are you telling me, Herr Colonel, that you've
turned us into simple thieves?"

I watched my master raise his head a bit, a muscle twitching in his cheek, and I felt my heart begin to pound, and
the sweat was gathering in my palms.

"Are you *telling* me, Colonel Himmel," Friedrich growled,
"that the objective of this mission was no more than a crime,
with desertion at its end?" The captain leaned now on the
balls of his feet, his fingers curling round the metal of his
Schmeisser.

"Be careful, boy," Himmel warned, and I could see his
fingers balling tight as suddenly his character was there, and
bare, as if someone had flashed a mirror up before his soul.

"After years of following your orders, my Colonel,"
Friedrich seethed with scorn. "Years of killing and dying
at your whim, do you think that now you can snap your
fingers, and lead us all into *disgrace*?"

And then, the captain snorted hard and spit upon the
ground. His eyes were wild as he swept the spittle from his
lips with the back of his hand.

"You are a *traitor*, Colonel Erich Himmel," he snarled.
"To the Waffen SS, and to *Germany*!"

And Himmel shot him, right there from the hip, the
short burst smashing into Friedrich's chest and splaying
him flat out upon the grass. The men leaped back as if the
ground had been split open by an earthquake, and they
stared at Friedrich as he twitched just once, and then at

Himmel's smoking Schmeisser barrel. There was an agonizing moment of frozen horror.

"Are there any other objections?" the Colonel asked at
last.

"Mine!" I shouted, disbelieving the sound of my own
voice. My pistol had somehow leaped into my hand. My feet
propelled me forward, and I stamped to a stop much closer
to him now, my right arm stiff and quaking, the weapon's
foresight slotted on his face. He slowly turned his head and
looked at me, though he did not move his gun.

"Very good, Brandt." His voice was soft again, and he
added a minor smile. "I suppose I can guess at what you
want."

"Only your life, for our captain's," I said, "though his
was worth much more." And I was trembling not from
fear, but with my rage at everything he'd wasted. Himmel's
smile cracked and faded then, and he shifted on his feet, and
every nerve within me jangled warnings. "I'll kill you if
you more than breathe," I said. "And maybe just for that."

No one moved, at least that I could see, for I dared not
take my eyes off of my master's form. My left hand joined
my right to steady it, and someone murmured, *"Mein Gott."*
Lieutenant Gans drifted into my periphery.

"Take the men and go, Gans," I said.

"He wants the money," Himmel growled, meaning me
as he glanced down at the lockers.

"I don't care if it's fucking *coal* in there, you *swine*," I
yelled, and my master's eye blazed at me furiously.

And then I calmed myself, to better offer reason to the
men.

"Be gone, Gans," I whispered. "All of you. If you're wise,

you'll soon surrender to the Allies, and become prisoners of freedom. But if you have to fight, then find our men in Caen and join them. There's nothing for you here but dishonor now. Or the executioner, later."

I heard some murmurs, and then the gathering of weapons as they slung them, but my eyes and gunsight never left my master as I waited. Someone neared and touched my shoulder and I flinched, and Gans's fingers squeezed my neck as he said quietly to me, "Find us, someday, Brandt."

"I shall," I said, and they were gone.

We stood alone, together, my master and I. My breaths poured from my nostrils like a bull's, yet his posture remained relaxed and poised, and nothing moved around us but the ripples in the stream and the flames that danced up from our car. Himmel slowly raised his gloves to let the Schmeisser hang, turning to me very carefully.

"Quite excellent." He smiled. "That makes us all the richer."

But I said nothing as my finger twitched around the trigger, and though I tried to summon every reason not to kill him, they were so weak and few. His eye flicked over to our flank, the Kübelwagen's flames glinting in his black orb.

"My God, I don't believe it," he whispered.

Yet I was not so foolish to be duped that way and kept my pistol sighted. And then I heard the beat of hooves, the snap of reins, a heavy snort, and some rider dismounting from a saddle. My heart began to pound even harder and my elbows trembled more, but I dared not turn my head away from him.

"How in hell's name did you find us?" Himmel marveled.

"Edward told me where you would be."

It was Gabrielle's voice, and it pierced me as no bullet
could. I could not fathom why she'd come, and hearing her,
I wanted just to crumble there and weep within her arms.
Yet I did not turn to her or move, as the tears spilled over
from my eyes and she still spoke, so evenly, to Himmel.

"I summered here as a child, Erich. This place is half a
home to me, and you are careless with your maps."

Himmel grinned and let his hands begin to lower. I
quickly swiped my glove across my eyes and took another
step, which he ignored. "And where is my errant driver?"
he asked as if we'd rendezvoused here for a picnic.

"Still asleep, I think," she said. "The sisters' wine is very
strong."

I felt her touch me on my shoulder. I did not *want* her
there. I feared so much she'd break this spell and there we'd
be again, the three of us together, woven in eternal torture.

"He killed our captain, Gabrielle," I whispered hoarsely.

"I see that, Shtefan," she said, and she laid her fingers
on my outstretched arm. I glanced to see she wore a German soldier's tunic, likely from a corpse, and Edward's field
cap, her hair tucked up beneath it. And her hand stroked
slowly toward the pistol, and I knew I could not fire with
her there.

"Our boy is having quite a nervous night," said Himmel
in conspiracy. "I think he does not understand our kind,
mein Schatz."

"Perhaps not," she said, as her small hand curled about

my own, her fingers mirroring my grip. "But he does know one thing, Erich. That I promised you a night you'd not forget."

And I think he understood then, for his smile faltered just before she pulled the trigger. The barrel flashed lightning white and the bullet struck him in the throat, and his head snapped up as his glove snatched at the wound. But Gabrielle pulled once more, and then again, her finger welded to my own, and he stumbled back and fell into the stream.

Nothing of the world encroached upon us for some time. I had slumped onto my knees, and sat there looking at his body as the water lapped and turned him. I felt her arm around my shoulders and her fingers in my hair, and neither of us spoke until at last she rose and took my hand. We walked down to the pair of footlockers, and we looked at them and then at each other. I sighed and took my pistol from her hand, and she stepped back as I fired at one lock. She knelt and lifted up the cover, and she cocked her head, looked up at me, and smiled.

Half the case was full of currency, yet of a type few souls had ever seen before that night. There were packs and packs of banded, freshly printed notes, of strange square shapes and hues of pink and green and black. They were all French francs, marked *Serie De 1944*, and as I plucked one free and turned it in my still-quaking fingers, I felt the heated flush of comprehension flood my face.

They were, all of them, Allied Invasion Currency, intended only for the pockets of the troops who'd stormed ashore at Normandy. They had been printed strictly for this purpose, and useful only for barter with the grateful hands of liberated French. And they were worthless everywhere on earth, but here.

I dropped the single note. I would not be found with such a thing in my possession. If I were captured, the Allies might assume that I had killed one of their own to get it, and it could become an ace of spades of death. It fluttered to the stream and floated off.

The case's other half was full of books. Many of them, classics of all kinds, English pocket versions meant for resting troops, packed spine to spine. I nodded, knowing now why so few guards had been upon the train, and wondering if Himmel's brother had simply been misguided by his spies, or had secretly despised his older sibling. No treasure could have been more perfect, and even had it all been pure gold I would have left it there, just out of Himmel's grasp. I reached into the box and took one book and put it in my pocket, knowing how my father would have smiled.

And every year since then I read it still, and see and hear the flashes and the voices of that night...

AFTERWORD

ON THAT SUMMER night in 1944, Gabrielle and I were captured close to dawn.

We did not bury Noss and Friedrich, for I had no more strength for that. Instead, we laid them side by side beneath the gnarled tree, and used their bayonets to fashion crosses from its limbs, lashing them together with the leathers from their weapons. I pray that someone found them soon and put them properly to rest.

We never mounted Blitzkrieg, for he was lathered still and spent. We took his reins and walked him northward, side by side in silence, over fields that rumbled underneath our plodding feet and turned from black to mossy gray as morning rose. I stopped beside a crater filled with rain and plucked my Iron Cross from off my tunic, and Gabrielle slipped Frau Himmel's diamond from her finger. Perhaps those amulets still lay together underneath some flowered field.

We climbed a hill and saw the English Channel, lying flat and silver, swathed in fog beneath a windless light, the masts of many warships tilting in its swells. And then my spirit crashed, as cresting from the other side came seven battle-hardened SS troops, who loped so quickly to the top I had no time to think. It was the opposite of what we'd planned, and the horror I had feared. So close to freedom, just to be imprisoned once again.

"Was ist loss, hier?" their lieutenant snapped as he stopped before us, his finger tapping near the trigger of his machine pistol.

He was tall and blond, and his uniform and those of all his men appeared so fresh, I thought they surely must have just been flown in from Germany. He eyed me, from my cracked and muddy boots to my soaked and blood-streaked tunic. And then he turned his gaze on Gabrielle, as did his men. She had shed the German tunic, revealing a cream sweater above her muddied trousers, her hair half tumbled down from Edward's cap. My pistol was still loaded in my holster, and my right hand twitched, telling me that if they tried to take her, I would take as many of them first as I could manage. The lieutenant pointed over my shoulder.

"Our lines are that way, Corporal." He raised an eyebrow, perhaps because I'd forgotten my salute. "Who is your commander?"

"Colonel Erich Himmel," I said and felt my mouth tremble.

He turned to look at his own corporal.

"Kommandotruppe," the lower rank informed him. *"Das Reich."*

The lieutenant nodded and looked at Gabrielle again from nose to toe, and then at me.

"Are you deserting, my comrade?" he asked carefully. "Along with this French jewel?"

He cocked his head, but Gabrielle stepped up to me and gripped my arm, and Blitzkrieg whinnied as she raised her chin defiantly.

"He was a German war hero, but now he's done," she said. "And I am racially impure, so you'll want nothing of me. This war is over soon, and you would be wise to let us pass."

I nearly fainted with her fatal outburst, yet knowing full well what was next, I snapped my holster open with my thumb. But the lieutenant was quick, and he stilled me with his Schmeisser jutted toward Gabrielle's chest.

"A Jewess?" His tone was disbelieving.

"That's right," she said, and she reached inside her blouse and yanked a necklace out I'd never seen. It had a small gold Star of David dangling from it, and she thrust it forward as defiant proof.

The lieutenant slowly grinned from ear to ear. I did not understand. He laughed and looked around at all his men, who also smiled as if party to a private joke. And then, he slipped his hand inside his SS tunic, and like some sadistic magician, produced a chain and silver star that nearly matched her own, and said in perfect British English, "It looks rather like mine."

My eyes must have been large as saucers. The heavens spun and the earth swayed, and nothing in my world made sense. And seeing my expression caused these men to roll and shake their shoulders with laughter.

"We're Brits," the lieutenant finally announced, as he returned to speaking German. "We're commandos with the Jewish Brigade, just newly minted. But our tailors are Berliners, as were all of us, once."

Gabrielle clamped her hand over her mouth and looked at me. Tears sprang from her eyes and rolled over her fingers, yet I remained in shock and frozen with this madness and good fortune. She gripped my tunic in her fist and announced, "He's half a Jew as well!"

"Now *that* I don't believe," said the lieutenant.

"It's true," I whispered as I closed my eyes and nodded with impossible relief. And when I opened them, I found his gaze drifting down below my waist.

"He isn't cut," said Gabrielle in my defense, raising a maternal finger.

The lieutenant looked at her and blushed, and someone poked him from behind and said, "Neither are *you*, Froelich."

His cheeks flushed more, and then his eyes grew kinder and met mine as he gently reached out and gripped my shoulder.

"Come," he said. "Sometimes a man can find religion in strange places."

We stayed with them, those seven men I'd never dreamed of. They kept us close, perhaps as amulets of luck, as if the bond of love we'd forged amid a charnel house engendered hope that someday they too might find a treasure such as

Gabrielle, to mend their ravaged souls when all was done. Yet more than that, she was useful for her nursing skills, and I for what I knew. Throughout another year of war, so many times, her smile was the final blessed escort of an Allied boy en route to heaven's peace. And my voice was often that which shattered the composure of a captured Wehrmacht officer, who sensed that I'd mined blacker hearts, and his was easy prey.

Across the summer fields of France, the autumn battles in Alsace, a brutal Belgian winter and the springtime Rhine we flew. I'd shed my German tunic early, but it had stained my skin like purple wine, and sometimes when our seven British charges donned their SS smocks like Trojan horses, I gazed at them in longing cleaved with shame. There was no hiding it from Gabrielle, who knew and blessedly said nothing. In her eyes, and mine, judgments were for those who'd never tasted wars.

I never found my father, although his name was always at my lips, and I hunted for his eyes in those of every elder Viennese I met. And when at last we learned the fates of millions of my mother's kind, Lieutenant Froelich taught me something he called *Kaddish*, and she was placed to rest a stone's throw from my heart.

Blitzkrieg, at last, faltered in Bayern. We rode him one last time, and gently, across a field of summer grass powdered in white flowers. We kissed and hugged his chestnut neck and wept, then left his reins entwined between the fingers of a grateful, simple farmer. It was the hardest thing we'd ever done together.

I do not know what fate befell the boys of the Commando, nor of Edward, without whose careful tutelage our lives would have been lost. Yet once, among a thousand prisoners cramped behind barbed wire, I saw Lieutenant Gans. He'd shed his SS uniform for the tunic of a simple Wehrmacht soldier then, and our eyes met across a skein of memories, and we nodded and I left him to his luck. They were not me, and I not them, and I knew that there would never be, nor wanted, whispers of nostalgia in some dark saloon of reminiscence.

The war became another race for Gabrielle and me, against a clock of thundering cruelty and prayers to survive it. I had scant hope, and also thought that I had seen too much in Colonel Himmel's care, visions that could never be undone. Yet these strange creatures, these Jewish commandos, neither fish nor fowl, painted scenes for us from their imaginations.

They spoke of distant sun-drenched lands, of deserts they would make to bloom, of ships from Crete to welcome sands, and both of us learned once again to hunger for the future. The guns would still one day, they said, and those like us would find a place to live in freedom, if not peace. And so it was.

It has been countless years since then, yet no day of that other life has faded with my age. I never touched the tools of war again, nor offered explanation, but they were printed on my palms, and Colonel Erich Himmel's name stayed hushed behind my eyes. There have been many other trials, joys and sorrows, yes, but nothing like that tarnished trove which Gabrielle and I had locked away. Its truth, we chose, would not be told until our own eternities were imminent, and questions only whispered at our graves. Few, we knew, could understand, and all our children and theirs too have been respectful of our private pact, until this writing and this day.

She left, at last, though not of her volition, no. And not before our eyes had met a million times upon some breeze that carried scents of smoke, or thunders of man's making, or horse hooves in the fields that stirred a memory. Sometimes I wander up our hill in Galilee to sit near where she lies, and hold her hand once more, and hear her voice, and see her in the night.

And then I surely know that the great privilege of my life was in the living. And yes, at last to tell it has been very fine as well.

★ ★ ★ ★ ★

HISTORICAL NOTES

It is estimated that approximately 150,000 partial-Jews, or *Mischlinge*, served in various branches of the German military during WWII. Over the course of the war, many were killed in action, or, as racial laws intensified, expelled from their units and sent to concentration camps. Those whose skills were considered crucial to Germany's war effort were granted personal exemptions by Adolf Hitler, including a Wehrmacht field marshal and Kriegsmarine admiral. After the war, some of the survivors immigrated to what was soon to become the State of Israel and served in the Israeli army.

At the time of the Normandy Invasion, Winston Churchill had just approved the formation of the Jewish Brigade, a branch of the Allied forces that quickly grew to 6,000 men. However, prior to that, Jewish German and Austrian refugees had already been operating in the North African and European theaters as commandos and intelligence agents, at times disguised as

German troops. The most intrepid of these were attached to the British Army's No. 10 Inter-Allied Commando, including a top-secret contingent known as "X-Troop."

The German name Stefan is pronounced *Shtefan*. I have chosen to spell it thusly throughout so that the reader would hear it correctly.